WHEN NATURE CALLS

With thanks to Linda.
Never stop inspiring me

Foreword – here we are dearest reader, for the first time I type to a real human being and visualise the pulsing intellect behind those pupils. Perhaps you're opening this book and it's my first for you as well, it's a fresh copy with that new book smell I at least always lean into. It might be that this is a tattered old relic you've found battered behind an old Martian cooling unit while you're doing repairs, staring at some strange physical script you just can't interact with, and feeling dubious at the idea Earth was ever really a home-world…

Anyway, it's impossible to know where this book will end up, or who you are, but I find that exciting just as well, that irreplaceable sensation which cascades out of the power of the story, the great tale which wields your escapism for a short time and firing an imagination which might make you leap even further into the Humanity series than this one tale, and *beyond.*

1: I'D RATHER TALK TO THE SQUIRREL

Squirrels are very forgetful animals, and with all the nuts they bury away, they'll be happy to catch half of them. For every nut they miss, a tree will grow. Sometimes it pays to forget.

It didn't matter how many times they called Ellis weird, they wouldn't change. It wasn't because he was defiant or putting on a brave face. Nor was that the reason Ellis spent so much time with just nature's calls. No, the adults might have worried about them and every strange, cautious step Ellis took. Some of them listened to Ellis' high-pitched giggle which came out like a chortling little engine and wandered if they needed some serious help.

The problem was that everyone thought everyone else around them felt and thought the same way. Ellis could see them typing and browsing and endless connecting, but it didn't stop Ellis looking at the rest of the world around them. It didn't prevent Ellis looking at nature whenever they could, grasping at the fun and inventiveness of all those little personalities.

In fact, Ellis just felt happy and ran after any sense of excitement they could find, they'd only walked out in front of a car once before and was fine afterwards anyway. The parents though, they thought something very serious was happening, they always looked to the worst, and with that came this weird night, a night where the normal schedule of reading and playing after homework had stopped. Ellis knew something strange was going on, but it was OK, he trusted Daddy without thinking. Yes, everyone else was calling their Daddy "Dad" by now. Ellis didn't care, why change something which was so perfectly OK already, and a little bit fun? Change was usually a violent thing, and whenever it happened, at least Ellis had Jacob and Daddy to cling to. Like grabbing onto a piece of wood while a whirlpool grabs at you.

Ellis didn't want to recall the fact it was just like that when Mum stopped coming home and Daddy turned sad and angry and started to find enemies in a world where he had only ever seen happiness and friends.

-

"Hey, cricket, do you want to come over here?" It was the kind and solid depth of a voice Daddy always used when something was a bit wrong, but he wanted to pretend he was still fun. He paused between each comma like it was a new word, but Ellis wouldn't have had any idea what that meant. As always, he was staring out into the trees and smiling at the way the branches fluttered in the breeze, just about seeing the memories of faces.

Ellis couldn't be any more focused than he was right now, especially when he was in the comfort of home, quietly laughing to himself about the robin that bounded among the little branches quite close to a bird house he had built obsessively with Jacob, his best and only friend.

It had taken a few weeks, but their new house had a

friend. Every time the bird jumped or flicked its head, Ellis's eyes enlarged, and he paused completely when it started to sing, silently trying to sing along. Whenever Ellis was this close to the animals, they were completely silent, completely transfixed by its sharp movements. The robin considered the window of that little house again and Ellis stopped, a statue, not even looking the bird in the eye. Just in case.

"Cricket...?" When Daddy stood so close behind Ellis, their size difference became obvious.

Their GP had wandered once if Ellis's age was right, for fifteen he was constantly mistaken for a much smaller child, and on more than once occasion had ended up in the wrong group for a school trip just because the teachers hadn't noticed. Ellis had tried following a fun trail with the little animals they could pet, but they'd have to learn about the farming machines instead. Ellis could never sulk though, there had been a kingfisher that day – the first one ever - and the chance with inspiration, to paint a picture of it sometime soon.

Ellis' Dad was a larger man, the kind of strong build where other people wouldn't ask if he could pick up a sofa or carry all the shopping. Ellis had watched him move a whole chest of drawers and he didn't even drag it along the floor. He picked it up, just as easily as he still threw Ellis up into the air. Ellis wanted the same invincibility, and kept trying to pick up those cold weights in the basement, but it didn't work.

Every now and then Ellis could imagine and sense something strong in the back of their mind, but it didn't matter what they did, nothing went right and there Ellis stood, straining and trying before sitting down tired and panting, frowning at the obstacle in front, the great weight. Most of all, they wandered if the time when their body would "fill in" was going to happen anytime soon.

The best part about most days was the running away, so the best season of all was summer, just like it was now. That luscious bright light pushing through the trees was something Ellis couldn't forget. Nor could they forget the little smells and twinkling of sound all around as they wandered through the forest.

Each time, no matter how much Ellis tried to focus, the path felt different. The trees seemed to move about. There were weird new marks on the bark, and then quite quickly they weren't. There was a small valley where it had been a little hill, or maybe it was just the paths that was changing.

Ellis was convinced there were strange hoof marks, even if there hadn't been a horse around here for at least a hundred years. Or at least that's what Jacob said, but then he couldn't come up with a reason why the horse had come back. The biggest tree right in the middle always spoke to Ellis. Just about.

That's where they usually ended up, summoned, but no matter what Ellis tried, the tree wouldn't move or say a thing. Maybe it wasn't real after all. Even if it seemed to scream at the secrets which might be hidden just below the surface. Just in case he could lift it and run right underneath into the maze of roots and something else below.

"Tree trunksh are heavy..." Ellis muttered, leaning back against Daddy's big chest, as always, Ellis tried to roll into a ball like the cubs he'd seen on the TV, incapable of seeing Daddy as anything else than a strong bear. Ellis emphasised the lisps, even more so if you tried to teach Ellis not to, to try and change anyone's nature was.

Daddy had learned a lot through the years, so he whispered too, letting the small bird song from the last shreds of daylight be the loudest sound in their front room. With a smooth cupping of one large hand, Daddy pushed Ellis' face away from the window, smiling down at him in a reassuring way, just to make sure it was safe.

There were no bright lights, to keep Ellis calm and unstartled, and while the outside dimmed to evening darkness, a small lamp was the only little glow in the room now, the same deep yellow of a sunset. "Cricket... do you know what a bully might be?" Daddy nodded his head slowly while he spoke, knowing it would be an effort for Ellis to move away from the single track that their mind had been on. There would need to be encouragement, but he was happy to give Ellis a chance to try without being forced to, his son was growing up after all.

"... They're shtupid. If we were all animalsh in a shymbiotic ecology, it wouldn't happen. We can't wag our penishes at each other, sho shomething elshe had to happen." Ellis paused and made sure it was exactly the right thing, mouthing the words a second time, just to make sure.

7

"The kind of people who would laugh when I get losht. They find it funny if you make a mishtake. They don't lishten to reashon and I bet they'd kill a bee if they shaw it. Ish that right Daddy?" Sometimes Daddy forgot just how old his son had become, the way that his son giggled and moved, and Ellis' short height kept tricking people into thinking he son was still a child. Like any other animal, was always watching and much more aware of the world around, more than anyone would give them credit for.

"Cricket, that is a very righteous tune you're playing. They're not stupid, they just live in a pack like hyenas. The only problem is a lot of adults end up the same way. Have you noticed a lot of people changing recently? Before you say anything, I don't mean physically, I know you have forgotten that one – it hit you pretty hard!" He chuckled at the joke, knowing at the very least his son would get that joke when Ellis didn't get a lot of the other jokes and sarcasm was completely useless.

It was so much better to be direct. That was good when it came to having fun, but it was just as powerful when someone else learned how to use it for harm.

"Lotsh of them think they're all grown up now. They've shtopped calling the teacher shir or missh, and they think they're sho shtrong when they drink or shomething elshe new and dangeroush. They're already adult hyenash, but the worsht part ish, they've never quehstioned a thing, it feelsh like everyone elshe is on a leash nobody bothered to put around me."

Ellis had buckled over with the strain it always cost him

to think what another human might be feeling. Animals were so much easier, and at least then something very powerful happened, a religious experience most people would have said. This was not a person who thought any idea of being stuck in a pack gave the same claustrophobic squeeze any time inside brought out.

"Little cricket…it's was OK to say things like that a few years ago. It is not alright now when you'll be a man soon." The embrace between the two of them shattered almost immediately as Ellis ran, jumping and stomping against some hidden trauma, and as the click of the lock smashed against the door, Daddy knew he'd slipped up.

In the cabinet, next to their sofa was a cacophony of books Daddy had collected, and he cursed whoever had decided to take their mum away so early. She would have known what to say to a son who didn't even see themselves as a single person. Maybe not, but at she'd know what to say to calm him down. *Them* he thought, furrowing his brow even more. "Well, I guess we were right Christina, more than we knew. We got all the child we could ever need in our first. I'm not too proud to admit when we need help. I can't lose Ellis too. I can't."

Most men might have wept now, but being the ex-soldier, he was, Daddy would fight a challenge all the way.

Grabbing one ham-fisted book, his large hand man-handled the book "Your love is more important than whether he's a son or she's a daughter.", grasping at a thick wad of paper filled with spidery notes hoping to find out just what was happening to the son he so tenderly missed.

-

Parents lives always seem to move so slowly, everything somehow calmly just the same as they were last week. They seemed to have memories which harked back to a wilder time, and with it would come a warm smirk at what had been. Ellis had no idea how you could live like that. Everything was incredible and energising, full of dreamy possibility and an infinite count of interests. Ellis couldn't hold a storm of sulkiness for very long.

The slammed door was more than enough satisfaction, just one of those moments where Ellis performed and continued to be normal regardless of what the inside told them to do. It was just like playing dead, or when an animal might walk confidently by a skulking predator, well-aware it is hiding in the shadows, and well-aware of just where it is going to run if it must. Then the one-track mind would fuse to something else.

The sheets were spread over the thin window sill where Ellis had fallen asleep for the last month, transfixed at a whispering sound which was never quite clear enough to be ignored, like a smell that tickles the nostrils. Like the sound of that tree, an eternal calling which would never go away.

The best thing about that twinkling sound? It was not a noise. Ellis sniffed at that, a short snuffle of the usual nervous giggle erupting as they hopped across the floor and over the small sketches on mismatched stretches of paper, and with a flick, hopping up to the sill, chuckling

10

with a strange anxiety they couldn't quite explain, at the prospect of playing with this strange sound.

Before you ask, and you shouldn't just in case you might get a sulking run of your own. It's not an easy thing, growing up, but with consistent defiance, Ellis wanted to make it more difficult for themselves. Even with growing up hitting so hard, Ellis wasn't filled with the same wants as all the other students.

Those other students flew along like small flies; every conversation was filled with one divine word "fancy". Who fancied who, why did they fancy you? Ellis knew it meant posh or OTT, not something you did. Nobody spoke to Ellis about it though, after they'd ran away from the sex education. Those other students thought it was fear, but it was the noise and nonsense, no idea why the idea of a vagina was a funny thing at all, had nobody seen Attenborough before?!

Ellis had run away then, and there the first twinkles of low mumbling had first caught their attention.

Well, more like a sharp kick to the leg.

Ellis went over that every day, just before they focused on whether the little song was continuing outside. For a second, a sweet trill had cracked out, like a bird-song but not the sharp bursts of noise, a long bounding note. It almost became a vowel. It was so close to becoming a word.

Ellis was a careful runner, they'd been running through forests since they could walk, and you look down and all around as you run, make sure you keep your legs up and you won't trip up. Somehow though, a branch had reached out and clacked with a bang against their leg.

It was a shame they hadn't got any further, Ellis just struggled back home and tried as hard as possible not to limp.

No, Ellis didn't find anyone cute or beautiful. If a girl bent in front of them for some accidental reason, while every other boy was ogling, Ellis would be watching the nearest tree, imagining and exploring what those noises might have meant, or maybe trying to grab Jacob's gaze. Just because something had flashed into their mind, and nobody else would be interested.

Daddy had tried to confront the idea of growing up, but Ellis had no idea why that had to involve "chasing skirt" as Daddy had put it. "I'd rather talk to a squirrel", they'd mumbled and giggled, they were not ready for breeding yet, whichever animal Ellis saw themselves as at the time, it was always the young.

"Right now, I'm a bat. Perfect." Content, they leaned against the sill and waited for the whispering to start. With a small effort, Ellis pushed their ears back and forth just a little, trying to look at the wafting ears before they closed their eyes and listened as hard as they could.

2: RIDICULOUS, IMPOSSIBLE, AND FAR AWAY FROM ORDINARY

Bats have the best hearing in the world. Every time they speak, it's at a higher pitch than any other animal. It's so powerful, they use it to find where their prey is while they fly. If someone is quiet and a bit different, you never know just how special they are.

It didn't take long this time for the whispering to start. Ellis had tried once to tell Daddy about it, but it was thrown away as just a dreamy stupidity, something which couldn't have been. As usual, the parents seemed to throw their own rules on everything that happened, just as if anything that had been or could be was already nicely tucked up in a compartment somewhere.

Anyone who spends long enough listening gets used to the groans and squeaks of their little world around them. Ellis leaned against the window, pushing it open as much as the safety catch would let them. Their eyes were half-crossed in that focussed way people concentrated on something else except what they could see. Their large, light blue eyes flickered softly from side to side as they tried to just hear one that one, sweet sound.

It was impossible of course.

Have you ever tried to just look at a butterfly as it flutters by, surrounded by the lights of a city? You've tried, but just like Ellis was finding right now, it was impossible to just hear one thing. As usual the noise of the world tried to crush the trills of nature in the background.

The house looked out to their one tree in the garden, the robin long gone, but behind that stood the shadows of a town. You had to walk up a short hill first before you got underneath where the whispering waved from. It was like a soft waft of a sweet smell, just the hints of something you could recognise and wanted to know more about.

The sound had been following Ellis around for a long time, but the way it twinkled, it was never a sound you could quite ignore. Ellis didn't even realise but in fact it was only the kind of sound a child could hear. The adults' ears had all dulled to the point of deafness to higher notes. They'd winced from the sounds of alarms more than once while Daddy walked on nonplussed.

They leaned a little further, pushing against the cold frame of the glass and feeling a quick sprint of wind whoosh through their long, blond hair, unkempt when Ellis relaxed after they had come home. Every small house was filled with the glow of electrics, entertainment forced on the other children's laps. Ellis could never sit still long enough, and the world itself was a far more interesting place anyway, just imagining and challenging yourself to find out what made birds murmurate or any of another thousand questions.

If you ever started to think the sound might have gone away, it always felt as if then the whispering song would start again, tantalisingly close.

Cars roared by on the nearby motorway, two men laughed at each other somewhere in the lights. An alarm buzzed from a car even closer than that, it always seemed to be the same one. Ellis listened a little harder, leaning even more.

They were concentrating too much to notice the window wasn't stopping, it was still yawning open slowly.

The sounds of some muffled groaning, a few houses away from that the grunts of an argument and the clatter of a plate smashing against a wall. That was quite ordinary as well, adults never seemed to like it when something new happened. Ellis couldn't wait for the next time something else might go unexpectedly, what fun.

An owl hooted far away, and with that the whistling was the only sound, fizzling just above the breathy moans of the wind, just like when Ellis had tried to do the high notes in the last music class. The notes never quite made it, hovering around the right sound and just sounding slightly off.

The wind seemed to build, but it glided through the branches, not fighting against them for once. It went completely silent, as if it was taking a long overdue breath.

"Ell...is"

Ellis jumped, flicking their head back from what they thought would be a solid glass pane. A sweet perfume they could barely remember stroked their nostrils and disappeared just as soon. The window simply clicked and opened softly. Just in the edge of their eye, Ellis could see the flicker of a feather knocked away from some little creature, twittering as it ran around the corner of their ceiling, clattering against a loose tile, which rolled further toward a crashing tumble.

With a note that just cut at the very top of Ellis' ears, the tile stopped in mid-air, flicking back up into its position with a quick flare.

Ellis didn't care, they were fixated on one thing. Someone had chosen to speak to him, and it wasn't Daddy. Without thinking, they crept slowly out the window, balancing delicately along the fence, pulled as if on a string toward that tempting whisper. *"Ell…is"* it whispered again, a little louder this time as the wind slowly closed that window behind them.

With flowing hair rocking in the wind as it grew again, anyone would have been excused for thinking the ghosts of the forests had made their way outside, just like all the tales said.

-

The cold was starting to just twinkle as the night time faded in. It was just a little dark now with the coming evening. Ellis thought they'd never seen the dark because they always went to bed early, and Daddy wanted them close. Ellis didn't realise they could always see in the dark.

Not like you or me.

We can pick up the faint impressions of buildings, the flashes of some shadow passing us by, just a dark grey screen on the pitch black of darkness. Tonight, there were deep clouds, but Ellis still walked down confidently among the darkness and the shadows. Almost swaggering, trying not to dance too much, just the odd little flicker

Fearless.

When it's daytime, there's no way you can hide away from the attack of sharp eyes looking at every little movement you make. They'd lived under the attack of bullies for a long enough time now, that it had quietened them Ellis down, every little insult pushing the volume of their own voice down a little. It made them consider themselves a little more. Most people walked by Ellis without noticing them, if they were new in school, the quiet one which was always watching and thinking. Ellis didn't find the normal day of rumour interesting enough, and most slang walked straight past them.

Everyone of course, but Jacob.

In the clarity of the night, Ellis could no longer feel vulnerable with nobody watching. Somehow a few hours had gone past listening to the small swishes of words, and from the faint evening, it was a harsh darkness all around them. A black and white day for Ellis, but still filled with tiny noises. A hushed conversation in the middle distance you could almost catch. Ellis kept walking, the wind seemed to be kicking them on now.

The bleak evening had just a hush of a distant moped whining toward the lengths of lights that made up the sets of apartment towers. There were always lights on in those buildings, but it just made Ellis think of a huge bee's nest, something always working away, the building buzzing with a strange energy. They were walking down an alleyway now, as the crow flies ambling along with fences either side of them.

The whispering had stopped, and it was now a stroking wind, if Ellis paused it kicked behind them again and pushed them forward a bit, trying to encourage them to just keep walking.

-

They'd been wandering for a short while, driven by a sense of direction Ellis always felt, but what had been a quiet wander turned into a short jog. Even a fox snuffling in the bins where a crossroads of these alleyways connected didn't stop them now. Ellis could not only see the smoke whispering in the air, in a half second just the smallest impression of a crackling branch.

It was time to get running, tripping and scraping against a fence with a sharp wince while the fox ran the other way. They both seemed to whimper at each other as they collided. Ellis knew it would be another bruise they'd have to hide, but the outside was an honest place, even if it did hurt.

If you put that place of wonder in danger, then you had a child who gained a lot of the animals' fury with them. This was not an animal that was made to run when instincts took over, they fought.

They kept walking, feeling less and less clustered as they wandered further away from the houses, and out into the forest, walking faster and faster with the anticipation of what the voice was saying, regardless of the fire.

They stopped.

It wasn't a fire, it was a twinkling flame.

Ellis paused like a statue, pouted lips left open, gawping at the burning smoke wrapped around some strange wiring of some kind. It was smoking as it burned, flicking to and fro, fidgeting just like Ellis did sometimes when someone was watching. With just long enough time gone, the burning thing ran away, burning at the small branches as it disappeared into the forest. "*Ellis*", it was a sharp sneeze of a small yell this time, and a booming crack echoed as if there was thunder even if it wasn't raining.

A branch hit the back of Ellis' head, and then the wind whooshed past. While they were thrown forward, the odd brain-ache of something not quite being right flickered their eyebrow up and down as they fell to the ground. If the wind was the only thing that made a branch move, how did that happen?

With small shuffling steps, another feathery creature walked just out of sight as Ellis stumbled into a place they would never forget. That one branch, they tumbled down the thorns of a deep, ugly trail, and they pushed their hands over their face, just as they rolled down the ditch and into the darkness. A moment no matter how many years passed, it would be as bright as a dreamed you'd just woken from. Of course, if you thought about it, then it would fade just like all those dreams before it.

Not this time though.

-

Rumours are a powerful thing, and falling into the forest ditch made Ellis freeze rather than just stand up. Sure, most things could be explained, but nobody went in the forest anymore, it had been a long time since anyone had played in here. The fact anyone even called this place a forest showed just how strong rumours were. At best, it was a patch of ugly trees, even in the brightest day that madness of trees was a deep shadow.

Anyone that looked there long enough saw the small figures of something wandering in there. The disappearances had only made those rumours spark like fireworks.

It was lucky if you ran around the forest, especially if you held your breath. If you looked hard enough you might see the small puffs of smoke, and the only things that could live in a forest that dense had to be witches. That's what some said, building tales of just what those witches looked like, and that they were hungry for children, that's where they went.

There were lots of tales, but Ellis saw through them all, how did you get a survival story from someone if there's a monster that's going to eat them all? If they'd seen a knife or watched a snarling beast wait for anyone who'd tripped down this ugly valley.

Ellis might have been done here before, but that was in the day time. Things are so much easier when the daylight is bright and shining. No matter how well you can see. No matter how much you try to believe the logic of Jacob and see the world without its pressing whispers. When you can see the top of the small valley, just seeing a small prickly edge of barbed wire, and the pebbled path back up the steep ramp.

Not in the dark though, this was just like being

swallowed by a great monster, surrounded by the grunting moans a forest always seemed to strain with under the torrent of wind.

 With all that noise, it would be impossible to know if something was creeping up behind you or not. Ellis couldn't bring their eyes open under the impact, leaning into the warm, kind touch of rest. Somehow pushing against the branches without effort, those strange creatures pulled Ellis away from the outside of the trees, just far enough for the moon's glow to disappear and a blanket of black to stretch across their bruised face.

-

Stretching, one hand walked slowly along the cold soil, spidery and cautious with the blurry, waking feeling where the world won't quite come back fast enough. Ellis was crushed under a weight of confusion and fear, nearly panting with the force of it as they woke up.

 That hand struggled and worked over the little pumps of soil, the tiny flickers of branches, and pausing against the cold of something solid. The hand snapped back, but it was pulled forward anyway, needing to know where that voice was coming from. The solid thing was nearly frozen, but it was moving slowly, springing back… and for the shortest second Ellis thought it might be the button to a dungeon.

 This might be how they got you, whispering and hinting at sweet smells, leaving you with something that pushed everyone else away, and then one day, there you are in the forest and all alone, out in the dark when everyone else has gone to bed.

A huge RIIIING splattered out from where Ellis' hand had been, and they sprung up, stepping bodily away from the noise and yelling out without even a glimmer of the old giggle. Smoke fizzed in their nostril, and suddenly it was far too obvious the way out had disappeared.

Just pick a direction and run, they thought, wounded feet screaming in pain as they started to run, feeling the press of heat coming higher and higher. The voice behind it was lost from the snap and crackle of the wood as it buckled under the heat. Their eyes squinted in the smoke, and it was all around them. That crystal must have been summoned by a witch, just to make a fire when the child fell into the pit.

The sure strides turned into struggling steps, flicking and limping as the roots seemed to reach up to spite them. Ellis ducked and huffed, not seeing they were turning around again where the valley started. A length of wood kicked into their stomach, and they leaned against the trunk, like a cornered animal their eyes flicked from side to side just to see if there was a way out.

The branches moved in.

Not fast this time, but slowly and in a single group like one great, endlessly fingered hand.

A cold breath pushed away at the flame, and the wind swelled, but still the flames were biting, and the air was running out. "Please help" Ellis whispered, unable to shift the feeling they were being looked at even in this much danger.

They turned to run, one more time with all the energy they could muster tripping on another driving root and flipping forward, banging their head a second time with a small groan.

With one fell swoop, a tree uprooted itself, grunted and kicked the strange, metal flame up and out of the valley.

A sea of cool air rested back from the flame's wrath.

In a booming groan of an echo that exploded out of the very air, and up from the moist floor, something shouted: "We've finally found one chosen with the art of true Hearing. Thank the Gods you've arrived, Ellis."

-

Try to hold your arm in the air and keep it there. Hold it as still as possible for as long as you can. It starts to hurt quickly, and I bet you can't hold it for more than a couple of minutes. Those great and ancient trees had been holding their arms up for centuries, always groaning and hoping for the wind to move their arm, then groaning a little more.

They would grow leaves so the birds could land and massage them, and when the nights came they could stretch. If you were a brave enough tree, you might wander in the day, or swap places with other trees, talking about the centuries you've been through, and whispering, just in case.

They were mumbling in tree-speak, as was there way, hoping maybe this time they really would be saved by someone with Hearing they'd almost given up on. The young trees that were only a hundred years old were full of hope, jumping around and laughing. Their laughing sounded just like a thousand leaves whistling in the breeze, and when they shook it almost woke Ellis up, and in a gruff voice the eldest tree shook the top of its trunk, waving a branch about and pointing at the feathered people who walked and flew among the trees.

Purple and yellow shots of light burst from the ditch, and in a flash the scene was still.

There were people coming, and they were shouting that they had lost Ellis. The trees felt sad before they hid, remembering the time when anyone would have bowed before they entered a land of greenery. They might even have prayed.

An adult kicked at a thorny bramble to try and find Ellis, punching and pushing back at the woodwork in front of them in their anger, shining torches in faces which shrunk away just in time. There Daddy caught Ellis, bruised and restful, with just the hint of a smile on their face.

It was time to go home, and now Ellis had proved themselves, the Trees and all that served them wouldn't be letting them go.

3: A CUDDLE TO STAY FREE

It is not just people that talk to each other. We have seen Chimps that have their own sign language to each other, with signs which can ask for apology and food. If you take the time, you can teach gorillas human language through sign, they're smart enough. It's always worth talking about anything that makes you feel sad, or anything you might need.

It was a cold room, even Ellis could pick that up. It was not the kind of cold which hit you in a sharp shiver or numbed you completely. It was the type which just struck you in little spikes of small, fussy fidgeting as if you were just trying to catch some warmth. Ellis didn't question things, there was just enough energy to focus on everything and remember it, just about keeping up with what everyone else just experienced with good humour and ease.

Being the only child in the cold, sterile waiting room, Ellis allowed just a little bit of normal behaviour to come through in small giggles while a small conversation seemed to bubble silently with just that high giggle popping from the sweeping feet which signified complete happiness, not even checking around to see if anyone else had come in the room.

Their ears twitched like a rabbit, and every couple of seconds, their nose sniffled too. Yet outside of Ellis' notice, the smooth shuffling of a psychiatrists' sandals stroked along the floor's surface. The beak of a nose flicked back from Ellis in a flinch of some other giggly answer, startling them both. The doctor was much quicker to recover, a long, toothy smile stretching out from below two sharp, hopeful eyes. He was squinting just a little as his sharp gaze swept upon even the smallest indication or subtlest behaviour.

A thin eyebrow curved up with Ellis' quick scan scrolling along his white name tag, and down along the white overalls and back up directly into the doctors' eyes. Ellis did not blink first, the doctor did, who was already realising he'd lost the initiative.

"Freddy doeshn't shound like a shurname, what forename do you have which shtarts with 'A'?"

"You are right sonny, but those name tags are expensive, and the people who write them make a few mistakes. Just like any of us might. They didn't know how to spell my name. I tried to tell them it was F-R-E-D-E, which is Fred with an 'E'. I can only guess the connection must have been bad. It seems you've forgotten you can call me Albert. Please, come in as it's time I spoke to you, I can't learn everything about you from Daddy."

Albert hummed as he walked away, shuffling a little as he walked, grabbing both hands behind his back, and humming in a comforting way Ellis couldn't help but follow. It reminded Ellis of something else he'd thought so impossible which had faded over the last few days, and inspired, Ellis skipped just a little before entering the room.

The medical room was filled with smiling pictures and

health advice on white cabinets. Ellis liked it simply for the green glow that came from the nearby tree they looked out on. His parents knew why, but nobody else knew how taking him away from the greenery made him sick. Albert hadn't given up like the others, he kept trying to understand what made Ellis tick. Ellis always gifted him with a smile just to show how much that meant.

"Sonny, you might forget my name, but I know actions are far louder to you than anything. Especially the fun ones." The smirk Albert tried to share was mirrored for a second, but Ellis didn't feel like telling them about the impossible was a good idea, something was telling them not to. "Please take me through the strongest moment of your last month in your view. Your Daddy told me you ran away. I know the truth. You were running toward something, and the curiosity got the better of you. Take your time, and tell me everything just as you saw it."

Ellis couldn't see the gap between their dream, or the real thing in the dull evening. Both were flashes of strange feathered things, the huge trees exuding age and power, and far more birds than they'd ever seen in one place before. Ellis didn't know, but I can tell you the dreams weren't their own, running to something in the sky. It pulsed out of the sky like the leaves grow, skipping and then flying right to the top of some beautiful spire.

Then there was the memory of following the flashes of whispering, the running figures just out of sight when Ellis looked straight at them. Elis had learned one thing with this strange man though, nothing they said was true, it was all just dreams. Ellis didn't mind though, this time it was something so real, something they had reached out and touched, how could Freddy deny that?

Ellis did their usual trick, staring down at albert in a cautious way, side on just like a deer might, wary and only just in their seat.

"Ellis? I need something from you, sonny"

This time, Ellis couldn't storm out. This time they weren't allowed to show feelings that were too strong, they couldn't express themselves too strongly, or Albert would have another firm word with Daddy and he'd look scared again. Scared as if the end of the world was just about to happen, but of course he couldn't tell you anything about it, he would just stare hard at the middle distance, and take a little longer to do something that usual, as if a huge weight was pressing down on his back.

Ellis stared, unable to look away from the long, stretching nose that made up most of Albert's face. It was the kind of face you can only get with the sheer weight of years, the deep wrinkles and a balding head sparked at Ellis' mind. There was no other animal. It was impossible to get away from it.

Albert was a vulture.

An ugly vulture at that.

Ellis held their breath, trying to come up with a sensible way to explain it as the doctor's face seemed to morph and stretch. Just a trick of the light seemed to be what Daddy always said whenever there was a story about another ghost sighting, close to the ditch or that forest people didn't even gossip about anymore. No, that wouldn't be enough. The pause was enough of a giveaway, and the vulture was leaning further and further forward in his seat, waiting for his prey to say something.

Albert had such short, stubby hands. Not like the long, stretching fingers Ellis had. No, they were just long enough to grab rabbits and bits of meat, but not enough to hug you. Just enough to hurt. Elis tried as hard as they could to sound sensible, forcing away the lisp and concentrating so hard, they had to close their eyes, just to be sure exactly the right words came out.

To make sure at least the vulture would be dazed enough, he might have to think about his answer, not drone on about what must have been a dream.

"You were right, I was running toward something. You won't believe me, but I had help. The most I can tell is they must have been fairies or something else that opened my window, though maybe its catch was just broken. They wouldn't let me see them for long enough, they know I'm smart enough to name a bird just from its call, so I'd know they weren't any kind of animal far too quickly. They helped me out because something out in the woods kept whispering at me, and it's still whispering now. It might be something in the wind though." The loud sigh came from Albert so quickly when Ellis started, it could have almost started before they talked, just as if every child might say something silly just by opening their mouths. It just made Ellis think about how funny it was even a vulture didn't like the taste of something.

Ellis giggled to himself, and Albert sat back, hoping he was past the fun and games.

"So, I kept walking toward it, there was a small puff of smoke coming from the trees now and I wanted to run and get it, it was an evil flame and I didn't like it. I don't know what happened in between, but I fell into a ditch, and ran from the flame when I was in there. The flame was coming closer, you've hurt about the fire. It wasn't hot or burning, I could tell it was thinking and hungry, feeding on the air in front of me.

"I tried to run again, but that time I was knocked down I didn't try and get back up. A tree pulled itself out of the roots, groaned and kicked the flame right out the woods, telling me how happy it was I had finally listened. I almost forgot, they were calling my name too. You've told me before though, all about what can happen when you hit your head."

Albert left the room, and slammed his arty chair onto the floor in a spark of inspiration. Ellis followed, and was shocked to see Daddy sat in a seat, squeezed right into the cushions with strained shoulders. One small tear stained the top corner of his right cheek, but Ellis just wandered if it was a trick of the light. It had been a long time since Daddy had let himself cry. *Why is he staring so hard at me? I've never seen him frowning like that since Mum disappeared,* Ellis thought, scrambling for their own seat and feeling just as weak as they had when the sharp glow of that flame had pushed against their cheek.

-

Ellis didn't understand what was supposed to have happened, even if they had been sat there, the words hadn't made any sense. It was meant to be something important and very serious, but all they knew was Daddy wasn't the same as before, the frown hadn't gone anywhere, hours later that night. The great thing about people Ellis found was they were just like animals when they were responding to somebody's wounds. A quick hug and everything was going to be OK. Ellis couldn't help it, but they would even coo just a little at whatever he was hugging, the other person, or the nervous animal wouldn't say anything, but it was obvious to Ellis they were happier for it.

Daddy even sighed this time.

The last time he had sighed, Mum wasn't with them anymore.

Now, he was saying something about Ellis not going away, and having to behave just like the other children. Ellis had started to sulk, they'd seen these pills before and all it did was kill any senses and cool the days to be nothing but the boring feelings just the adults must feel in their entire lives. Ellis couldn't think anything about what might happen in the future when they had to be like that.

They stared down at the pills and knew there was no choice, the way Daddy kept saying this was their "last chance", and no matter what that was supposed to mean, it was impossible to ignore the threat. Honestly, Ellis had tried to listen, tried to concentrate for once, but there was a squirrel out there on the tree.

Well, there had been no other way, Ellis had been stuck staring at the squirrel, learning its behaviours, and checking it against all the other squirrels. No two moved the same, and this one was a steady, silent type. It even seemed to pause and stand on the branches, staring out along the winds while they blew, leaning into the breaths of wind, as if it was patiently waiting for something.

Ellis was happy to just think it was thinking about all its life's problems.

Most of all, Ellis was waiting for one of those other friends to come back and play, something else to get them away from the storm of an argument that grew behind them. Elis kept hearing their name, not thinking what the problem might be, but knowing it was their fault, just like before when Mum was ill, and before she disappeared everyone else would tell them they were doing too much, they were too loud with far too much energy for someone that wasn't well.

Ellis had tried these pills, but for once it was impossible to get away from the coming enemies,

That's what Daddy made it feel like sometimes, just like he was now, while they walked to school. They never shared a journey to school together, Ellis walked himself to school now they were all grown up. Daddy made sure of it this time though, he even held hands with Ellis to make sure they didn't walk too far apart. Just to make sure they wouldn't wander off, as if lateness couldn't possibly be alright today.

Ellis felt another twist in their stomach, the same worry which came every time they looked down at the pink pills and shook them, knowing it was time to taste another bitter piece of medicine. They just hoped Jacob would be there, without him Ellis was lost, and all the bullies felt a lot more confident when it was just one person left behind.

Ellis grunted at a blow to their arm, someone walking the other way finding out just what happens if you get in the way of Daddy when he has one thing on his mind. All that Ellis could work out was from that vulture poking at their bruises and asking why it was happening, at just what they really meant from the whispering, and always as if Ellis was hiding behind games of imagining.

They weren't supposed to talk about it now. Ellis had been told two things, and Daddy was making sure the day would start that way anyway. "Don't tell anyone about the dreams you've been having, and make sure you try to be as much like the other children as you can. Otherwise, I can't help what might happen next." He had shaken his head while he said it, just to show stupid he thought it was, but hoping Ellis would understand the weight he would have to shoulder, just to keeping being special.

Ellis would try his hardest, but there were things waiting to make sure Ellis wasn't deaf to their voices, driven by blind hope. They stayed away from the cold, concrete path Ellis walked down, sprinting and leaping to keep up. Ellis half-ran while Daddy pulled them forward. He was just making sure they were not late this time. Making sure they were as normal as possible.

Those strange creatures had been called a lot of things

33

before; fairies, spirits, sprites, elves, pixies, maybe even angels, and far more words besides. Most of those words were lost in languages lost in time. As Ellis walked, and tried as hard as they could to look around and take in the overhanging trees, the little sprites ran delicately along the branches. Keeping up, but keeping out of sight.

The little sprites, hiding behind leaves, jumped along, flipping and diving without bumping the branches at all. Just trying to catch Ellis's attention, just enough to let them know something dangerous was coming to get them, but Ellis was far too busy to hear it, and then so soon they were at the school.

Daddy hugged Ellis again, right outside the school, embracing gruffly this time with a firm handshake. Daddy tried his hardest to pass the bag of pills between the two of them quietly between the handshake, but they tumbled to the ground. In that small moment, feeling sharp eyes on them both, Ellis was locked into the school world now, so far apart from swaggering just two nights ago.

The sprites hovered on the edge of the gate where the trees ended, one of the old oaks that stood right at the ornate entrance shaking itself from the sprites feet pushing against its trunk. There were a hundred other students rushing in, always a storm of noise that seemed to be far too many children for one school. Under all that rumbling, the ancient tree could tell those sprites off quietly enough.

For anyone without the old Hearing, it just sounded like

autumn was coming far too early, as a flurry of leaves slowly fell to the ground. Ellis waved at Daddy, making sure to force a smile, but not make it too obvious it was forced. As usual, Ellis failed at that, looking like a clown, or someone that was far too cold not to have a strange expression where only Ellis's mouth moved in a sign of joy.

It was school after all.

No matter how good school could be, it couldn't beat the weekend.

4: THERE ARE NO WRONG ANSWERS

When humans and apes are very young, they can recognise both species just as easily. With time, all apes – or all people – end up looking the same. Which one just depends on which one brings you up more!

"Class, calmly now if you can. Let's keep everything under control now…", Ellis always wondered if the teachers really thought they had anything under control, or if they just couldn't help but say it. Like a cow saying "Moo.". They were skulking at the back, staring out the window and waiting for everyone else to go quiet. Ellis had accepted the bullies taking their pills, most of the exchanges were quick and harsh now. They had some hidden anyway.

That usually happened with fun new things, especially if you learned to hide them. Jacob was there today, so they didn't try to find any money on them, Daddy paid that monthly straight to the school. Ellis had stopped bringing nice shoes, they'd swapped those long ago.

Ellis scrambled about with the worst pens, not even tutting this time as the ink spilt across a small sketch of what they could just remember from that one night.

Only Jacob would believe them, they just needed an opportunity to do something together. School would have to be over first, at least it was their last lesson now. Ellis looked over at Jacob, trying to do something else with a set of paperclips, Ellis knew he was trying to build a bridge. It didn't matter that they liked different things,

Jacob cared.

"Today, we are learning about the dangers of the outside world, and why we shouldn't wander away from the paths you've had marked out for you. I don't want to alarm anybody too much, but you must have heard the stories about the children who have gone missing. Some of them have ended up in hospital. We still haven't found them all.

"The most important thing for this school is that you don't become one of those children. Yes, there are stories, but as you grow up, you should learn about the real world. Just to be prepared." It was a special teacher. One that whispered when she spoke. It was such a soft voice, it was impossible for every student to pay any attention, and at least one of them would not stay awake.

All she had to say was "missing children", and it made everyone alert though, they leaned forward, waiting to find out just what they were supposed to be learning this time.

There might have been stories, but for a few weeks now, everyone couldn't help but notice how close the idea of danger was getting for places of fun when they were all just children. Anything to help them would be something they could not ignore. The hubbub grew again as the substitute teacher, Mrs Hill, grabbed for a video player, pulling at the heavy box to get it into the room.

One of her hands slapped up to catch the heavy screen as it almost flicked off the stand, and with a few more tumbling clicks, the TV was ready.

"Don't worry about taking notes, just like all my lessons there isn't a test, just a few exercises to see how close you are to the views you're about to see. Just like with any opinion, you can't get anything wrong, just give us an answer which isn't the best. Then we can talk all about where your differences might be.

"I know some of you struggle with this, that's OK. It's better to find it hard now than when you're confronted with the situation out there. I'm not there to talk in your ear.

"One final thing before I forget", her head snapped a little oddly to the side, as if something was whispering in her ear, and Ellis noticed how strangely yellow her eyes were, "please remember the competition to name one of our new statues is still open, so any suggestions can be given. If you win, you get a chance to go to the big city where they are all being made."

-

The television fizzled and sparked a little, just a black and white mess squeaking to a fun pop, and everyone jumped back a little in a show of fright. Were they really scared? Of course not, they were just pretending just playing so that the teacher would ask the question which came next.

"Do any of you know why this TV is broken? The last class I was in watched a film just fine, and now something's wrong. What did we learn last week, class?"

"You should never lie", the class repeated, every pupil but Ellis and Jacob had a small smile on their face. They knew what would happen next.

One hand rose confidently from the back of the class, and the teacher focussed on the student, one eyebrow creeping up and up for a couple of seconds just before she said, "Do you have something you need to tell me, Sandra?"

They all did, and even if the class was now quietly giggling to itself, the teacher didn't seem to notice or question why, she was just wanting a simple answer and a way out of this issue being her fault.

"I saw Jacob playing near the TV when we came in from lunch time. I don't know what pointy things he was using, but he has broken some things before." Another student, Harry, kicked at the back of Jacob's chair, and he stumbled in his seat, kicking away at a small model he'd been making out of paperclips, while he tried gruffly to hide it away.

Jacob just mumbled "sorry", knowing what was coming next, detention. The teacher shuffled along, back behind the TV and pushing it away. Jacob skulked and turned behind him, shaking his head at Ellis and ignoring the jibes aimed at him, focussing on a tunnel of friendship as the best thing they had in a school of wild people.

-

"OK class, with the TV down, we will have to try an old-fashioned route. I am going to set you a question, and I want you to pick one of the options. You can chat amongst yourselves. The most important thing is you think about the current situation, and those missing children. What your parents have taught you about the dangers of the wild world out there, and people we can't trust." Her voice wasn't quite as whispering now, her voice had gotten cold, and sharp.

As she walked from side to side, she placed a green sheet of A5 paper onto Jacob's desk, planting it with one hand quite firmly down on the desk, with a slam that surprised even her. She stepped back a little, looking up at the class. Her eyes glowed strangely again.

"Please push your desks out into a circle, and we will start when you are ready." The students stood up, nearly in unison, glad to be up and free to talk for a few seconds. Most of them lifted their desks easily, placing them to the edge of the long room, and standing in the middle.

Ellis was struggling with their desk, as usual, not quite able to pick it up or work out how they were supposed to be picked up so easily, it was a solid weight, and Ellis was always surprised at times like these when they just didn't have the power a lot of other people just seemed to naturally have.

Thankfully, this time they hadn't noticed, they weren't interested in that, given the time to chat to each other, and Ellis found it impossible not to compare the behaviour to chimps. At least this time they weren't waving their butts at each other. He chuckled a tiny bit, completely sure in themselves, Jacob would be here soon enough.

Ellis was reminded of Daddy when he just saw Jacob's hands. They were solid potato wedges, usually with a few burn marks cursing the pale skin. Ellis was tanned from all the running around outside where Jacob was pale. The big hands grasped the other side of the two-person desk, both Jacob and Ellis were the only ones that didn't have a partner to sit next to. The teachers always thought it was because of the mess they made.

They were told not to push Ellis and Jacob together, you wouldn't get any focus out of them. They filled the mess of books, notes, clips and anything else to try and hide there was a space between them and the next table. In the middle of the tables there was usually an aisle, so it was much harder to talk to anyone else. Not that anyone but Jacob would talk to them anyway.

Together, they pulled the desk to the edge, and sat down on it, skulking down and laughing to one another with the fascination Ellis had with a butterfly he could make with his two hands. Jacob still couldn't do it. That was still funny.

The rest of the class turned away from him, and kept in their closer circles of friends, loudly laughing at each other, loudly exclaiming names across the spaces, and even if they noticed, pointing at Jacob and Ellis and laughing at something which they'd done wrong.

Fashions moved along, and right now all of them were standing and relaxing with upturned shirt sleeves and no socks. Ellis and Jacob just followed the uniform, and didn't understand any reason to change that just because some other pupil was doing it. They laughed as Ellis sat back and revealed of all things, he was wearing the black socks you were supposed to.

While Mrs Hill gathered her notes, Ellis and Jacob

played the shortest game of snap. They'd both collected detention slips, Ellis would not cut into an animal to learn anything. Especially because it was already in a book. Neither of them wanted these lessons, if you knew how to manage life's challenges yourself, are you still supposed to listen to the teacher?

The answer is yes, but Ellis and Jacob just couldn't change their mind to see the world the way the teachers wanted. As Mrs Hill stood demanding silence, they both sighed and looked at each other. They knew they were going to get this wrong.

-

"OK, it doesn't seem like we are all getting the message I'm trying to explain. Teachers and Policemen are people you should trust. Staying in groups is the best thing you can do. If you are ever confused or scared you should look for an adult, you know and can trust. They will help you, but the best choice of all is to stay away from anything dangerous.

"There is little need to put yourself in danger, when there are so many other good things you could be doing. Like your homework!" She tried a joke, and most of the group groaned at the comment. Ellis and Jacob were still struggling with the question. Somehow the right answer to seeing a bare wire was not to just walk around the trail and through the woods.

Nor was it to walk carefully past the wire, maybe even trying to fix it.

No, you were supposed to run away and tell the

authorities all about it.

They were given the chance to change their mind. They went from option 2 to the first option, Jacob having been taught more about nature than he had told Ellis about electrics. They still got it wrong. Two people in the big crowd laughed, and the teacher only tutted and shook her head with a little smirk. All to get rid of the sound, dismissing the bullying as if everything that is ever mocked is in on the joke.

Both Ellis and Jacob had spent many hours talking about their choices to Mrs Hill, Mr Walker and the head of the year Miss Courtney. No teacher believed they were destroying their children, leaving them vulnerable to the predators out there. The world wasn't like that, there weren't really any brave heroes, and they would answer the questions the same as the students, it was OK to depend on the state and the people in power.

It was careers week soon, and they had a test coming up to determine where they would be when they were an adult. Every time they got one of these lessons wrong, they were just told they just needed to think.

"The problem is the rest of you don't" Jacob had stated. For once, he hadn't mumbled. Yes, it cost him a week of detention, but from his smirk, it was obvious he didn't care.

Between each question, Ellis and Jacob tried to find out what might have been wrong with people, why did the teacher have to go back to her computer to check the right answer? Why did creative thinking become something wrong, when last year it was encouraged?

They had started with laughter at how strange things were, just like you were on your own little adventure. Even more odd how people didn't even notice what was happening. They'd started the year telling everyone to be themselves, dreaming to be the best they could, and to take control of their life.

The little giggles turned to frowns and groaning to themselves when they got another question wrong, shrinking a little bit more each time. While they waited for what must have been the last question, they leaned against the side of a desk, overwhelmed by it all. Always aware of being the only two to get it wrong.

"This will be the last question, and it has effected a few of you recently. If you hear a policeman yell, and you walk around the path to see there is a big animal growling at the policeman who is holding his hand in pain. What should you do next?

"Is it 1, don't engage with the situation, turn around? 2, make sure you protect the animal, it would only be growling to protect itself? Or finally 3, scare the animal off and guide the policeman to the nearest A&E?"

In each corner of the room was a big number stuck to the wall, in a simple triangle, and most of the group walked to the corner marked "1".

Ellis and Jacob were still standing in the middle of the room. Jacob was defiant now. It was something they didn't have in common, Ellis would rather skulk and walk to the right answer, but when Jacob was defiant, they squeezed each other's hands for a short second, and as Ellis's heart fluttered, he felt strong enough to stand there too.

Ellis was learning animals could behave differently, against their specie. He'd seen lions running away from their prey, and parrots which wouldn't talk back to you no matter how much you trained them. The school seemed to try and make him like the rest of his pack, but in one gesture he showed the two of them were enough of a pack.

Ellis raised a "4" shakily in the air with his fingers. "4, it is imposshible. The shituation wouldn't happen, and you're not letting anyone ashk a question about why it had happened.

"Animalsh either stay away from you, or they are domeshticated. If they are domeshtic, they won't bite you, unless you do shomething wrong. If it bit you then it would either shulk with its ears down, or it would run. Animalsh don't just jump out of the dark to a human to attack it, you told me there are no monsters out there. They know we're the biggest predator."

Ellis was shaking from all the eyes looking at them, but their voice had held. Without realising it, they hid just a little behind Jacob who was must closer to raising a fist. Ellis's voice had shaken and squeaked by the end, but at least it hadn't disappeared. That was the most anyone had heard from either of them. The fact he lisped made the students lose themselves in a hysteric fit of silent giggles, just behind Mrs Hill.

Ellis sat down from the impact of it, the teacher could only do one thing. "We'll talk about this while you're in detention, I'm glad the rest of you have learned to be safe. The bell is just about to ring, if you don't have any detentions or further questions, you may go."

Mrs Hill was not looking away from the two of them, when they were together though, you wouldn't catch them looking away or backing down. Jacob put one hand behind himself, and Ellis slapped it in a gesture of companionship. With a little jump, they walked together to detention.

You couldn't put out a fire by ignoring it, or putting it in a room for a short time.

5: TIME TOGETHER IS TWICE AS GOOD

Dogs are secret superheroes, if you've ever used a whistle for dogs, you're not going to hear it, but the dog will react. They can learn to do a lot of tricks like dancing and flips. Some dogs out there have a sense of smell 100,000 times more powerful than your own. If you have a dog, see how many tricks you can teach it!

Detention. Daddy wouldn't mind because he wouldn't know. They could just say they'd been playing but Ellis would make sure to call it "hanging out" so Daddy smiled, and didn't need to question the idea anymore. The other students had walked past, back by and along again, laughing and mocking with shrill voices for anything Jacob and Ellis had done that day.

That was punishment enough, Ellis hated being in a cage like this, but even if it wasn't their detention this time, those two friends would share everything. There were a group of tough kids at the front of the class, and a strict teacher reading a book. The funniest part was the only punishment the school thought they needed to just be bored for long enough and they'd be taught a lesson. When you came into the room your phones were taken off you, and they listened for any chatter.

It always took Jacob and Ellis longer to get through, the teacher never believed they didn't have a phone until they showed her all their empty pockets. All you had to do was sit, they wouldn't even let you do homework, you just had to sit in silence and that was all you were left with.

Jacob and Ellis whispered to each other, they were just quiet enough to stop the teacher watching. Just until the teacher fell asleep of course, it didn't take her very long and Ellis always wondered why she kept trying to read that same book every time if it just sent her asleep. Neither Ellis or Jacob could remember the last time she'd turned a page.

This time, it was Ellis who had something to talk about, and they nearly buzzed with excitement there was someone to share the mystery with. Ellis looked at the clock as it turned to 16:00. It was time for another calming pill.

The whole day had been a slow, groggy one. Ellis hadn't been able to hear any whispering, or even feel anything. Not even a second had been spent staring outside. The best part had been the pushing and name-calling hadn't hurt, and Ellis had easily ignored it for once. In a horrible way, each time they could just hear the voices, and then the time came to take more medicine, and everything disappeared again behind a thick fog. Ellis was just glad the last lesson had happened while the medicine was wearing off.

Ellis span in their chair, looking at Jacob bending over his paperclips again, they had been allowed into the room, because what reason would you have for banning someone access just because they had a wad of paperclips in a bag? Jacob was working away impatiently, bending right over the little clips.

Ellis stood next to Jacob, staring down at the bridge he

was trying to build. With just a small tap, Jacob was aware, and they were looking right at each other. They both smiled at the fact they just had some more time together. Especially time away from those bullies.

Being quiet they crept toward the window, led by Ellis as they flicked their head to the window subtly, and Jacob was happy for the challenge.

Where Ellis was made for nature and all its creatures, Jacob was made for machines, and getting past any human inventions that got in their way. They saw the world completely differently, Ellis as a moving, emotional world full of meaning and strength. Jacob saw the world as a solid structure of rules and laws that couldn't be broken. Just manipulated.

Jacob kneeled against the high window, and while Ellis stared at some feathered creature watching him, the tablets were forgotten. Instead, Ellis was convinced it was more than just a fidgeting bird. Jacob was looking at the lock instead, imagining the inside of it. He could see the whole mechanism, and he was pushed to try and get out with Ellis back to normal, seeing the spark back in their eyes.

The two friends struggled sometimes to understand how the other one saw the world. They were happy to try, and they allowed each other to get things wrong, they enjoyed how different the two of them were. It was a fun challenge to learn. Right now, it was another time for fun, just another adventure, and as usual they didn't feel the need to ask questions to each other, the trust was strong enough for them.

Jacob had a great mind's eye, staring into space just like Ellis did when he was listening for that whisper. In fact, Ellis was listening right now, just trying to find the voices, and he was looking out at the field and further which surrounded the school.

If you were looking in at them from the window outside, they wouldn't have noticed you.

Jacob straightened a clip with one hand, dexterously dragging the thin metal into a small spike. He did it over and over, and then with his small blade he pinched it all together, and it all fell to the window sill. Some of it rolled into the sink of the science lab, and Ellis was quick to help. Jacob was already bending back over his desk.

At the front, the teacher, Mrs Crow, a name that was very true, and a student were lost in an argument. It was the same student as every other time. Her name was Crystal, and she made sure to shine as much as she could for all to see. You would know just where she was from the shrill arguments that came out of her, the harsh crying which always came as an answer to any kind of control.

Ellis heard her in the same ways as a barking dog, their owner trying to get the dog to calm down, but it just kept barking without listening to you. Ellis would mumble just that, and was woken up from their imagining by the sheer force of a clawed slap as Crystal became more theatrical. All that did was keep the idea stuck in Ellis's mind of a dog that needed more training.

Jacob was just glad of it, he smirked at the same game

being played out just like every other time, at least this time the two good friends are finally getting somewhere. With a little clasp of another clip, Jacob stared at the little hook he'd made, admiring it not because he'd made it, but a strange feeling he got sometimes this was exactly what the window was waiting for, and some other being was telling him this was just right.

The hook clipped into the small key slot, and with a fiddle, Jacob's tongue poked out as he really concentrated. The lock clicked, and as the window struggled open and Jacob leaned out, they were both ever so glad Crystal slammed her bag down to the floor. She had decided it was time to shout and yelp about some great injustice this detention must obviously be for such a lovely girl as herself.

They were free as the window opened quickly with a tight, single squeak. Even Jacob could hear the whistle catching the wind through the branches. They might have seen the sound differently, but it didn't make them any less interested than each other.

-

"You're the only one I can trusht with thish..." Ellis stated simply while they hid in the small trees just outside the school's playground. Ellis was shaking a little from the cold, as they pulled the school shirt unsteadily up. Cold under the small light under the trees. Mostly though, they shook for the sheer nerves of showing the bruises they hadn't bothered to cover.

The dark bruises on their face could be easily covered by their hair. In one motion as they walked away from the school, their hair had gone up into a tight ponytail, clasped tightly behind them, and the bruise shone quite brightly. Ellis had gotten into a lot of fights over the last few weeks, and it was something they all ignored.

Now though, Ellis clasped their shirt by their neck, tight with anxiety and closing their eyes at what Jacob might say. "What happened?" he gruffly mumbled, most of his words coming out in a noise quite like an engine that hadn't quite got going. Jacob knew Ellis was thin, so the little bump of their ribs didn't surprise him.

Ellis pulled the shirt down, tucked it in and flicked a hand forward in an act of dismission, saying it was nothing. They had walked quickly to the far edge of the playground and those trees, but now it was time to completely escape. Grabbing at the weak metal fence and bending the space open for each other, disappearing as they'd seen many students do before in lunch time, or a particularly annoying lesson.

They were in a tight alleyway of branches and thorns, an old bike wheel spinning as Jacob kicked it, a flurry of playing balls and frisbees in the green light were tripping hazards. The whole space would be far too small for any adult to walk through, it would be the kind of place where they would give up on following you, and hope they could walk around to find you.

The two of them walked through, dodging the sharp thorns and slowly stepping through, knowing they'd pop out just by the busy shops. Imagining it was a game, they both bent down as they left the greenery, shedding leaves and throwing a Frisbee between each other. It was a shiny one that glowed in the sunlight.

They ran when they saw an adult, hiding and panting and laughing. It was a fun game to make, but the tension in Ellis's heart was growing as they came closer to that ditch again. It was a hard thing to prove yourself in front of a friend, even if you trusted them. Jacob enjoyed following rules, and he didn't enjoy going against them unless he knew why. They were both pulling each other on while they crept and ran, pushed on by pure nervous energy and trust.

So, they kept wandering, pausing by every tree, and trying to look any odd-looking branch and find the creatures Ellis talked about in small, breathy statements. Jacob was trying to explain away the idea of those magical trees. "Maybe you were too tired that day, and you went wandering into the woods? Maybe it was just the wind playing games?" Jacob would wander, but most of the time he would stop himself talking. He knew how much Ellis disliked those kinds of questions.

They were both thinking about the missing children, both in small hiccups of hope thinking perhaps they'd be the ones to save the missing. They'd heard a lot of things about the huge forest further away to the north, so close to the mysterious city. Neither of them were going to walk that way this time, Jacob was only going to do go there if two things became true.

Only if Ellis was there, and only if he sees enough proof this magic is real. He had an open mind, it was just far less open than Ellis. Plenty of times it had stopped the two of them doing something mad, just from Jacob taking the time to check the river wasn't too rampant before they swam.

Jacob didn't say it, but the only reason he thought Ellis had this dream was from being without him.

As they ran, both saw things they weren't quite sure of, small glimpses that while the adults were busy, the magic of the world might be happy to show itself. When you play to hide and run about, together, they had a system that you had to take it in turns to look away from cover, and just check that the coast is clear. Just for fun, as they got more nervous they started to make each other jump, and whispered in the background "Did you see that?"

They would run and play that the other was being abandoned, they were going to be caught, and each had their plan to get away.

Jacob was ready to download himself into a computer, Ellis would always giggle so much from the idea of him being a page you could browse to. Ellis had found a CD once on one of these days away, and shook it in Jacob's face, comparing them for size and giggling all the way.

Jacob still had it in his bag, just in case.

Even though Jacob had told himself it was just a lie, he'd watched a dog being walked, and gaped for a second as a tree trunk seemed quite quickly to have light just underneath where the trunk had been. The sunlight seemed to be stronger than the usual light, a green glow, and with a shake and small rumble the tree must have moved. He hadn't leaned out behind a hedge with the sun in his eyes.

Ellis would run into the forest and commune with the animals, even though they both laughed about it, Ellis was sure it was possible they could do it. Nature always felt like the most comfortable place in the world. The further Ellis ran, the more they felt happy and warmer on the inside.

By the end, Ellis was incapable of not smiling by the time they were looking at the ditch, the entrance just a small flurry of hedges sprouting out of what anybody who lived here would know was the witch's ditch.

All the rumours and stories came back at them then, just like pushing your door after you've come back from holiday, too much information to take in at one point.

They both sat down, feigning tiredness even if they had run more than ten miles multiple times before, just for fun. They were shackled by the potential of what could be coming. It was worse because from the angle of their town, you could see the small ditch which was like the opening of someone's mouth if they'd dug themselves a hole. More than just that though, you could see beyond, and up a tall hill behind that was a deeper, dark forest.

They both had the imagination to turn the two clumps on that great big hill into huge, gawping eyes. There were small vibrations in the ground below, from a factory nearby. Looking out at the face in front of them, it felt as if it was grumbling, just to try and get up and talk. It made Ellis and Jacob feel very small.

-

A long way away, a ringing pulse was keeping dogs up at night. It was a noise a lot like the sound a fly makes as it flies past you. Not the loud buzz you'd get if it was right up against your face, but the little whisper you get when it's the other side of the room.

Just enough of a noise to wake you, and make you flick at your head. Not loud enough to tell you where the fly was though. It whined and built up to a high crescendo, only to disappear again. Every time it whined, the note was longer and higher pitched.

There was no way the dogs were going to sleep.

This far away, there wasn't a few houses in a small town, it was the city. This was a city in the middle of the towns, and when Ellis walked to the top of the hills that surrounded GreenView where they lived, you could see the glow of the city from there, just on the horizon as a row of twinkling lights.

If you looked hard enough, you'd notice one of the reds glowed red for just half a second, off for three seconds or so, and then it flashed with the flicker of light.

It was as regular as a baby's pulse.

That's just what it was.

The high tower of a skyscraper flickered like this in a small corner. Just as the building bent up like a swan's neck, it sat and flashed, hiding in a glowing nest just out of sight. It was time for the small animal inside to wake up.

At early evening, people are too busy to believe themselves if they see something fly against the starlight. This time it was just the same, just as the wings flapped past a relaxing taxi driver felt the sharp waft of wind rush past him.

He looked up, patting and shaking his head. He frowned up at the darkness, guessing maybe the small yelp could have been a plane, or trying some way to tell himself nothing strange was happening.

The dark thing flew and flapped its small wings, uncertain and waiting for its parent to answer their small calls. Each question was another whine, and the dogs whined back with their own bark, confused and running back and forth in confusion.

Soon enough, the sound disappeared as the winged animal fled, driven by instinct to get away from the bright lights and find somewhere comfortable to grow and learn.

Deep down in the city, another rumble swelled and shook, and the little thing was glad to hear its parent telling it this way was safe.

As it broke free of the city, it began to burn with its bright tail light, small twinkles of strange purple and green sparks glowing bright and shining. It was running right for the forest of GreenView, hearing the small calls of its fellow beasts, and happily burning a firework behind it. Just as small crystals and other creatures welcomed it home. The trees shook in anger at this attack, but they had to bide their time.

The Hearer was weak right now, but they would learn just how strong they could be with time.

The bird called and whispered to its friends, looking at the green sprites which ran away. It jumped up, trying to chase the small creature through the forest. The trees gave it no space, an ancient oak groaning as it burned from a small wound. The ugly bird fell from the branch and groaned, stretching out and growing under its own flaming, small creatures.

They flew right over Ellis and Jacob, as they played neither realised just what they were stepping into.

The ancient trees were the parents, and even those sages couldn't hear the approaching monster growing hungrier every day, pushing at the very ceiling of the earth around him. Very quickly, another two red lights twinkled in the city, and this time it was just the bats that would be annoyed.

The Unholy -as this monster was named - was growing smarter.

-

It had been two days since Ellis had last been there in the darkness, but Ellis had a sense of direction that wasn't going anywhere, and they stood just above the ditch. Both leaned forward a little bit, just to make them feel a bit sicker at the vertigo.

"Don't you think leaning like thish ish fun? "Ellis said, having stopped just before the edge of what right now looked like a deep valley. Jacob shook his head slowly. He was strong and sure of himself, so long as his feet were on solid ground.

"Are you ready…?" Ellis teased, leaning forward a little more, and running just as gravity tried to make him fall.

The ditch had a safe side with a nice gentle ramp, but nobody who wanted to have fun would run down that another path. In fact, it was the clearer of the two paths, if you wanted to go the other way, you had to avoid the nettles, this way you could slide right down, and just the pebbles might hurt you.

Jacob sat down and slid, being the most careful he could, pushing himself off his hands and pushing at the little stones with his feet while Ellis ran. They were both in their own little worlds, squinting just a little in the sun as it peaked out from the clouds, just as it set.

The fall was over before they realised. Once you were down in the witch's ditch, it was its own world with its own strange noises and a breathy scent of ash. Something growled in the distance while they knocked the dust away from their legs and arms, and they didn't hear a thing while they chuckled at each other, a long way away from the lesson at school.

6: TRUST ME, I CAN WHISTLE

Crows and squirrels are both much smarter than you might think. If you put a seed or a nut inside a puzzle, the squirrel will use its balance to get to the food, and crows can use sticks and blades of grass as tools. Never underestimate someone without knowing them.

There were burn marks, that was undeniable, but Ellis couldn't see anything else, only a soft and sweet breeze which wasn't anywhere in the huge ditch. It looked small from the outside, but from the inside, it felt like a huge maze, "It's a lot like if the whole forest was an animal, this would be its armpit." Was all Jacob could say, after they had slowly wandered around for nearly an hour.

The time down there wandered away from them though, they'd been following the sounds of something big. It took them much longer than if it was Jacob introducing Ellis to something, he would have marched forward, driven and confident as usual. He hadn't learned everything he knew about machines by accident.

No, for Ellis it was a slow and ambling walk, looking at the small flitter of a butterfly and laughing at Jacob who still couldn't quite get it, "Butterfliesh just don't fly like that, look." Ellis said, suddenly very close, and flicking their hair over their ear and smirking as Jacob frowned with an exaggerated firmness, "You justh have to – ", a branch snapped in half, not the quiet snap of being stepped on, then the silence as something crept away as if it had made a mistake. Another ugly slam. It was the sound of something angry enough to break a branch in two.

They both stopped, but they weren't shrinking back this time. Jacob didn't know why you ever would, and Ellis couldn't down here. No matter how strange you might think it was, Ellis couldn't ignore this feeling they were being watched, and they couldn't let down those who seemed so happy someone had finally listened.

A shadow walked among the trees, in a small path made by the footfalls of hundreds of different people, swallowing the small light that reflected on all the rubbish scraps. It was a hunched figure, but with the rectangle shape of someone so strong, it was impossible to hide that. Something shiny reflected the thick, green light under all these trees, and it Jacob's shoulder, the white reflection of his shirt making Jacob feel uncertain if he shouldn't just hide.

The beast might not have seen them.

If it was a man, it would have called out by now, surely? It would have said something, even if it was a swear, something to scare them off? Even now, neither of them wouldn't have ran to tell the authorities, they would just say they were "investigating" which meant doing nothing.

The shadow didn't say a thing, just slowly moving forward and scraping its claws along an ugly, hooked knife. It pushed a huge paw against a trunk of one tree, pushing the tree back a little, and Ellis could see its leaves were rattling a little in annoyance at this intruder, just catching the edge of strange speech jumping from it.

The stinging smell of smoke hit them both, and then they noticed the beast was glowing from a small play of flames which rattled around its other paw. No facial features glowed back. It stood still, seeming to think. It pushed the burning paw into the tree, grumbling in satisfaction at the scalded wound.

Ellis felt sick at that.

The thick neck clicked dully as it turned from side to side, seeming to check if they were alone. Jacob tapped Ellis's back, pointing a little shakily at the school jumpers tied together to make the beast a kind of coat, it was hung from a branch high up for now, but the sheer size of it would only fit that thing, it was far too big for a grown man.

"It is a shame you do no listen to your elders. My Queen will make sure you are both forgotten." it growled. It wasn't talking like a man would, it was speaking with the gruff sound somewhere between a snuffling pig and a cat's hiss. The only thing between Jacob and Ellis and this beast was open space now. It had walked through the trees and they could see the hint of long, dented fangs in a heavy smile. They could already smell the horrible breath which itself still burned from a smoking mouth.

"Ugh", Ellis sighed, surprising themselves with the slight boom of their voice. The beast stopped, the other children by now had tried to run away, tried to find their sense of direction and the easy path out. It sniffed the air, and nodded at some distant command. Ellis felt those words like a sharp knife to the back, and winced through their teeth.

It moved faster than it should have, moving behind a different tree and grunting, snapping another low, heavy branch. It flew back, fur flying up in the air and burning with the beast losing its control. It was still stepping back, losing its balance on roots that were all over the place.

Roots that hadn't been there a moment ago.

Jacob coughed, eyes wider than they had ever been before. He could see the roots reaching up and biting at those huge legs. Legs bigger than Jacob's chest. Against a hundred small roots, it was impossible for it to stay stood up.

It was knocked to the floor, burning and laughing all the way. Both friends coughed as the smoke kept growing, but it was dark ochre and seemed to bite at the trees around it, the wood cracking and rattling from the vengeance.

The trees rattled, and a sea of leaves started to fall. They were arguing, but it was a note so deep both Jacob and Ellis looked up at the sky just in case this was thunder on the way.

Any sky they could see was bright blue.

A kingfisher sat calmly down, Jacob and Ellis were focused on the beast, waiting for the next fantastic thing to explode, but they didn't notice the tiny sprite climb off, grow and tap at the tree incessantly.

A kingfisher is a bright, glowing bird of bright metallic blue with a brash orange chest. Its call is a very high whistle of single, punching notes.

This one ignored that.

It was a small song playing out, a little like Morse code. It was a small packet of sound, over and over.

The beast was struggling against the roots again, fighting against each bind. As it destroyed one root, two more reached out, tangling around its fur.

Ellis gawped up at the bird.

Ellis couldn't help it, for years, they'd always copied animals, always hoped for that time when they might talk back. Now, Ellis could feel something burning their heart, a rushing heartbeat and in a rush of chills, suddenly Ellis was inspired.

In a practised trill, Ellis copied the tune of the Kingfisher as well as they could. It went silent, in one moment the two of them were looking at each other, and the bird nodded.

Something had been decided. A second test of fearlessness in the face of that great enemy passed far sooner than they had thought possible.

The kingfisher launched itself at the beast, and it threw itself out of the way, moving in one flash up and behind the two friends. Jacob turned, still not able to close his mouth after watching Ellis's moment.

He didn't have anything with him to beat the beast.

Sighing, Jacob moved closer to Ellis, looking for something to save them, trying to stop himself working out just how strong this thing was if it could break branches and through trunks without thinking about it.

The beast growled, they could see two sharp ochre

eyes below all the fur, funny fuzzy ears twitching in the quiet. That gaze, that colour chilled Ellis, but there was no time to think about it. The beast brushed at the feathers, gargling half a word, but stopping as if something had told it to stop.

It leaned forward, snapping a quick, ugly, gurgling noise as it leapt forward. A blur of hungry fur and claws.

THWACK!

A thick branch swung down and smashed it clean in the face. It reached up with those great claws, grabbing at the wood and clasping. It bit at the air, pushing its feet down into the floor, trying to flap away at a new flurry of roots. This time they were the thick roots right at the base of a tree.

This time the tree in the way wasn't an ordinary one, taken over by the ancient, sages of trees. This time it was a sage, and though they were slow to anger, it was something you would not forget.

A longer gargling note rang out, sounding far away, but Jacob could see more black shadows of those beasts in the distance. He grabbed for Ellis, but they reached out to each other, grabbing hands and in the sheer panic not having the time to flinch away from that touch.

The tree behind them was grunting, croaking like trees do in a heavy wind. Both friends didn't have time to watch it rise and smash the beast to the ground, it was now the panicking animal, trying hard to bend wood it has easily destroyed before. Now it just stayed still, and seemed to grow as it was struck. The yellow infection was pushed to the leaves, and they fell in a rainfall now.

Jacob and Ellis were running, pushing their legs across the obstacles and leaving, tumbling a little as the ground shook from the force of a tree uprooting itself, which you couldn't see from outside the ditch.

They climbed and climbed, not having the time to joke or play around. The burning bird circled the scene below it, running back to its family and calling out to their huge parent to wake up. Ellis flinched just a little at the sound, as they ran, checking the leaves they'd grabbed were still there, stuffed into their pockets.

They stopped just after the big face of the forest was gone, hearing the comforting sound of cars beeping their horns while they rushed to get home from work. They were panting, but Ellis was more alive than he'd ever been.

"You were right, if it had been me, I would have wanted to find you too. I'm not a fan of surprises, but that one took the biscuit" Jacob mumbled, his mind racing about how he could have helped, but from the smile he was getting from Ellis he could see he'd given Ellis the strength to not always lean on him now.

"There'sh sho much more, trusht me." Ellis nearly sang. Where Jacob was confused and insecure, Ellis felt like the dream of more of this amazing world opening itself up, was coming earlier than they could have wished. Ellis didn't feel in danger.

Jacob smiled, amazed, as they stepped apart, knowing now they'd have to go home. "The trees needed you, I couldn't trust you more." He said simply, for once not ending it with a joke. They embraced hard for a couple of seconds.

Neither of them noticed the feathered green sprites watching them, one had just made it back from another site where the adults had come and cut down all the danger from the forest. They knew they had chosen well.

The friends parted ways, knowing they couldn't trust anyone with this. Neither thought the other people's way was right, to just run away and hope everything will work itself out. Ellis had unlocked something, and though the whispering had stopped, something more was sitting in his brain now, slowly letting them know just what the world was really made of.

Ellis whistled to themselves quietly, not noticing how the trees moved when they hit the highest notes, how the leaves seemed to glow.

Sandra stood leaning against a lamppost in Ellis's way.

She seemed to do it, just to wait for Ellis to walk by so she could say something mean, something to bring Ellis down just as they were getting away from school for a short time. She might have been on her phone, but she kept looking up as Ellis sauntered down the alleyway between the backs of houses, checking they were coming her way, and reading the best jokes from her phones her friends were sending her.

"Is the rumour true your mother grew tired of your silly gender, and that's why she died?" Ellis was different now, they didn't shrink back and nearly cry. Instead they smiled at Sandra, sticking their tongue out, and walking past as if nothing had happened, whistling all the louder.

-

An hour might have passed, it could have been two, but Ellis's heart was still racing. They were thankful Daddy believed them when he checked the pills. Just the right amount had been taken that day. Ellis felt very guilty, Daddy didn't even check. He just smiled in the small way he did, staring down at his book again, then smiling up fully as he saw Ellis without scruff on their uniform.

The shirt was neat and tucked in, the sweat had dried on Ellis's back, but they had kept their bag on this whole time, walking up the stairs quietly and calmly, as if everything was under control. Ellis didn't question where the scratches had gone. The smoke had disappeared, and scuffed knees were beautifully clean.

In their heart, Ellis's heart was racing, and for the first time they took three steps at a time, nearly leaping up the steps, almost falling at the top. Their heart raced with the same leaning madness when your gravity runs away from you, but recovering quickly enough, and with a little skip, they leapt just in front of their door.

Ellis scrambled for the lock.

For the first time in a long time, they looked around their room with a new alertness, taking the time to take in where they were, feeling guilty of the mess for once, but the leaves were calling, talking and hoping for something more to happen.

Ellis looked around, shaking their head in annoyance, nowhere was clear, the bed was still folded up into the wall. The wall still had boxes moved into the way, old notes and pictures so they could get to their desk.

The drawers were spilling with old clothes. Books and other messes flowed along the floor, the desk was a smash of other sketches and pictures. The books were always nature stories, ready and waiting for more and more knowledge, more and more of the amazing sights and intelligence the natural world gave away with just a moment spent learning about it.

With one fell swoop, Ellis pushed the papers to one side, careful to avoid the art supplies and a neat pile of paper for a particularly exciting adventure into the deep Ellis had been taking. Still open on a huge picture of the Giant Squid wrapping itself around a camera it thought was prey. That picture had been grabbing at Ellis for a long time. Just to one corner, the book had a silhouette of the squid compared with a human.

It was three times as long as the average man, and above it, the huger colossal squid imagined against that size, and it was a great monster that was just the kraken people had talked about before. Ellis must have been rushing and panting for this time alone, but they still paused at that picture, grabbed by it again. Looking out at the evening which had spread slowly across the sky.

Something tapped the window as it turned to run away from their eyes, and Ellis couldn't help but smile. This was the first time they had felt special and chosen, the first time there had been something more than just the faces moving away from theirs in school, or the opposite as that bullying crowd attacked him with growling faces.

The beautiful moment passed as it trilled, just catching a small golden shadow as it left. Ellis pushed his wheeled chair behind them, grabbing onto the chair as it slid back and pushing back forward to sit down. The leaves crunched under them as they sat down. They stood up and pushed the chair back again, fighting with the paper to get close enough to the desk, growling a little just to be able to lean over the desk and try to find the next clue.

The whispering conversation was still silent, and Ellis looked at the window one more time, just wandering if something had gone wrong. Thinking of that flame and the beast coming again, maybe one was controlling the other, maybe they were both part of the same thing?

It was a bad night to be thinking about things like that, there was a fog growing across the town now. A thick, grey sheet spreading slowly along the houses and making the world close in. It crept across the town, moving under someone's will. Ellis normally slept with a sight to the stars, but that was hidden away behind the same sheet, and Ellis squinted, trying to see something. Still feeling like they were being watched

Shadows moved out there, most of them becoming clear as boring adult things the moment they came into the shrinking clear part, but some waited on the edges, waiting and growling just a little.

Ellis's mind rushed, and with one quick pull, the curtains were pulled across the window. Without the bedroom light on, Ellis jumped across the bed and back onto their chair.

Daddy was used to Ellis jumping around, he didn't react to the noise. Ellis wasn't just an active sleep walker, they tried to hide any anger from the day just in their room, anywhere else and they would seem calm and collected.

Ellis pulled at the lamp and switched the bright beam on, bending right the leaves and waiting for something to happen. Each leaf was carefully splayed out, patted down and set out in a nice order. As each one sat prim in its own little space as Ellis pushed at their warmth. Some of them splayed on their own, the whispering seemed to grow, louder than before and trying to say something.

Ells couldn't understand what they were saying, and they blocked the sound out, just like you might from your ears by using both hands. Ellis was focussing, the veins on the leaves glowing under the bright light.

Just like following those whispers, Ellis was feeling brave and powerful, ready to take on anything which might come their way.

If only they'd listened, they might not have been so calm.

"Danger" the trees kept trying to say, but each time the trees felt the cold from the harsh fires of a burning touch cutting them off. They could do nothing in this fog, the new town was confusing, and only the birds could tell them the way.

Those birds disappeared in a flurry of fangs and black. Even they wouldn't risk coming out at night. Especially with the Ash Queen on the hunt.

7: UNTAMED, FEARLESS AND MORE THAN A LITTLE GREEDY

I'm not sure how much time you've spent deep underwater in the dark and mystery, but before you do go down there, I have one tip. If you see a pretty, dangling white light, don't stay still. It is pretty, and it might be the only light for miles. Stay still for too long and a great monster will appear. Long fangs and big, hungry eyes will appear from the gloom, that bright light stretching from its harsh brow. If something looks good, it might not be true, be careful.

It was thick, slimy fog outside now, a bleak emptiness which squeezed against anything, making all the surfaces wet and harsh to the touch. It was the perfect time for the Ash Queen to walk in a town.

She had been sneering for centuries, but with the weather under her control, and the flames finally making progress again, for once a small smile was growing on one lip.

For centuries, she had been sleeping and resting. There were strange memories and thoughts of modern life, but she ignored those, biding her time from the old war and hoping soon enough the time would come when all the precious power and beauty others saw in nature disappeared. The time when they might fear the dark and not embrace it.

Then the beasts had woken her, waiting and festering they had finally thought it time to wake her up, time to learn what she knew, waiting for her plans together after all that waiting.

From those beast's memories, she had been staring at the new towns and cities, the beams of light which never went away. It always felt like it was nearly time, and as the humans pulled more and more trees from the ground, her eyes glowed with a glee where others would feel sadness for the suffering of those old trees.

Not her. The more they suffered, the more she smiled.

Over the newest years, something had been changing. Now the people were outside less, they were stuck in the machines and obsessed by some new message, some new calling riding itself along the winds. They were listening to her whisperings and it was sweet to watch.

The Ash Queen was not a powerhouse, she was not the conjurer of this power, but as always, she was watching and trying to learn. She plotted, deep purple crystals were her eyes. Grey and short spikes were her hair. Thin, steel lengths were her arms and legs, solid with muscle but looking like it could barely hold her up.

She was standing on the edge of Greenview, chuckling quietly to herself, and thinking how this ugly hamlet had grown. It was her habit to get stuck in the past when the biggest moments were coming. She blinked to try and hold back her racing heart. Just as she had conjured them to, in subtle words and playful nightmares, everyone had stayed inside, away from the fog.

"The one with the True Hearing is out there. I grow tired forcing this fog to grow, and we need to move quickly. The time has finally come, and the 'city' is calling to me. I know out there. The great King, the Unholy, is calling to me. Now, we must strike."

She spoke in the same hissing voice, like a car driving along stones, trying to park. It had a feminine edge to it, a small trill at the end of some words. She noticed a tall beast staring at her, as her voice rose out of her control.

She gulped, with her old, wrinkled hands pushing their scratched and burned fingers away from her. In one fell swoop, the town was coated in an even thicker fog, a smog so thick you would have to push to get through it.

She sat, crossing her legs and smoking at a pretend flame, she formed it from clicking two fingers together. She liked to play and grin when a plan was coming together. She chuckled loudly, and hummed a jolly tune in an irregular rhythm, tapping her feet in the air. Just for a high giggle erupted out of her, but she shook, and her eyes faded from their bright blue back to the deep purple with a lash right along her back.

She'd sat the same way years before, just as they were taking the last with True Hearing away, and into their cages. Sat on the hill, she couldn't help but clap twice, just as a beast brushed past her, remembering the little firecracker of a child it had once been.

The smog sank even more, the streetlights faded down to pools of dull light, just the small yells from people as they jumped at the strange shapes which ran past them, at the other weirder, whirring noises.

-

The trees might have had their sprites, small and

delicate, joyfully embracing the flowers and birds around them. The anti-sprites of that Ash Queen flew with a sloppy noise. They were always burning, scowling round faces squinting from underneath the flaps of moist feathers.

The beasts were bigger in the frost, they dragged at the spaces between buildings, jumping along the roofs and chatting at the moon in hate as they ran. They moved together, other things lurking in the dark and yelling out when they saw another one of their kind. The people obediently turned up their TVs to make sure they could say why they hadn't heard a thing.

If you were to look outside right now, you might think a troop of bears was set free, or that some huge monster was breaking down the whole town in its tireless hunger. Devourers burrowed at the earth, feeding on the soil, destroying a shed with the sheer force of their biting. For just one second, a sea of teeth could be seen, swallowing all that wood and every tool without pausing.

Ellis let out a sharp whistle, trying something at the leaves, and frowning as nothing happened. For just the smallest moment, a flash of bright green twinkled. It was just like a traffic light, here and then gone again. The beasts looked up, waving their ugly paws at one another.

They were scared.

In their own language, they grunted and gurgled at each other, angry and yet trying to show they were the powerful one. Maybe they were too powerful, too much of an asset to be the person that would run forward.

To run out of the fog with all these people around.

Even though the fog was being pushed and forced forward, on an energy of its own now, it didn't quite reach the window of Ellis's room.

The light from the inside was like a beam of yellow, and the Ash Queen could not get out of its way. She pushed her burning hand right into the grass, twisting and grunting at the greenery as it fought back. Her other hand came down, crashing down on the grass and squealing as the roots seemed to fight back. A small vine flicked up, and she frowned, along the cloth of her old clothes a tattoo of rampant flames danced for just a second.

With a waft of angry breaths, the fire left a heavy circle behind, the mark of a huge fist crushing all the life from a half-mile all around her. Her humming ended, and in one quick spin, she flicked forward, right amongst the bending, growling beasts yelping at each other on the rooftops right near the window.

She stared up at the huge figures, barely reaching up to their shoulders, to the hugest one whose elbows were higher than her scalded black hair.

It didn't stop them flinching back though.

"I know what your problem is. You've never fought a battle, you're the last of hundreds of generations just waiting to fight. One of you has already disappeared. I'm here to put that to a stop.

"You..." The fog swirled around her then, her whole body leaning forward with a single focus. The fog grabbed at her body, swelling her power and making those two eyes sharp needles facing the smallest beastly mess that stood before her. It shook at the impact of her focus, but it wouldn't shrink back.

The Ash Queen was superstitious, knowing the branches and roots were everywhere, she pushed herself just a little off the ground. All she had to do was think about it. Somehow already, her Burning King in the city was sending her powers which for so long had been dreams.

-

Ellis was usually patient with this kind of thing, normally completely in control and more than happy to wait the long trip. They'd spent hours and hours waiting for a bird to show itself, jumping from a branch. They'd taken pictures, and if the focus had missed, would wait for it all to happen again. This was different though.

It was just like having the bird sat right in front of you, perfect, in focus and waiting for the picture to be taken. Yet, the picture can't be taken, all the instructions are Japanese, always changing and impossible to work out.

Ellis stood up, groaning and pushing both hands against their back. Their hair was thrown behind their face, tied together with one of the many bands they kept stuck around their wrist. "You can be brave" the yellow band said, as Ellis forced it around their long hair, trying a few times to keep it all under control, but growing flustered even at that.

They blew out of both nostrils, and stared down at the leaf again. The light was still throbbing from the last time, when it looked like every leaf was about to do something incredible. Then some boom had shaken the walls, and most of the leaves had gone dark.

Just one stayed glowing, just keeping touch with a light blue shine. There were strange lines coming out of it, just parts of the leaves veins. Ellis stood on the other side of the room, a hundred little pictures of animals staring up at them, and something clicked.

Ellis normally felt afraid, on the spot and right in front of the staring eyes of everyone. Right now, though, the world felt like it had just taken a breath, waiting for them to move again, waiting for them to push the world a little more so it could keep spinning. For a short moment, Ellis could feel the Earth spinning, the room disappeared from their mind, fading until just the glows of the houses were lost, until the Earth itself was just a ball in the air, hanging up there by seemingly nothing, but still dangling there.

Just like standing at the top of the stairs, balance disappeared, and Ellis reached out a hand to the desk's side. The world was OK, it was beating with an ancient pulse, a fading steady tone they could feel through their toes. Ellis was still, just the tumbling, huge spin which just felt like some immeasurable power had thrown the whole world along.

Ellis was feeling the very heart of life those trees felt, Ellis couldn't escape these sensations now, this world was theirs. The huge spinning force started to make sense, and Ellis stood unaided. Both blue eyes slammed open, more open than ever and not needing to blink anymore.

One single note squeezed between their lips, to anyone, it would have looked like Ellis was just pretending to whistle.

The leaves knew otherwise, the beasts outside too.

With one huge swirl of force, the leaves threw themselves up into the air, standing still in the air as if they were part of a great tree. It was a chaotic rush of brush strokes. Ellis stared, whistling more. The room was glowing green, and Ellis was overwhelmed by this light.

They flayed with their hands, but the leaves were making a message of their own. A beacon of green slammed out of the room, the street shaking along that light.

The small beast which scrambled along the rooftops, pausing twice to check the Ash Queen was still there froze in the air.

The green pulse smashed through the animal, rolling across the black, matted feathers and shocking its body. As if it was held up by kind hands, the beast was dropped down to the path just behind Ellis's house.

As the light twirled and fought against the beast's black and matted fur. Under the explosion of light, pale skin came back instead, the smudge of torn trousers and a crying face. One of the lost children spluttered and shivered, staring from side to side, and without thinking pushing a burned hand into dirty pockets, and onto their phone. The Ash Queen hissed, flicking a small firework into the air, and with one fell spin, disappearing away, finding some way to the city and more powers than ever before.

The beasts skulked away, hiding in small alcoves while the child wept, nodding and walking to the nearest road, trying to work out just where on earth they were. The parents ran out from their room, still holding the phone with shaking hands. After a few seconds, they could see each other.

Sam, the newly free child, didn't care about being embarrassed or playing it cool. They ran the whole distance overcome by the joy of finding their parents again, laughing as their dog wagged its tail and barked at them. Some people stared out from their windows, ready to be angry and tell the stupid animal off. When they saw a lost child had returned.

-

"Cricket…?" Daddy always tapped at the door first, he didn't mind how long Ellis stayed awake, and whatever he was doing. So long as Ellis was up on time, everything would be OK. Ellis snapped awake, and it was just as if they hadn't been asleep. Without the huge pressure which seemed to come from the window last time, the sound of impatient breathing just behind the curtain.

"OK, I'm wide awake. I'll be there in a minute. Don't worry Daddy, everything's great." No lisp today, everything felt clearer than before. Ellis breathed back out hard, like they'd been forgetting to do that overnight. For just a moment some of their skin glowed white, as Ellis reached for the curtain to pull it back.

Small scratches marked the glass, but Ellis wasn't

looking at that now. With one quick movement, Ellis ran to the door, flicked the door open, smirked at Daddy and pointed fully with both hands to their garden, still running.

Yesterday there had been one, small tree. Maybe just enough for two birds to sit on and not disturb each other. Just in front of their back gate though, a huge tree now stood, one clump of leaves missing, standing taller than even the house.

Both Daddy and Ellis craned their necks up at the tree, one bemused, the other feeling even more overwhelmed at this gift. "Well, at least I know what all that noise was last night!" Daddy chuckled, ruffling Ellis's hair for the first time in years. There was some huge shadow in his head about that evening, and he just accepted this new realty without question, squinting his eyes at a searing pain which came whenever he questioned if the tree had been there all along.

8: WE'RE ELASTIC, YOU CAN'T PULL US APART

There is a kind of ant so clever that it can build boats and bridges out of itself, anything to overcome any obstacle that comes their way. It's OK to ask for help, people can be much stronger together, so long as they work as a team

"I know some of you don't enjoy my lessons, maybe you don't think they're as important as some of the other subjects, but this test is a very important one. There are no right answers, just pick the answer that agrees with what you feel.

"This is a test to determine where you will end up in life. I know it isn't easy for some of you to understand, but this time you're spending in school is just a small part of your life. I hope you know the end of your school life is coming up, and we must start thinking about what comes next.

"In silence, start as soon as you can, and answer the questions honestly."

Ellis and Jacob sat next to each other, and as Mrs Hill said the last part, they moved away from each other, and back to the computers. They unclasped their hands, undoing the close grip, not quite realising why they were so anxious at the idea of being apart, but knowing they didn't want it regardless.

They looked at each other quickly, nodding a little to try and show just how impossible being apart was, and Ellis was so thankful for their adventure together, unable to understand just how happy Jacob was to have this excuse to be together too.

They stared at the machines, both knowing just how strange the questions would be. For just another half-minute, Ellis stared at the glass of the window, which this time was clear of any scratches. Ellis was comforted by the edge of a tree, shaking in the daylight.

-

Hours had passed, "Your test results are in this envelope, please take it home, and have a talk with your parents to understand just what you want to be. This test took a long time, so you are free to go home for lunchtime today.

I hope this will let you think about your futures seriously now. Huh!" Mrs Hill dodged a ball which threw through the air, tutting and waving her hand away at the students already stood up and ready to leave. Waiting for each other at the back of the glass, Jacob and Ellis took each other's papers, filled with the nerves that came from what they might say about their life to come.

"Engineering. Robotics. Architecture." The three words were scrolled down with thick lines separating each. There might have been other writing around those words. Ellis flashed their eyes up and back down, just in case something was wrong, throwing the paper onto the desk. They stared out the window, hoping for some comfort while they hid away from the words.

It was a strange, squeezing feeling, stabbing in their stomach. Impending doom getting closer with a great weight behind it. Life was pushing everything to the edge of some horrid cliff, the space between now and that drop getting closer and closer.

Jacob folded the paper back, looking out at the same trees with a frown. He was quietly cursing the tree, having no idea if this was supposed to be something that could hear his thoughts, whether it would just hear him if he shouted. He sat down too, reaching out a hand to feel a little closer to what was happening right now.

Both Ellis and Jacob felt how important the other person was, and both couldn't help but want to get out of that room, to escape and be part of something else. It didn't matter if that other thing was dangerous or frightening, so long as it wasn't this solid weight of menace.

The teacher smiled, and it felt cruel. She was happy to see the facts of life play along all her students faces, already knowing that most of them wouldn't talk to their parents at all. It would be something to bring up on their next parents evening at least.

The students were shuffling, and with a nod of her head, she let the class leave, knowing the summer holidays were close enough for the students to want it now. She didn't admit it to anyone, but she felt just the same. Ellis and Jacob didn't walk past her, she knew they'd snuck out as always, and she shook her head, wandering why they wouldn't act the same as all the other children, why they couldn't try at least.

The screen fizzed in the corner of her eye, some strange writing and a set of eyes. The strange face shook and looked around, seeming to become aware it had been seen. In the corner of the screen, a claw patted at the screen's display, disappearing behind the class notes.

On another screen, it stared at the skulking form of the Ash Queen, just hiding to the edge of the forest. The ochre eyes of the Burning King's servant were glad its Queen was coming back home.

-

If you stood behind the Ash Queen, it looked like she was smoking. Not an ordinary cigarette, but a big cigar, with the puff of smoke that whirled around her small body. It wasn't something she was smoking, she was the thing which smoked in thick plumes, like an old fire.

For the first time in centuries, she was nervous, surrounded by too many different sounds and sights she couldn't quite understand. It took her long enough to understand the car. At the beginning, she had stared at them, trying to see how it was controlled, and what it had been.

The last kind of vehicle she had seen was a man on a horse, travelling with the animal between his legs. The car was something else, and twice she had tried the old gesture to sit in one of the cars. They had sped straight past, a loud noise from the horn making the Ash Mother jump.

A cacophony of sounds was all around her, the beeping and slamming noises, and all that chatter. She walked past the smell and fizzling of a hundred different food stops, her groaning stomach saying enough, but she couldn't stop here. When you've lived so long, the days merge, and though the Ash Queen had walked for days, she would not stop now.

She pushed her face down with every person that passed, driven by a sense of direction toward somewhere she couldn't remember. The Burning King had told her where to go, but wouldn't say what it was. Something in the Ash Queen's memory was giddy with a memory of strong arms wrapped around her.

A memory of burning castles, pushed back as she might move her hair. Huge ships crushed in the hands of something out from the ocean. Never being able to see it, but always being able to speak with it. She was given power back then, but while she had slept, this monster had been feeding and learning.

She panted, leaning against another wall, trying to find some signpost to help her on her way. All the cars and people pulled her eyes away from those signs, all her life spent in a wild world. She was in the exact middle of the city, and a buzz of electric shock knocked along her spine.

To anyone else, the building might have looked like a huge, solid structure, but where the Ash Queen stood, the wall started to move. It made a huge, grinding sound, as if a thousand stomachs were hungry and grumbling. Nobody looked up at the wall, as it unfolded like hands slowly folding back.

A thirty-foot space opened, glowing blue, as the Ash Queen stepped in, she was happy to see nobody noticing, they were all bent down on their phones as they walked, and even for those people that were looking, they looked through and then past it. As if something was telling them to look away.

Wires reached around the Ash Queen, quite calmly she smiled, used to the feeling of what everyone else saw as a monster. That was the best word they could use to describe him and the huge things he commanded. The Ash Queen knew him only as her husband.

The wires pulled hard on her shoulders, and with a small laugh, she disappeared into the building, kicking her feet as she went.

-

What was happening to the people you ask? If you're outside somewhere, have a look around and tell me what they are doing. I'm imagining they are looking at a screen. If they are, just guess what might happen if those screens had been taken over, if just like the natural sprites keeping you in their world, something was trying to keep you in its world. Something that thought your health, happiness and safety was less important, but just wanted you under their control.

There had been a group trying this for as long as there had been a group of sprites protecting nature. For so long now, nature had been feeling weaker, trees had been cut down, and no prayers had been given. So many of the sprites and their ancient trees had left for the heaves, escaping to the golden city just above with a great effort.

They could feel the tide of conflict turning to the old ways, the times of all that building long ago, all that war.

They sorely missed the peaceful praying times, when animals were sacred and everyday people stood quietly holding hands.

Years ago, they had lost their place in the cities, there were new trees there, young ones who couldn't take the spirits of those ancient beings, they were trimmed so much, no carrier spirit could take the pain. The birds were pushed away, spikes were put on all the buildings, so they couldn't sit. People used to come out and play in the nearby forests. The cities were growing bigger, and all their life was lost in the city.

The trees could not stop talking about Ellis and Jacob, the way that two children looked at them and didn't run past. The way they ran into the forests, not to make fires and hide, but to see everything they could. The wars were the oldest conversation, the pain they had felt so many times before was a constant one of wounds and fear.

All they could ever do was wait and hope and prepare. Ellis would have powers soon enough that would eclipse anything the machines could do. In their desperation, the trees had left Ellis a map behind, an ancient trick to push their powers further forward than they would have imagined possible.

A brave sprite was out there though, a bird of prey swirling off the thermal winds, riding up and hovering Watching just like it did when it was hoping to find prey. It saw the smoke wafting away from its great heights, and with zooming sight, just caught the moment the Ash Queen disappeared.

A living drone sat just behind it, turning just out of sight and waiting for something to change, waiting for the animal to turn back, and show them just where the nature sprites were hiding. The huge trees should have been easy to see, but everything the machines had tried just would not work. It was as if they weren't allowed to see them.

Nothing realised the golden heavens had chosen their side, and just as the bird of prey turned to go back home, the sprite riding it yelping in their seat, a bold of gold light shot from the air and killed the drone with one blow. Its power was overwhelmed, shot through with far too much power.

A tiny silhouette, looking like a child floating from the machine, swimming in the air. A gold beam grabbed the figure as it started to panic, pulling it up and away into the true target of these two worlds at war.

The ground shook, that great monster angered and shaking in his building, stopping himself before a full attack as it had done before. His wife was nearby, and he wouldn't want to hurt her. That was the only thing he would admit to being afraid of. A statue almost seemed to stand up, but it was just shaking its muscles to get rid of the pain in its legs. Nobody noticed of course.

It was a living city, but nobody had realised quite what had been looking for life in the bowels of the city. Those bowels where wires for the internet and tunnels for huge trains had been built. The Ash Queen thought about it as she fell, remembering the men as they burst into her home.

She'd see some of them soon enough.

-

"It's so good to be in the presence of people who haven't forgotten that's the only way to greet me." The Ash Queen purred. She was having to squint in the dull light, but she could see the figures bowing in front of her. "You recognise your queen, no matter how small and weak I might be."

She stared at herself then, ignoring the beasts and the metal lengths which had been statues. They both guarded the scene, most walking from one command to the other, trailing wires and screens on their shoulders, or dragging them behind.

The whole corridor was filled with energy, one small burning sprite lighting a waving hand in the air down the corridor, running ahead in the shape of a small fox. The fox stopped, tilting its head to one side as the Ash Queen paused, staring at a bright screen. The screen was a growing red haze, reaching out from the bright eye at the centre where they stood.

Small green bubbles danced across the map, most of them surrounded by this red sea, and the Ash Queen scratched at one mark, free of red, and growing with small strikes at the red. The Ash Queen gulped, groaning as the glass of the screen fought back at her, she was getting weaker even from the short walk here.

She turned away, feeling a wave of panic as she breathed heavily. She stared at the fox, running after it shakily, panting. She leapt where a huge void stood just in front of her, pushing her hands out to be caught. She

90

couldn't help it, her eyes closed from the rush of such a fast descent. Just as the great monster glowed before her, she was ashamed to meet him again closing her eyes in fear.

"You have returned. Their fate is sealed. The world is ours." Every word was a thunderclap, shaking the room and breathing a rush of small flames with it. The huge figure of a man slowly rose from the void. There was a reason the monster had a huge skyscraper built around him. It was the only thing large enough to house his true form, wings and all.

All around her, as she fell, images of burning trees popped out of the darkness. Pictures of dangerous animals. Poisonous snakes, rats.

It showed machines performing surgeries, a robot fighting fires on its own. A driverless car avoiding two human drivers, crashing into each other. The Ash Queen giggled, having no idea this was the message the Burning King had been building, picking the fear in everyone and turning it into a new trust. Something new to prey on and hope for.

The pictures changed to a heart, beating in the bright lights of a lab. It was not a human heart, but one that had been printed, a little silver showing the fine fabric of the work. People really were starting to live forever, but they didn't realise what they were signing off.

"So long ago, we had told the humans to burn the world. We had shown them in the darkness there could be light, and they had seen factories. They did not know how they would wound this land. They could not see they look for us to come to the rescue again. That is when I left them, growing strong on their need, and all the energy they spilled in their eternal wastage." The king's growls grew stronger, all around the city, machines stabilised the buildings, and more people prayed thanks than ever to the machines which saved them.

Each prayer, each connection of hopeful data made the Burning Father all the stronger. As the Ash Queen approached, he still glowed, pushing down the great form, the great wings, and a huge mass of muscle receded, the bulk of a hundred men pushed back into just his single, mortal form. The room vibrated with the sheer force of his wrapping.

The wires which had been pushed right into his system for so long cascaded down to the side of the huge tower, scratching and grinding at the walls. He stepped slowly forward, waiting for his Queen to arrive.

His Queen was falling to the ground without fear, even if her feet were starting to burn from the vacuums grasp, with just a simple gesture of the King's upturned hand, she slowed down and settled into a smooth descent. As always, she was in awe of his incomparable power.

The Ash Queen landed on a small platform, seeing the Burning King, her husband all this time, turning back to his human form. She knew he wouldn't approve, but she ran toward him all the same. It was time the final blow was dealt to their oldest enemy. Humanity would be there's.

9: FURTHER DOWN AND INTO THE DARKEST DARK

The funniest underground animal of all is a star-nosed mole. It has a big, star shaped nose on the front of its face which is five times more sensitive than your hand. It can eat faster too, it takes it less than a second to find out if something is food. Please, don't judge anything on its appearance.

"It must hurt to be that stupid", Crystal yelped. As usual, she pushed her face right up to Ellis's, knowing they'd react. This time Ellis didn't pull back. Jacob was waiting just to the edge of the school. He was just past the gate and ready to jump in just in case something escalated.

Just in case Ellis needed a little strength to back them up, Ellis would almost seem to lean on something and that would be enough of a sign. This time, Ellis stood straight up, leaning over them and standing a little taller than before. It wold normally be a tally of insults, and as Ellis tried to get away, then the group of other people would throw at Ellis as they ran away.

This time, Ellis walked away, together Jacob and they had faced monsters and once you've seen the worst things the world can throw at you, it's hard to look at a bully and feel any fear. The group of bullies were confused and didn't know what to do, they laughed at each other at what was wrong with Ellis's look, but it wasn't good enough for them.

The crowd still had a can of drink from all the rubbish

they had spilt, and Sandra gleefully threw the empty can. She was just hoping Ellis might trip as usual, or wince far more than they should. The can spun through the air, that crowd leaning forward a little, just for something they could exaggerate and turn into a big story for everyone tomorrow.

Ellis caught the can, taking it with them to the nearest bin, and never even bothering to look back, not even listening to the yells about their mum, or animals being the only people Ellis could get on with. Normally Jacob would have been gone, but he felt something strong, pulling him back to Ellis's house. He kept behind though, knowing how protective their Dad was becoming.

Jacob didn't want to seem like Ellis's dog, only making Ellis confident by being close.

After a short time, he jogged to catch up, just in time to stop Ellis stepping out into traffic as a car rushed past. The small car honked its horn, and Ellis flicked back, both jumping together at the sharp sound in their own focused state. The sunlight glowed through Jacob's hand as it was held up to block the light, so he could see who was shouting, but he looked away at the roaring face.

"There is something amazing I have to show you." Ellis slowly struggled to say, pointing with their thin fingers at the way those veins splayed out. Without thinking about it, Ellis kept their hand fused to Jacob's, and they were running back home together now. Inspiration had struck its lightning bolt, and Ellis was fixed on it, there was no letting go.

Jacob always followed rules and orders, everything fitting into its place and calmly staying there as neatly as it could be. He always felt strongest when he worked through an issue and dissected it. He grabbed at his bag, while Ellis tried anything. Whistling, or something else to get the trees leaves on that tree to work with this next magic madness.

So, he continued to look through the bag, kneeling and grabbing at his laptop, while placing two pens to the side of him, pushing down a notepad into the grass, and smiling at the neat outlines it created. Ellis whistled at his highest pitch, pushing it through the leaves, and Jacob looked down at his phone, writing down the pitch as the little app told him it. Grabbing onto the smallest sense of reality, just as the leaves danced against this new, huge tree.

Right now, he was just in one of those moments he had where he just gawped forward, trying to understand what he could.

There was a light from the leaves that shimmered much brighter than the daylight. It was a huge green beacon, and a million little veins spread out from the leaves. It didn't spread the way it usually would in a leave, or a tree, straight to the core. It was something different, and Jacob almost fell over from leaning too far forward.

He grabbed a small camera with him, a little ball grabbed and joining him as he jumped up and stared into the light. It was a 3D camera, and Jacob felt much more comfortable inside this weirdness, at least that way he could learn something too. Every part of the light was gold glitter, dazzling as the bright droplets fell around him.

The hand was white with his tight grip, he was happy to be pulled back to the real world by Ellis, whistling again and trying something to make the tree do even more. Jacob leaned forward, staring at the footage through a strange program that tried as hard as it could to make some sense of all the flickering lights.

Time disappeared then, Ellis trying different sounds and sharp claps, rubbing leaves together and whistling at all sorts of different locations, not knowing which part of all this glowing green miasma was the source of its brightness. Ellis tried four times to make the tree jump, grabbing a harmonica from the dusty space just behind a chest of drawers and nearly falling as they ran down again. Nothing more had happened, at least every time they tired, the golden light exploded again. Each time, they sighed in amazement, failing to hide the disappointment at the way the light grew more and more dull over time.

Jacob's leg shouted with pins and needles, and he hopped up, standing with a yelp. It was nearly dark, and Daddy would be there soon. The only sound for a moment was Ellis's panting, as they breathed out, just a small whistle but Ellis was sitting down in the next second.

"Thish might be it…" Ellis whispered, in the squeaky childish way they usually kept for their inside voice.

Jacob shook his head, it stood against every difference the two of them had, Ellis could always see more meaning and romance in the world than most, always wandering at the relationship they were playing with, and hoping this time would feel right. Jacob saw everything with a clear definition you could learn from with enough time. He had spent so much time proving the power of data and research in everything Jacob depended on, and he loved to learn more.

His heart was pounding; this was something new he could finally attack with all the gadgets he'd found and built. All that pocket money would come together for something. Jacob sprang up again, this time with the laptop balanced on just one hand, the other reaching out to Ellis.

"We can do this together", he grumbled, squeezing Ellis's shoulder to try and settle them, just as they sighed and sat down with a sulk. Jacob spent days and days watching and learning about the latest, magic technologies. He had spent hours aggravated with no progress at all, just staring at the screen, and then in a moment he could understand what someone meant by a "neural network".

"Look," he snapped, never quite able to grasp just how someone could get so confused by these machines, he was just glad these apps always came with clear, flashy displays to show Ellis. When they got confused, Jacob had to fight just to get Ellis's attention back, they'd be off, running after another adventure.

They stepped away from the huge lights, Ellis started

to lean back, staring at it again, but Jacob pushed their head down, showing the lines, his computer had drawn across the picture of that outline.

It was a hard thing to try and explain, so he didn't bother. "The machine has thought about it, and from everything the internet knows, this is the best it can come up with."

The golden light had turned black and white, the sprawling madness of all those lines turned into something far nicer, ordered and sectioned off. "It's gone to the internet to ask it just what language this might be, or if it could be a painting. It has to be something real, nobody would take this amount of time to just show off." Jacob looked down at Ellis then, they were leaning forward and staring at the screen, trying to work it all out.

"It took a while, but they look like old runes, Celtic or something. I'm not even sure it's right, but it makes more sense than the whole thing being random," Jacob tutted, Ellis stubbed a finger at the screen where it hadn't turned black and white, it had just ignored the light completely, guessing it was nothing.

"That could be a map, but it only knew what parts of it were, and they were far too small to be sure. Whatever map this is, it has long gone. He tutted again, Ellis was staring at his head, and seeking for some greater truth in the world than there could be. The hours the two of them had spent arguing about God. What a lot of wasted time.

"Can I tell you what it thinks these lights are telling you?" Jacob's voice had taken on that depth he usually saved just before he was going to fight someone, just before all the empathy he was supposed to have disappeared. This time, it was just the pain of feeling like he was standing on the other side of a bridge to Ellis, and they might never be close enough.

Then Ellis looked right at him, and something glowed in his heart. He couldn't help but smile then, taking on his clearer, speaking voice. "Last of the Blessed walk among us. Those who are not blinded. Tread with care below. Run if you must. Follow the path you fear. Do not stare the captured in the eye. That twinkle of silver may tempt you. Be pure. Fight it. You are the gift. The blind shall see. The harm shall stop. Do not give in. When the blessed are none, life as a free spirit is over."

-

The Queen and her King ran toward each other, in the darkness and surrounded by the echo of so many yelping voices, they were deaf to it all. The platform was deep in the silver depths of this tower, surrounded by small lights and the echoes of other creatures still trying to learn the ways of the Burning King.

They embraced, kissing and not moving for just a second. She burned with the touch, electric sparks flashing from her bleak eyes. She might have been held in just one of the Burning King's arms, but she had all but disappeared. She might have been tall for a woman in the human world, but he was very large for a bear, with hands that could cover her face with space left.

They butted heads as softly as it was possible to, he grunted a little at the closeness. The fact she was one of the only people strong enough to not just wince and hide from the onslaught that was his touch.

"It has been far too many lifetimes…" She whispered, her snake tongue just tickling his arm as they stared at each other. The Burning King flicked a little blood from one hand, chuckling at his Queen.

"It seems you haven't grown tired of hiding behind this image?" His voice when it was suspicious shook the walls, it was a thunderous, ugly tone, rocks tumbling from a cliff. "I had promised you I would burn the world, you would own everything that came after this. You should not let that green fool see you so clearly!"

The bone of her arm cracked, but the Queen didn't wince, she smiled, curing herself as he loosened his grip. He was far too used to cruelty and power, he hugged her again, picking her up with his second hand just to stare at her hard for a second.

The metal of their platform started to groan from the heat, just before the Ash Queen took a step back, shocked at how much he had grown in power. She knew this was just like someone else relaxing, not unleashing their anger, but just letting go of his own control for the shortest time.

"That is why we don't rest, my King." She played at curtsying, always popping back up onto her legs just as she did it, "I'm allergic to that!" she laughed, flicked her tongue as she giggled. Small, blue flames popped from her skin as she healed it again, eyes still fizzling.

For just a moment her old wings bloomed, and she felt the rush of air from those years of victory so long ago.

She cracked her neck from her sprinting heart, how she always felt nervous in front of him. It took enough not to just stop and watch him forever.

"The green fool is growing mad. She has taken so many forms in both our worlds, every leaf and beast can remember her name." she flicked both claws up at the air, grabbing her arm from that pain. She could see the loving, young partner just behind the burning face. Right now, though, the wrath of an endless war was the only thing she could see.

"My foolish sister, she splits and splits herself, pulling her life-force further and further into more beings. Every time he burns, every seed grows in a rush. There is one beast she cannot control. They are learning it is best to love me."

"For once, I find myself agreeing with a beast. Please, tell me there is something I can see. Please, tell me I can see a place where your sister isn't in the air I breathe?" She giggled in a high pitch then, the same pitch she had hear Ellis use, again not knowing why she laughed like that at times, and she anxiously tried to silence these flinching habits. The same pitch she had used to destroy a sprite, trying desperately to hide from her gaze. She had spent centuries running from assassins, no sound could get past her.

"The humans, they were the key. Let me show you just how much they have changed from their praying days in the trees. They gladly give me everything they can. Soon all their life will be turned. The world might be dying, but they aren't thinking about that, just their love of me, and what next they might give up."

Smaller beasts grabbed at the wires, trying to control the power, black and silver sprites of machinery and shadow. They grabbed old, rusted claws around the power. Each screeched to a crescendo as the King and Queen went to see the true length of their power. Nobody in the city realised quite why they were doing staring into those screens all that time.

-

They had spent a day thinking about it, both very differently trying to solve the problem. Ellis prayed again with a little giggle at all these characters, grabbing at the old pagan books and finding all kinds of Gods to ask for help. They spent a long time by the local farm, staring and thinking about taking the goat. Maybe a sacrifice was what they needed. They couldn't bring themselves anywhere near taking the goat other than just standing at the gate and staring.

If they had to kill the goat, they would rather the adventure silenced itself forever.

Jacob had tried to find some old maps, tried to grab at the idea maybe this area had been an old fort, but there were no records of how it looked. There were records of a huge battle, a haunted tale of witches and fire that lived on its own energy.

He had slammed the book closed in a start of fear, and filled with embarrassment, left the library at that second. They weren't even surprised when they bumped into each other, neither of them were following the normal route home, but still they nearly bumped right into each other. They'd been able to talk and sit in the grass all of lunch time, twice watching Sandra and Crystal walk toward them, then watch them turn away as if something important had interrupted them.

"Normal day? Not a sound." Ellis chuckled the words out, sensing Jacob's energy, "You ", Ellis stopped, surprised at Jacob for grabbing their hand, Jacob's eyes burning with that twinkle they always glowed with when he had just had an inspired moment. They ran to Ellis's home, they'd grown used to just calling it home, Jacob didn't want to speak about his, and Ellis was OK with that, especially since they'd starting spending this much time together.

Something had been troubling Jacob, but now he'd been give the fire of life to get going and live again.

Ellis steered him with their grip, having to lean their own body as if they were pulling a horse at times, they were running that fast. They ran past the front of the house, having to back on themselves, and up through a little shortcut, just between two other buildings.

Then before they realised it, both were in the garden again. Ellis took a short breath, inside happy the tree was still there, Daddy had been in such a rush before about some assessment, they hadn't been able to check it was there in the morning.

"Wait." Jacob commanded, and Ellis stood still, trying to hold the ball of air in their lungs while Jacob fiddled with his phone. Ellis thought if there was one picture to define them both, it might be this moment. Ellis was just about to create magic and Jacob was spending his time looking at the data of the act, never believing the amazing thing he'd just missed.

Ellis didn't realise how Jacob had been thinking about the sound, about how the high whistle must be like one half of a key, just enough to wake something in this world up. Not quite enough to really keep it listening. He'd watched the frequency of Ellis whistling, and from the most average sound a person could hear, made a deep pulse of a noise himself, right in the other direction of pitch.

Jacob quickly held the phone up as if it was his own whistle, smiling a little at the fact he couldn't just whistle himself. "You can do it now. Can't you tell they're waiting for us?" The last part came out almost like a song, but it was hard for Jacob to contain his excitement.

Ellis let the breath out, focussing on making the purest sound they could. It was a huge noise, it pushed Jacob back a little, and the leaves and branches stood upright from the force of it. A group of birds circling nearby in the setting sun started to fly away, and a deep crack started to form.

For a second, they both felt the crushing fear of the beast coming closer. Then the sunlight grew stronger, and Jacob knew what was happening sooner than Ellis, who had to close their eyes for the sound to come out so powerfully. The sunlight had been blocked by the tree, but now it was shining brighter, the tree tilting back like the oldest mouth opening, a yawn it had been waiting a long time for.

The two sounds had played in the air, dancing and

colliding with each other until the notes resonated perfectly. The sound collided and became physical, working its way right into the barrel of some old mechanism. It turned a weight, which swung and knocked a bigger weight, growing bigger as the sound kept hitting the workings between the tree and the floor it had chosen to stand on.

"They are so amazing…" Jacob tried to whisper it, but in the loudness, Ellis heard it, and stopped. Jacob skipped forward from the sharp jump, laughing at the sign Ellis gave he was so happy to be understood by someone.

"Tread with care below. Run if you must." Jacob whispered to himself. They both stepped forward, bending into the entrance, and staring into the tunnel that was filled with howling. A rushing breath of rotten eggs pushed past them both, hot enough for them both to shake their heads.

Jacob was never as careful walking through the forests as Ellis, he always found the little roots to trip on, the branches to hit his head. Nothing had changed. He tripped on a tangle of roots, grabbing for the moist wall as he fell, the huge door behind them closed. As if a giant was thumping at the roof, they both were forced to crouch as the tree shuffled slowly away, hidden by the talents of its ancient brother trees.

The roots stabbed at the ceiling, grasping and stabbing through the loose soil. Both coughed and spat. Jacob yelped at a rat which skittered away. The booming faded, and it was so quiet they could hear each other panting. A torch flicked on, still just casting a misty grey glow in the soil smoke.

"We haven't got a choice now. You're the Blessed one with the Hearing, maybe you should go first?" Jacob whispered. Any fear they might have had melted away as they play-fought to decide who might go first. They didn't think about it too much, but the tunnel was just the right size for them to walk side by side. They didn't have to duck.

-

It was a huge tunnel, and even Ellis couldn't remember where they had been going after a short while. The worst problem was not knowing how long it had been or where they were. Sometimes they would stop for a breath and a car would whizz by, rumbling at the earth and nearly covering them with all the torrent of earth shards, slamming down roots and metal scraps.

A long time later, it was hard to tell if the grumbling was the trees, monsters, or just their stomachs. The noise had been rumbling along for so long. They were bruised now, grunting through each step, old spears and rocks would pop up, right in their way. They kept going though, there was no other choice. The first time they had come to a turning, they had both stopped, and stared at each other.

Jacob believed in Ellis and their sense of direction. Ellis just thought Jacob might have had another plan.

They very quickly learned two things; a sense of direction comes from seeing where you've been and where you're going, and batteries really don't last if they should on a smart phone. Jacob was reminded of a labyrinth with a rampaging minotaur. "if we always go left, we'll find a way out."

He almost shouted that one, succeeding in scaring himself and realising any adventure had faded with the torchlight. Soon enough they were nearly blind. Ellis could see even to guide Jacob along, but even they were struggling in the soil and the mess.

They shrank away from the sharp points or the wet pits. Even Ellis had stopped feeling curious about what life might be out there, it all felt like it could be watching them. The worst part of all was somehow it was getting loud and warm, all at the same time. Just like they were walking into the back of an oven in a very busy kitchen.

The only difference was even from here they could hear the buying and feeding. Ellis couldn't argue with the logic of following the left, but twice had been convinced with a sinking feeling they were walking past the same old path again.

It had been too many times now, and the horrible, dizzy feeling of being lost and helpless crept up on them both in kicking bites, and faded as they thought a path was just ahead of them, before all the clarity disappeared.

The whole plan had been for Jacob to feel his way along, Ellis just behind, guiding him around any sharp parts and looking for the end of the tunnel, for any hint of light. To keep going left you must keep in touch with the wall.

Jacob kept stepping slowly forward, shuffling now really after all those steps, trying to hold in the panting panic, and giving up. He took another shuffle forward, dragging himself a little further on his right foot.

The ground gave way, seeming to disappear into a complete void.

Jacob skipped back, losing his grip on a loose root and tumbling into the middle. Ellis fell too, knocking into him and sending them both spinning, knocking the phone to the ground too. "Which way ish left? WHERE are you?!" Ellis pushed out, shaking a little with the fear. A sea of chewing and biting came from nowhere, and they both realised just how loud Ellis had been, trying to find him in the dark.

Jacob was relieved Ellis had said it first. The growing roar of some huge beast stopped any questions though, and they both stood up, trying to run. Then they paused and stood, facing a hard cliff full of jagged rocks. The chewing roar came closer and closer, its growling echoing with the echo of an evil laugh.

10: IT CAN'T SEE US IF WE'RE IN ITS MOUTH

There are animals out there – small fish, and little birds called plovers – who live off feeding from the food in other animal's mouths. The first one swoops near a shark and cleans its teeth, the birds sitting in the mouths of crocodile and feeding while the crocs relax with their mouths wide open. Being fearless is amazing, so long as you're fast.

The funny thing about the fight or flight instinct is if you can't run, the need to fight becomes even more powerful than it might normally be. Both Jacob and Ellis roared, trying to sound loud and scary in the huge space. They failed. Ellis worst of all, the nerves bringing out sharp hiccups. Jacob could only struggle out a small note before he stopped too.

Something far bigger and far hungrier was roaring back. For once, they didn't need the dark to add to their imagination, the booming groan was enough. In the background, they could hear huge bumps, more and more ground falling around them from this massive thing shaking in the ground.

"Maybe...", Jacob shouted against the sea of sound, already correcting himself, they had gone down too many steps for the vibration to get right to the surface. The booming grew louder, from some light out there, the yellow glow of long fangs glowed, and it was obvious which way the mouth was moving.

"We have to run at it! Then we'll have to get past it.

Now! As fast as we can!" Jacob shouted, wincing as he watched Ellis try to shrink and lean back into the rocks, both hands scrambling for some hidden exit. Ellis was whistling quietly, holding that firm face which told you one thing, they were struggling to hold back tears.

Jacob grabbed both hands of Ellis's, staring into their eyes. Everything stopped for a second, as the roof just over them started to collapse, Jacob pulled and nearly threw Ellis in front of him. He only let go off one hand, they were in the dark after all. Ellis couldn't help but giggle as they spun, that touch of light was enough for them to avoid any little spikes. As Ellis unspun back the other way, they skipped a little, still trailing that hand behind them.

"So long as you're coming?" Ellis yelped, starting to run as the whole world started to fall apart. The ceiling fell in huge flaps, and they had to punch at them while they fell. Then the pieces of soil grew bigger, big clumps of grass knocking them to the side.

With that, they started to kick as they ran. Suddenly they were jumping, just judging the gaps between the broken ground. The ground was now only stilts of stronger earth left behind. They sprinted, nearly falling over and grabbing at each other while they almost fell. They grasped at one another's hands, finding the walls falling apart from any touch.

The roaring was all around them, just as Jacob was preparing to leap further forward, Ellis grabbed at him with as much strength as they could muster, just pulling him back as a sea of fangs destroyed the world in front of them. They both balanced on a small stretch of land, kicking at the soil, staring down as it kept falling away from them.

The sea of biting fangs sped past, taking more than a minute to pass in its hugeness. As it passed, the light from the daytime glowed down, but the friends barely have time to recover. They leapt at the soil, scrambling across this huge space and climbing on the soil.

They fell together, hearing the rumbling of this creature grow, both trying to work out what this monster was doing, and thinking it as they sprinted and crashed against the roots. They kept running, seeing just the smallest hint of light. Not knowing where they were going, they ran up an old gate with strange runes scratched across the huge walls. They climbed up the steep steps of this broken ramp cascaded behind them and the whole tunnel was decimated. The King had tried to trap them, but they had gotten out of the trap just in time.

They stopped, just as if they had stepped right into a wall of glass. A searing heat hit them, the deep green light of the forest glowing red from just a little to their right. The forest so many people had been staring at, feeling a sinking fear stood at the top of an old hill. As Ellis and Jacob looked around themselves, they could see Greenview below them.

They both gulped, pushing themselves against a nearby tree as huge shadows walked past them. A trumpet blew harshly out, and as they shivered from the sharp note, they realised something had seen them.

Dark red eyes stared down at them from the tree above. Ellis couldn't explain it, but they could feel the emptiness without a listening tree nearby, or even a small sprite to smile up at.

"Surrender", the burning bird grunted, stabbing its sharp wing at the closest flames as a wave of gurgling answered in agreement, the darkness waving a little in the sheer weight of all those creatures.

-

The metal of their tight cages bit at the skin, and their hearts wouldn't stop beating from the rush of running. The huge, tunnelling creatures disappeared to the depths of earth, waiting instruction. They had been working hard, and Jacob kept staring down at the black beasts they'd ran from before. There were a group of them, walking down the tunnel in one large troop.

Two of them pushed up at the roof of the tunnel, most of them scraping at the earth, and just two grasping at some strange bags of material behind them. One of the big bags dragged against the earth, some little points reaching out to the little roots. One of the dark beasts growled at the bag, but it held on.

The bag was torn into, little hands trying to work their way out, and Jacob tapped at Ellis while the child tried to escape, fighting and then scrambling out of the bag, pushing up and running as fast as she could. The beast howled, chasing after him, as the little child hit behind the tree, scrambling further up the hill.

Jacob turned to Ellis, trying to work out everything that was going on, hoping they might be able to tell him the way out. There was a group of them stuck in the cage, too many than was comfortable, stabbing pains from an elbow knocking into his chest, and if he moved, someone else might groan back in the bleak darkness.

Ellis wasn't there.

Jacob was powerless, staring at Ellis as they ran toward the child, and looking all around, just to see how they had done that so quickly. He climbed up, taller than the other children in the cage. Those children were still crying, no idea of anything around them, each staring at the fires and the beasts.

Jacob grunted as he tried to climb the tree the cage had been wrapped around, the roof of the cage was only build for small children. With his heart still racing, he grabbed for the roots of the tree. "Same as always" he grumbled, kicking at the bark of the tree while he fell back down in the cage, just about fitting his leg through a gap between two other people, not hitting into them. Never quite able to find his centre of balance.

He scraped his knees and arms, still bending down at the metal floor of the cage instead. At least he could break that. From his pocket in a pocket, he grabbed at a little swiss army knife. Tiny scissors unfolded, and with the clarity he could always get in crises, with a few snips, they fell to the floor in a pile, Jacob didn't mention it, but he was glad for someone breaking his fall.

The kids jumped up from the blow, some of them spluttering feathers as they ran. Jacob had more important things to look after. He just made sure none of the beasts had noticed. No, Ellis was staring them down.

That sharp, whistling note echoing against the trees. None of them moved, this was not a magic place.

Jacob ran to Ellis's side, grabbing at his phone to make the low note which might make something happen. The groaning echoed again, pushing away at the trees with the force of something answering their noise. The ground rumbled, beasts grumbling as they tried to run back out of the tunnel. Jacob pushed his hand against Ellis's back, feeling like they might have done something to stop this evil.

The tunnel slammed closed, and Ellis ran out of breath. The silence grew. Flames started to whisper and float toward them both, smoking in the air as they danced. They both tried to knock back the flames, afraid of what they might do if they caught on the branches. The searing heat was growing stronger, bigger than either of them. It almost seemed to form the outline of a person, and then it all faded away again.

They both stood there, in the dark which the fire did not beat back, the only sound the deep breathing of those beasts, as they worked to surround them both. "These trees aren't listening; do you know what to do?" Jacob whispered, grabbing for Ellis's hand in the dark, feeling the rush of air as a beast snorted nearby, flinching as its wet, thick arm stroked past their face, trying to grab at them in the endless shadow.

A huge sea of flame blew at them, rushing something right in front of them. They both blinked in the sudden light while the darkness disappeared. They were staring straight at a burning woman, not knowing her as the Ash

Queen. They were rooted to the spot in fear, staring around them, and trying to think of something.

They crept around a nearby tree, trying to catch a clearer sight of the flames on their own while they calmed. The woman was barking at the beasts, yelling at them to catch the children. Something just behind her whirled, showing just the hint of a city nearby. She snapped straight in front of them, smiling with a dagger in one hand, and the other curled up in a sharp claw.

"This is a land of fire and ash. I can't let you go and tattle on me now, can I?"

-

It was hard to say where the flames began, and where the person was, or people. Faces and arms swirled in the ash of this indescribable mess of fire and heat, burning at the leaves around it. The leaves fell as if caught in a horrible wind, both Jacob and Ellis were wincing from the acidic touch of it. In the distance, the yelp of children echoed along the trees.

In all this chaos, Ellis sat down. Their friends might have been away from them, but one sprite did watch from above. They had felt Ellis disappear in the tunnels, a cursed place they hadn't been in for so long. They could only catch the hint of their blonde hair, just as they sat down. As the branches blew a chaos of leaves around them all, burning as they rose.

Jacob stood next to Ellis, running toward the Ash Queen, trying to distract her for a second, but there was no water, nothing to stop this burning woman from advancing. She stepped closer, whispering to herself and growing bigger, pushing back at the trees in her way. Jacob was quick to work out this had been the source of all that smoke Ellis had ran after.

A buzz grew behind him, a sound coming from two places in a high buzz which could only be coming from Ellis. It had a power to it, and as Jacob ran from the monster, he couldn't find the strength to life Ellis up. Ellis who was screaming with an open mouth, one hand seeming to hold onto that other sound, as it opened the noise grew louder. They were stuck to the floor, hands closed together with white knuckles, almost shaking with the force of their emotion.

As it grew louder, Ellis started to float. Slowly at first, then pushing half-way between the roof of the trees and the soil. The soil floated with him, and the fire couldn't touch the growing yell. The whole place had been made as a trap to make new beasts, and the Ash Queen knew the power of fear. She just hoped that nothing would come among this world and destroy its corruption.

Ellis breathed in, and with their eyes open and glowing bright blue, pushed out with this tamed force, slamming the high note against every tree. The fire nearly stopped, the Ash Queen crouching under this attack. She snapped her fingers together, but nothing happened. One of the burning birds swooped down, igniting her hands, and flapping wildly toward the beasts they would need to fight against this storm.

That same black corruption fell away from the old trees, and they groaned bodily while they cracked to the floor. The branches unfurled, growing yellow from the

116

attack. She slammed both hands down onto the grass, burning away at the strands of green and blooming a huge cloud of fire and smoke.

Ellis crashed to the ground, dazed but glowing just a little from the sunlight that had come out of them, ignoring the fact it was the night. It was a gold light, and with it, a silhouette of wings shimmered just behind Ellis as they stood back up. Jacob ran to their side, grabbing their hand and staring at the growing figure swelling from the burning remains of those destroyed trees.

The ash smoked high in the air, but from a distance, something was hiding the chaos and it worked to push down the gap it had let through. The gold light was beaming down, it was only the afternoon, these enemies and beasts were trying as hard as possible to make fear. The Ash Queen spat magma and burned at the forest in front of her, breaking down the trees as she grew stronger.

Beasts ran toward the huge mass, and while they growled and bit at each other preparing for a charge, Jacob slung his arms underneath Ellis. They started to run. Soon enough Ellis could see what was happening, but was so drained they could only lean against Jacob as they tried to get away, nearly crawling at times, but just finding a way out, and down to the safety of the other trees below.

-

Jacob and Ellis just kept running, pushing through something strange and electric, jumping from the static, and seeing the outside of this chaos, just a small breath of smoke was all they saw. The sudden, hard rain slowed them down, but they couldn't stop, knowing what lurked amongst those trees. Jacob panted in the ditch, recovering under a tree which seemed to lean even more to cover him from the fire.

Ellis was nowhere to be seen.

Jacob ran back, thinking the worst may have happened, or that Ellis might have had enough and just lie there in the cold. In fact, as usual, Ellis was talking to the magic of the world, with a strange figure grown right out of a few raindrops hovered in front of them, waving its hands at Ellis in some strange way they seemed to remember. Other sprites in a stormy wave, ran at the forest throwing themselves at the beastly thing that pushed at the roof of the forest.

Jacob fidgeted as the electric shock passed through him again, some strange screen passing him by. For just a second on the edge of his sight, strange metal lines ran by, but then quickly it was gone again while the other half of the screen ran past, fizzling as it went. As it rained, he watched as a thousand small figures laughed and glittered past him, small faces chuckling with shining eyes. He leant back, looking up at the huge hand of water rushing past.

There was just the hush of words for that short moment, the river running as fast as it could toward the forest. He hadn't realised it, but the sound of smoke had been a huge noise, and now it had gone, it was like a breath had been taken out of the world with a soft groan. Trees crackled and died, pushing out of the ditch and surrounding Jacob as he walked toward Ellis.

The energy of the expanse seemed to shift to announce something else was about to happen, something they wouldn't forget for such a long time. Ellis was still talking to the sprite, teary eyed as they usually became in the presence of nature, but Jacob knew something was different. In the distance, the Ash Queen yelled at the falling rain, starting to squeal as the darkness disappeared.

It had turned to a whirlpool, pushing down at that cursed part of the trees, the only sound soon enough was a strange whirring noise, like an old fan had been left alone, and Jacob wandered where the sounds of the town had gone, and what that fizzing might have been.

He didn't have long to think about it though, Ellis grasped his hand tightly, with much more force than Jacob thought they could. "It can sign," he said, struggling through the tears. Jacob shook his head as he stood next to Ellis, watching them talk to one another quietly with the sign language, something telling him that was a huge moment, but not telling him why. "The only other person I've known that could sign was Mum, what does it mean?"

For once, Jacob didn't know what to say.

-

"Up?" They were both sat down now, quizzically staring at the figure who'd stayed behind, even after the fire had gone out, and only the grunting of the beasts sometimes interrupted their guessing. The fizzing feeling had gone past one more time, and Jacob had tried to grab onto it.

He could remember a lot of things, if he held onto the idea for long enough, then he'd happily analyse it later.

It was a perfect memory, but it could only really work if the thing he was remembering made any sense. This didn't. Now the fizzling, strange light had gone past, all they could see was a small smoke from the forest. While the monster had been struggling, it had reached up and pulled at the old trees, pounding away at the long stretches of wood and burning them.

There were no scald marks in the floor anymore, nothing to say what a huge monster had cursed the land and not even the hint of the beasts or the running marks left by the children who had retreated and scraped their way back to the town. He was so tired, he could just see the hint of sunlight reaching out below the hill.

"Like this…? Why not?" Ellis grumbled, flopping back down to the grass again in exhaustion, trying to find some answer to why standing up or jumping wasn't quite right. Ellis looked around them, trying to find anything above them they could scream at, but in their exhaustion, not even thinking that was real anymore.

The little water sprite chuckled, and pointed its tiny hand at the sky. It was floating in the air, and it was only a quarter as tall as either Ellis or Jacob. It still wobbled in the air with energy, and for just a moment it was lost to them both. It was staring at the sky, and whistling in a strange noise, just like rain pattering against a tin roof, a high note.

The sky began to open, a golden light Jacob just recognised through the smoky haze of the last evening, and he coughed at the memory of it, his mind was so linked to the experience. In the early morning sky, the hint of some strange city echoed in the golden light, the sharp knife-strikes of silver star-light, there was a centre of blinding brightness. Ellis and Jacob stared up to it, just about seeing the edges of graceful buildings of glass. Around them the trees groaned, seeming to chuckle themselves just a little too.

The whining noise of a fly just far enough away that you can't hit it grew louder, and even the branches of the trees shook. Around them, a small golden light was growing, but any time they moved, it grew weaker again. Summoning them from the heavens above.

From the top of the hill, a strange metal shape ran toward them, fizzling through that odd screen. It didn't move with one foot in front of the other, but almost seemed to roll and tumble. "An anti-sprite", the largest tree groaned, and with that, the water sprite shook its arms at the golden light, waving its small hands at the beam.

The metal thing was getting closer, a bright screen where its face should have been, the rest of it made from the scraps of old wires and tubes. One leg was a strange tangle of aerials, the other a long wheel. It gurgled, and as it came closer, the inside of it was one of those curved statues, the pyramid face hidden behind a screen that wouldn't stop smiling.

The beam started to work, pulling them all up, roots and all. No matter what the water sprite tried to do with its waves of water, it only created sparks. The branches fell against the space where the anti-sprite had been. They were all going up together. Jacob and Ellis rested under the waft of warmth which covered them both.

11: HIGH ABOVE AND OUT OF REACH

Most birds can only sing one note, different rhythms but other than that they are stuck. Then there are special birds who can do even more than these ones. The Mockingjay can make the sound of any bird it wants, changing note easily. Then there is the Lyrebird which can make any sound it wants, just like a beatbox. They've been seen making the sound of a chainsaw, a camera and even a car alarm. Look up in the skies and the trees, who knows what you might see.

The Burning King walked briskly past his wonders. They were huge metal statues, built to show each age of mankind, all the way back to when they first met the King. The first statue stood with a spear, hunched and covered in furs. He and his Queen walked through, passing each statue quickly. The vaulted ceiling was filled with thin, white lights, and they snapped out of each metal statue, adding to the moodiness of the sombre room.

The Queen kept chasing after him, captured by each picture, and pulled forward to not be too far away from her loved King. She had been spending so long away from him, wandering if he was coming back, or had really fallen as the people said.

It seemed he had been spending his time watching the world go by. They stopped at the last statue, a huge grin spreading on his face. He had been ready for a show, and a cloth was thrown over the last monument.

The one just before showed a man walking on his books, stepping into the air just as if he was reaching to the very top of some heavenly point of knowledge. "Guess what this is," he growled, always pleased by how much taller than her he was, right now the way the light was eclipsed by him, and she stared up in the dark.

"I think you'll show me them being taken by surprise?!" She laughed in a small jump of excitement, knowing this would be the time when he would show her all his strength and wrath, the kind of lethal time when she was far too precious to be out there while the world fell apart.

"Damn, I forget just how well we know each other." He grumbled, the lingering smile making it so obvious how much he didn't mind. He grabbed the corner of the cloth, handing it to her with a flare. "You've been watching them for so long, you might as well ",

"Sir, sir, you have to come with me" a mechanical voice boomed, the only way it could show fear by the pace of its talking. Every word came out at the same tone and the King held back an old wrath. It was strange to be among people again, and not hunting through all those networks. There were so many radio signals, so much feedback in the chat across the internet.

Rolling for just a second in the sickness of that disconnect, he pushed one muscular hand to the side. He was trying to swipe away at this sickness. He missed, crashing into the small, metal statue that had ran to him. His slab of a hand smashed straight through the figure, the silver parts which had made it up dropping with a soft twinkling.

"Huh, I always enjoy watching this." His eyebrows rose in a theatrical awe while the small, glowing extensions crawled toward each other again, trying to make itself back again. "Try to be stronger this time." He growled, growing tired of the silly thing. Just as tired as he was of every person all around him. He sniffed the air, shaking his more burned hand.

The air in front of him squeezed into a thin, grey light, the line going straight past them at speed, and down some dark alleyway in the depths of the tower.

They followed it, the Ash Queen getting distracted, and running herself to catch up over and over. She skipped past another large, plastic door, a sharp right turn and she crashed straight into his back.

"Oops, "she squeaked, nearly drunk with the question which still waited. She squinted at the light of a huge screen, smiling at the small rose which glowed to the side in a deep red.

"The first thing is the green fool has cursed us to destroy the natural world around us. It makes people sick, it makes things worse. They thought it would only make us weaker, but they haven't realised the potential they unleashed."

He pushed that same burned hand into the screen, the fingers splayed open quickly, bubbling just a little as they fused with the display. A hundred small squares appeared around a middle, glowing as it rolled through each different view, rolling over and over.

It stopped fixing on the golden beam of Ellis escaping.

The screen cracked from his wrath, and that statuesque servant stood to his side, waiting for permission to start repairs. Without a word telling it what to do, the servant fused back into the wall. It had one small light in the middle of its pyramid head, listening to the noise of the next command.

This light rolled back up the walls, along a complex circuit and away to make more cameras, or some other task the King needed. He didn't take no as an answer.

"It started as an inner weakness, I know you felt the wounds and ran underground to our first home. So many of us fell, I say it easily, the best of us died first. They were the purest flames and strikes of light. There were different people though, like you and I, spread through the different tribes. We felt the pain and embraced it, learning to push it out as we had the fire.

"The most amazing part is they will learn about it right now." With a smash of force which crashed through the wall, nearly tipping him over, if the Queen hadn't tilted him back with her own powers. She watched Ellis and Jacob disappear, looking at a calm scene and frowning.

"They're running away, dearest, humans can't take it and they never turn up. Some of the green fools' oldest children are leaving the battle. Why are we so cross?" She whined, not quite able to keep up with the man she feared and loved so thrillingly.

Both his eyes glowed deep black, just the way they did for all his creatures, but with a shake of the head, his calm blue eyes glowed back instead, "They have the Hearing, and they were picked to go up there. One of our anti-sprites goes with them, and the war goes on. We must destroy everything they have, but the world has ruined my plans by creating two of those things which destroys us before. The fool's ways are always to rush away from us."

He sighed deeply, bending under the loss of all that time, and blinking heavily, his eyes flicking from side to side, weighing up a thousand things. Those he could say, and those he would not, those options he would always hold back just in case the flames needed to rest and calm for another thousand years. Even deeper, the darker horrors of anything he would do to silence every enemy in a wave of flames.

"I must throw my oldest tricks at these people, to jump up and reach those wonderful times when people ran in fear from my name, scraping the floor as they bowed before leaving. The second thing you must learn is that all these tricks, all these revelations humans have stumbled upon so unbelievably quickly. Every one of them has been fed through me.

"Sit back and watch." The statue unfolded out of the wall at that command, bending as a small chair for the two of them. They watched the pictures from the anti-sprite, the images struggling and wobbling as it moved to wherever that golden place was. Just under the gaze of the King the signal grew stronger. Pushed by the war rushing on, he closed his fist. The anti-sprite didn't need any more of a command than that.

In the smaller screens, hundreds of people walked by, looking down at their phones. Their statues walked onto their resting places, some growing larger while others flickered with electric power. Both the King's and the "green fools" powers wished for the humans to follow them, but only one group was prepared to try and take it by force.

-

Jacob woke in liquid starlight. It dripped onto his head, as he coughed and turned his heads as the twinkling liquid thrashed and played against his hair. He looked down at his hands and all around him, surrounded by everything that sparkled with the light of the stars. Jacob shook his head groggily, the bleariness from a deepest sleep.

His hands slowly moved. Not quite seeming to have control over his hands quite yet, watching the golden light twinkle and dazzle just in front of his face. He sat up slowly, staring at the beautiful world which glowed in front of him. The water sprite and Ellis had gone, but Jacob felt the warmth of knowing they would be together soon enough, knowing there was nothing that could stop them now.

The whole world was on their side.

He sat bolt upright, grabbed by a dazzling purple light which danced just in front of him and away, down past the impossible waterfalls. He tried not to look at them, they made him dizzy, but gawp he did. The deep blue spheres of ocean held themselves up, as if they were goldfish bowls. There were a hundred different ones, some steaming, some of them riddled with great icicles, and deep vibrations shook the bowls, tipping them further and further.

The bowls rolled, and the liquid flowed in whichever direction it wanted, the water glowing too just like glitter. It flowed and filled other globes. In one or two places, a long chain of tiny spheres filled up and sang out little notes as the water rumbled by. Jacob stood up, fascinated by the energy of these waters. He stared around him, following the flows of those colours.

He had been sleeping in another bowl, as it tipped under the water, he climbed out and into the avenue of huts and huge trees which marked down toward some white, glowing temple. It was blurry from the waves bustling past, and the clouds which slowly wafted by. He stepped forward uncertainly.

He wandered while he stared at the water, long rivers rolled and twirled like paper does if it's wound round and round a pencil. It twirled and danced, as he watched, one big surfing wave crashed into a cloud, exploding in a rich rainbow which splashed onto his face. It was such a thick vapour, he couldn't help but chew the rainbow light.

A massive cloud stopped in mid-air, it was shaped a little like a rabbit, just far fluffier. The head turned to look at Jacob, and with that the cloud started to run toward him. He hadn't noticed though, looking carefully at a strange rollercoaster of rich purple steam, little shadows jumped over a steep ramp, leaping through the glistening space, and he landed in a splash on the other side.

He crashed into a huge leg, for a second thinking it

was a house, or a skyscraper, but the huge length walked past. The foot of long roots kept going past, and he couldn't quite see the top of the tree, just small growths of green in the lowest branches. It stepped so slowly, he had walked a hundred winding steps before it rumbled with its other foot falling. He looked back to see a tree taller than any mountain or hill he had ever seen before, in the bark runes which must have been bigger than ten people spiralled around in bright, twinkling purple.

A bird called above him in a long and sweet note, circling past, and he had to squint in the sudden light. A colossal bird flew past, one flap of its wings pushing the clouds forward and keeping the water flowing. It had the wrinkles of a tortoise, the way the skin stretched, but its bright feathers hadn't stopped glowing, no matter how old it might have been.

For a short moment, at least one thing made sense, the huts. He had seen them in an old book at school, they were the first mud huts people had made right at the beginning, just about able to make shelter with mud and hay. "Are these the first trees we ever cut down?" He shook his head, that was not the most important thing to know. "Where am I? Where is Ellis? Hmmm"

He kept walking, but he caught a foot on a small stone, and looked down. Through the thin clouds, he could see the top of his own head, and a cloud hopping toward him, kicking its legs behind it as it flapped in the air. He moved one hand slowly again, they were so heavy, and his stomach grumbled, even louder this time.

What felt like a giant marshmallow squished into his side, and for a second all he could see was pink and fluff. All he could feel was wet, the only sound the same noise it might have made if he had dunked his head in a pool. He couldn't push his hands up, the cloud was far too excited, squishing him more and more.

He was lifted by his legs, pulled away from the little film of air that had been holding him. He just caught sight of that purple light he had been following, but now it was just twirling and running back into him. It looked just as confused as him. Out of the moist slurping and slapping, a giggle he knew far too well began. With a gasp, he pushed his head out of the cloud, and couldn't help but jump at the clump of cloud that was thrown right at his face, not as cold as a snowball but just as surprising.

Ellis sat in front of him, chewing on a tangle of the pink cloud, twirled around his head just like candy floss. Jacob raised one eyebrow as high as he could, trying to stop it moving up there again, it had done that so much these last few days it was starting to ache. "Don't worry, she doesn't mind." Ellis leaned over the sprite's seat, signing with one hand and only focussing on Jacob with one eye. "She says you're hungry, tuck in!"

To the amazement of Jacob, Ellis leaned back, completely relaxed as they flew straight into the swirling temple. It looked like a swirl of ice cream, instead of a flake of chocolate, a beam of that purple light shimmered instead. He grabbed at a clump of cloud, sighing at the sweet, filling taste just as they flew into the temple. They were both staring up and up a spiral with the most purple waterfall flowing gently down, lightly singing a calm nonsense.

-

The anti-sprite wasn't really an anti-sprite. It wasn't really the Ash Queen either, both forms had swirled from it in a blooming shock of electricity.

It was whatever it needed to be to make the most chaos possible. Anyone who might have found one called it a "Mirroring", because if you broke it then you had the worst luck for such a long time. It was hard to walk straight past, and it could only take a picture if there is something to reflect. Then it would have fun destroying whatever was looking at is.

The Mirroring is the madness of a volcano suddenly waking up, just to hiccup and go back to sleep. The moment every light turns off in a street and the power is gone, but no one can explain why. Even when somebody trips on nothing but their own foot, walking into a room and forgetting why you'd gone in there in the first place.

Once they were made from the chaos and magi, and a swelling madness, they'd normally start a fire or as the worst kind of earthquake. Sometimes they just exploded and rocked a long wave somewhere in the distance. That was only if they were set free and there was nobody to reflect. Then they would grow older, and the best they could do is make sure your seat was just a little further back than it was supposed to be.

Some people called it narcissism, but now that everyone was looking at the screens. The Burning King had lost count of all the little nuisances which had broken free. They had been unleashed from all those eyes staring, feeding on every piece of information they could. Most of them just being annoying, but this one had slumbered and trained with the Ash Queen.

As the children slept through the beam, it had cracked a whip of lightning strikes at the Mirroring, but they each bounced back. You either left these things alone, or you made it see its own reflection, then it wouldn't know what to do.

The water which flowed and rushed, the light that flashed and flickered past, made reflections. Each time, the Mirroring squeaked and hid. As they left the old world behind it reached a power the King nor the Queen would have worked out, once it had run away from the rules of direct attack of the acid it felt which the Mirroring felt where the trees had experienced life. Now, every limit went away.

it had been a strange mix of screens and metal, but now it tried to form just the hint of Jacob's face. Twinkling in the golden light and dancing in front of it, and still the forms struggled and flashed out in harsh spasms. It blew back from the force of that angry light, and became smaller and smaller. Still, the brothers all around these higher worlds were waking, and it was happy at the distant signals that answered its calls.

It grew tired from just staying up against this onslaught. It popped out of sight and became a sharp breath of wind, rushing and nearly unbalancing the little group. Each time it tried to grab onto the branches, they fought and slapped at the thing, just as anyone might against an insect, fighting without being able to help it.

As it grew more tired, it gripped onto the picture of Jacob, just glowing in the distance, barely grabbing onto the beam as everyone moved beyond. It stood in the space Jacob's reflection was supposed to be, looking for any moment when he might turn back to look at it, and then it would flinch straight at him.

-

The cloud bit away at the Mirroring while it rose, snipping and breaking it down. It knew when it was defeated and, so it leapt, and the transformation began. A whale sang in its long, drawn notes from some huge flowing river. Every other sound was a soft mumbling, or the snoring of ancient sprites, waiting for the moment when the mortal world might call on them again.

It fell to the floor, slobbering and spitting out from the acidic bites the thin, gold brightness hurt it with. It was popping up its arms and exploding like a row of zits, swelling and popping and squeaking to pop again. The noise started to echo, as the river flowed past its chuckling growths.

What's the best thing to fight away at the waters and soft clouds? Hard stone. So, like a pattern of sharp cliff rocks, the grunting laughter of this Mirroring grew and grew, snapping its rocky mouth back together. Jacob and Ellis wafted through the air, and no matter how much they tried to turn their cloud down back to this monster, it kept hopping up, pulling on the air with unstoppable speed.

The bright purple light twinkled and played as they got higher and higher, twirling up the strange cone, pulling at the strange rabbit while it charged up. Their laughter popped off the side of the walls, but the Mirroring was hungry and threw back the wall, slamming against the side of the huge tower.

It was knocked back again, booming with a loud horn at the fight coming toward it. The cloud rabbit kept trying to climb, trying to take them somewhere beyond. Ellis screamed, knowing only they could make them rise. Quickly enough they were pulled up, rising with the sheer force of their scream. It was still not enough though, the continuing attack grew stronger, and with a small look, the Mirroring saw the two of them, there was only thing it could do.

The huge hand reached around the cloud, pushing down on it while the fluff tried to grab at the whole thing. Jacob and Ellis hid, running into its chest, but the hard spikes were not going anywhere, and soon they were falling in the rain. The drops grabbed back together again, as the water sprite worked hard to come back to life, flowing through the spikes which fell, and racing to catch up with the falling children.

The air rushed past them, the little bits of light pushing them back up, little shocks running chills up them, but before long they couldn't help but look down. They tried to push toward each other, but the spikes kept falling, and the force was too much.

Jacob looked all around him, and still the spikes fell, and he tried to grab to one of the small points that dragged against the ruin while it fell. His hands strained, but he held on, then with more cruelty, the point sliced through his arm, and he screamed out. He jumped down, hearing the rumble of the building, but he couldn't see how to land.

The building shook, huge slabs falling past him, blocking out the light. It was just enough for them to both try and avoid the slabs, but soon enough under the chaos, and the reaching hands of the Mirroring, there didn't seem to be a way out. The purple light spans below them, swirling and grabbing at them. With a bright smash, both fell to the ground outside this destroyed building.

What felt like soft hands grabbed at them, and they fell behind large, glowing figures, still fighting with the Mirroring madness.

12: THERE'S NOTHING ELSE TO DO BUT RUN

You might think that at 61mph, the cheetah is the fastest animal on the planet. It is the fastest runner; much faster than even we can drive on most roads. The fastest though is the Peregrine Falcon, when it is hunting in a dive, it can go up to 200mph. Of course, humans have gone twice the speed of sound, so we can still do so much more.

The Mirroring screamed, slamming the scraps of that building behind it, gawping at the sea of spikes going up slowly to glowing light of that other place. The building boomed as it collapsed, the rubble a climbing frame for the beast, and it couldn't help but yell as it stepped over the tower of parts. Its feet feeding away at the rubble, and it grew even taller, until it could just grab up and bite at the swirling light.

The purple light began to change, turning darker. Ellis pushed past the glowing shapes, but one turned back, a soft face telling them to stand back. Each of the crowd of sprites were gesturing. Some threw torches of light at the Mirroring, each time it touched the monster, it grew smaller, and bent under the toll, throwing another piece of rubble and turning away.

They struggled, but the same beam shattered through the slab. Still others grabbed at the oceans around them, pulling on the waters. They were singing in high notes, a lot like Ellis's singing, but notes that danced and rolled over each other in a lovely harmony.

The water swelled strange shapes, and soon enough even the water sprite was singing along with Ellis and Jacob, as those massive creatures were coupled by sprites worked out of the light itself. These figures ran across the world, grabbing at the Mirroring while it grew and grew.

The light burned away at it, and each time, the rolling liquid flowed and pushed down, and with it the creatures sang past, striking through the Mirroring. It flickered and tried to reflect everything around it, flashing and changing, but growing all the weaker. With the will of those strange people, its spikes rolled back up and knocked it down, each one shining brightly.

With the unending attack, it popped into a thousand small parts, each trying to reflect a smaller and smaller figure. Soon enough, it exploded in one great boom, and with it, the group ran forward, mumbling in low notes now, some singing at the high note just as Ellis and Jacob had.

With that, the building started to shatter, and with it, the purple light flowed again, flowing out of the people too, just as they started frantically to look around them. Four or five of the people grabbed at them, feathers stroking their hands.

"You have to keep going, follow the daggers and find that monster. You will be safe with us here." As Jacob and Ellis grabbed at the assuring hands, they rose. Looking down, they could see small, spiked figures running wildly around, some jumping up to try and get to them, climbing a building which had learned to lash out by removing its walls.

A pink cloud covered them as they rose again, this time it was more of a rushed push that a relaxing rest to go even further beyond. "It was trying to change our birth world, where we came from. We can explain everything, but first we must protect that sacred land."

-

They were not human, that was for sure. They stood taller than an adult, but the grass' green glow was strange. Jacob was staring at them, trying to figure out if he was awake, but wincing from a heavy pinch in his head. Ellis walked around him, laughing and jumping with the tiny sprites that danced on this glowing, golden world.

Around them though, there was a sickness, and Jacob felt as if there would never be a time when they would be able to relax together, strange shining things in the distance more than just the spikes they had been running after. There was a deep blue light on this world, a blooming pulse which shimmered off strange figures which writhed and rolled across the grass. Every time it pulsed, that same pain racked itself through Jacob's skull, but that didn't stop him trying to move forward.

The feathered beings pushed the two of them back, tensing themselves to fight at the oncoming attack. It felt like the air around them breathed in and grew hard. With a deep gulp, the weird, fluid air rolled and rocked forward, pounding along in waves of fizzing shock. The green sprites pushed at this wave, working together to try and keep these things back, while the grass breathed in the attack, it grew stronger and popped with explosions of seedlings.

The odd metal Mirroring things leapt over the wave, just as it was pulled up to try and stop them. The sheer force nearly knocked everyone back, but while they held an electric bond which tensed like rope and held them up, both Jacob and Ellis fell back. They tried to stand up, grabbing at the air while the booming continued. They couldn't talk to each other, just reach out across the grass while they crawled toward each other, trying to hide but hold strong together,

The bond between the other group fell away, the shock exploding and making them all roll backward, just as they grabbed at the grass. There wasn't anything to hold onto, they kept rolling back. Feathers flipped past, scraping claws along the floor, and with a final screech, they all fell together against an absorbing wall, just like the wall of a bouncy castle. It was the only thing stopping them disappearing into a black infinity.

Jacob grabbed at the air, catching the shine of that conjuring, the wall glowing with little breaths across it, small lines of silver lace dancing along that strange screen. It seemed to talk to him, to tell him that there was one gesture just behind the need for something special to happen. He felt something deeper, and time itself seemed to slow down, each breath as a deep crumple like someone walking quietly over leaves.

He could see the silver Mirroring, and in their slowness, he watched as more forms pushed out of that ochre they had seen in the forest before, and though it looked like they jumped forward, they were feeding and biting on the world just in front of them, corrupting the very air as the ochre illness struck it. It spilled and tore through the air, breathing down on their haggard breaths and reaching out through the space it had taken up. Its hunger wouldn't stop.

The grass was burning below them, curving and turning darker as leaves do in winter. The Mirroring grew bigger. Just as the figures reached through the small gap between them and Jacob, some strange red world glowed in his mind's eye. He turned away from that, from here he could feel the heat pushing out of it, the deep smoke.

The silvery nonsense on this wall seemed to be fidgeting, trying to get a reaction from him, but he couldn't figure it out. There was so much noise on the screen, he waved a hand in front of him, alarmed by the scratches and little burns on his hands, and trailing up his arms.

At some point, maybe in the wind, his school shirt had torn away up to his shoulder on one side, a small burn as an ugly little mark on one of his legs. The trousers scuffed and torn up both legs, mostly where he had been rolling on the ground and running from the bites of that horrible cage. The deep drum beat of his heart followed slowly like a marching band, one beat lasting the time it took for him to look around.

He stopped, watching the memory of his hand pass by in the silver lacework that still flowed from this screen. He pushed his hand slowly again, watching as it glowed a little more. He pushed both hands, focussing on his heart beat, moving his hands out and shaking his fingers in time to the beat. It was the only thing that felt right, the silver light glowing brighter and firmer.

Time began to speed up, Ellis was trying to scream, but the air could not escape from them quickly enough. Jacob pushed his foot into the ground, twisting it just like those green sprites around him, so both feet stood at a right angle to each other, and for just a second the thrashing wind stopped. Instead, it filled Jacob up.

He felt the force of its breath rolling along his arms, pulse in his bones and pounding right along each hair, but it held back. The power of that driving breath rolled over his body twice and at the last time, it was too much. The feeling didn't quite escape him though, it felt like letting an animal loose and yet still feeling it under the command of your hands.

The booming force knocked back the other feathered figures, they had been trying to roll away from that attack, each of them turned a little as they noticed him fighting back. They pointed at his hand, one pushing him hard against the chest and forced him onto the ground, laughing loudly. Jacob didn't like that, there were too many memories of being knocked down liked this.

He stepped forward again, back into danger.

He shot up, but the same man now was tearful, still staring at his hands, staring at the little lengths of wood they needed to grasp, just for their tricks. "Eden," He yelled, needing to scream over the rushing wind. "She only told me one of you is blessed. One was the most hopeful she could be. Now, I can see it is both of you. Now, I can see we have a chance to keep on living forever!"

Two hands cracked him on the back as they faced the strange machines. They were still backing away though, there was still a sickness in the air and no matter what they did, they were still growing weaker.

"Hold your breath!" Jacob barked, seeing how much faster the metal things were moving now, they were leaping over each other and gasping at the air with a sea mouth that seemed to open and gnaw endlessly now, most of the way down their bodies. There was no void out there now, every millimetre was filled with enemies. He could feel his own breathing getting weaker, some of the other adult sprites had to stop and kneel for a second behind the fighting line, far too tired to move for just a little longer than last time.

Jacob had knocked the feeding tide back twice, but each time they fed on the wind and destroyed it a little more. Ellis was crinkled, whistling low and looking at a little figure which bounded in the grass a little away from them. Jacob didn't notice, he had his own plan. They all took one long breath as he gestured, and with that all the air disappeared. With that, Jacob, Ellis and all the surviving sprites rushed forward, keeping up with the sudden vacuum that exploded around them in a driven tide.

With nothing left to feed on, as they pushed past, every Mirroring fell to the ground. Exhausted himself. Jacob dropped to the ground now, looking at the dead grass as it grew back and glowed again. Looking at the small trees which grew and shook with excitement. A little one popped out of its roots and danced in the blue sky, tripping and quickly getting back up again.

Its face was made from the tiniest wrinkles, itty eyes twinkling while its small hands shook and played. It looked around, trying to find the little parents which it was supposed to be able to see. It tipped over again, turning far too quickly in the direction of something else which clattered behind it.

The Mirroring squirming remnants rose, this time as one being, collected together with a mess of faces tucked away in it. Ellis was the only one left smiling, the one who knew exactly what was happening right in front of them. It started like the soft fall of snowflakes, dancing among the chasing monster and that tiny little new born.

If it knew nothing else, it could feel that same sickness, but each time it tried to run, it fell. That only made it want to run all the faster. The snow grew harder, while the Mirroring grabbed at each snowflake and fed, the flakes pushed straight through it in a golden whisker.

Very soon, it was a growing blizzard, getting stronger and stronger. Each little breath of wind was a paw print, and a little shape in the distance dazzled in front of the monster. Another second passed, and the shape shifted to a small and white fox, sparkling like diamonds. The tail and ears were long twinkling lengths. Every piece of fur bristled with uncontrollable energy, almost blurring as it bounded toward them.

It shook and jumped in the way of the creature, copying

its steps forward, and making sure the creature couldn't run through as it blocked the lumbering monster again and again. The little tree clung to its back, hiding in the fox's fur. With one great bark, a snow drift pounded at the figure, exploding through the Mirroring, until just the impression of it remained, and soon enough even that was gone.

It looked at the group, huge purple eyes glowing at them. It even shook its head, seeming to smile at them, the great whiskers glistening while its shook its head to leave a little drift of snow just behind it. The fox looked away, fidgeted with its nose. After it scratched its head with one paw, and sniffed one more time, with a great kicker, it bounded away, tiny tree sat on top and waving its tiny green leaves through the air as they both disappeared.

Ellis had already started walking without thinking about it, that strange guardian fox leaping through the air with each little step disappeared past the horizon, the white sparkle of snow wafting heavily behind it with each step. Nobody watched as the metal shards crawled and covered the tiny pool which would let anyone escape.

-

The surviving children fled the Ash Queen and her cages as fast as they could, they kept running. They didn't have any phones on them, or anything to tell them where they were heading, or what they might find, but they ran toward the nearest light with as much exhausted hope as they could muster. They looked at each other through the darkness, and they felt just a little stronger.

Of course, they could do this.

Then the light they were following moved just a little, shifting in the strides of something much bigger. There were a few of them, walking toward the town, and all around them.

Without thinking, everyone ducked and crouched, most of them still sneaking to look through the hands they threw in the way. Pure fear at any movement from all that time with those slobbering beasts, less and less children every day.

Now they were escaping, maybe this would be those magic children again. Just like the movies. This was not like the movies though, and their panic forced them to keep running. Between the dark, giant metal legs they could see from the beam of light. If they had to, they would. They sprinted, stopping and running again as the harsh searchlights from those giant things rolled over them and disappeared.

Somehow, they ended up in the town, and they scrambled amongst the little lights of the shops, trying not to scream as a stupid, little fox ran by. The deep searchlights faded away as it scanned for something, pushing the line of light around each building. The immense stepping sleekly past, and staring at more and more of the town when it didn't find its prey. The children were all still together, forgetting any idea of difference, or whichever ones they were supposed to be bullying.

The statues didn't make a sound, their bodies had the shapes of people, but they stretched into a long, thin line. If they needed to step over anything, their bodies just stretched and stretched. Even if it was the huge 3 storey library, it didn't seem to matter. In the back of the town, the survivors ran and stopped, ran and stopped, finding their way carefully down the main road and back home. It was a long road down a hill with fields either way.

A vulnerable path, but one they took without thinking, just as if a wave of fire was right behind them. Just in case the searchlights clasped on them, and then who knew what beasts might be hungry for them that time.

In the day time, the view was lovely, but in the evening, it was just blackness at both ends, along a path where the street lights never worked. The children looked back for just a second again. With a statue lumbering onto the road with a grotesque, long hoot, they all ran toward their houses, this time they wouldn't stop running.

The children knew they had got the chance to name one of these statues, some of them would be famous children to show who had to be protected in all this peace. There had been such a long time without any wars, they only learned about them in their classrooms.

The statues moved slower than their Mirroring cousins, with perfect balance and poise it was a slow weapon. It had a few nicknames, be it the Unmoving, the Volcanic or even Finality, but Serpentine stuck. It didn't move and would just wait for its victims to start running, just so another Serpentine might strike at them.

The Serpentine had pretended to be trees for a long time, but the people had learned how to see a face in the shadows, how to capture anything which had lied and wasn't natural. Being made of stone was too slow and hard to control, and they had left those forms behind. This light steel was perfect, the Burning King was waiting to see their success.

Then the tide could begin.

From a thousand-little fire-pits, while the Mirroring waited for the reflections to capture, the statues were gathering. Some of them seeping into the walls as an art piece, just waiting for the next command. They felt the rumble of their Father in the city nearby, and they knew this was the time.

The Serpentine drifted into homes, pushing lightly on the doors or windows to find their way in. Some turned into tiny, little statues on a chest of drawers. Most of them stood on their pedestals, for so long the people had been told to build statues as a tribute to world peace, as a signal for everyone that there had been great people, and there would be again.

One child leapt across the darkness, landing in the small glow of his garden. Another ran and ran, but she'd grown so lost in the different houses, she couldn't find her way home. As a Serpentine walked over her back, and its sharp foot almost pressed down on her, a big sphere of light exploded in bright purple, and the Serpentine had to pirouette over the shockwave it created. Another child healed from heavy burns without realising it, running faster and faster, moving quicker than a light could, disappearing in a pop of bright light, and before anyone had blinked away the dazzling glow, he was already at home.

13: IN PLAIN SIGHT, BUT YOU CAN'T SEE ME COMING

Chameleons are most known for the two strangest parts of their appearance. Their eyes stick out on stalks and can move and look with each eye on their own. If they want, they can hide away just by thinking about it. It might seem magical, but nature makes everything possible.

The tower had gone silent, every statue slinking out to make their plan even more powerful. The Queen and King had rested, flinching as he felt the power of what he saw. His influence in all those wires, reaching out and grabbing at the people around him. The Queen pushed her hand to try and find the Burning King while she woke, but as with so many times in the old war, he was never here.

She groaned, never a morning person, but always feeling that pull from where he was, just where that flaming passion resided, and with that she wandered toward him. Her forming talents created a brand-new robe over her, always trying to find some new style. This one was a sharp silver artistic piece, draping down in long lines like a curtain, not the sharp shapes of combat.

She didn't think it would be good to be away from the plotting enemy for so long, but she still felt happy not to be waking up in the chill of an open field, or the skulked darkness of the shadow in another forest, chasing the trail of another person who someone had said was born with the Hearing. The disappointment of finding nothing to answer this scent, and on she ran, constantly keeping those beasts in control.

Instead, small white lights shimmered as she stepped, the soft whisper of her slippers rolling along the huge ceilinged arena, the lights pushing out across the high walls in small curving lines. It looked like a mockery of the strange runes, but she didn't want to crane her neck up. She contentedly marched forward, knowing in some small way he'd still be watching her.

He was hunching just a little to look at it even if he was stood over an eight-foot stone model. His back was thick with muscles, a thick crease on his brow, watching over the model and waiting for his Queen to come out and say "Hello". She knew this smouldering mood, it had been one she'd welcomed for a long time, one that had brought out the worst in him, but their best in being away from this hiding and torment.

To the top of the throne, and finally to be the ones in power and worshipped. This flaming gaze he fixed in the model was something that rooted her to the floor. He turned with a small but manic smile, and it swelled to a larger leer while his eyes flicked down and back up at the model.

"There isn't time to guess. There isn't time to plot and hope we might grab one of them. There isn't anything left when they've already found the way up and through to that ugly, green fool. The most powerful thing in the world we've built is data, and the strongest part of that is how they see it.

"Let's play show me tell me. You'll probably want to sit down." The Ash Queen didn't know quite how he had done it, but once again the King had become more powerful than her, as she sat down without telling her body to. She wasn't sure if being watched all the time was as good as it was meant to be. She felt happy ignoring that thought, there wasn't any time to try and figure out where that thought might have come from.

His claws pointed down at the model, and he seemed to be even bigger than he had been before, but she couldn't tell if it was a trick of the light which had seemed to run away, or if it was just him losing control of the monster within. Even though he just stepped forward a little to sit next to her, the floor around them crumpled and the lights groaned.

Every light was dimmed except for a couple that slammed into the model. She tried not to wince, she had hoped for a long time the people would pray to her. They would sit down and dream of her blessings, perhaps build temples in her name, but most of all adore her.

The model was the latest version of man, the next step they were taking without being able to escape it, and without knowing quite what it meant. The figure was bent over, nearly doubled over like the model a long time before it. This one was the first one not staring forward though, it was looking straight down at a glowing screen.

Its face was dropping just a little, and its eyes were huge circles. One hand scraped on the floor, and while the other people were in the middle of a long, loping stride, this one dragged its feet.

"It would have seemed ridiculous even five years ago, and the funniest part is while they slip they start watching the changes and talking about laws, controls. The only problem? Of course, it's still happening, and I let you back in for one reason: it's finally taken control of itself." He chuckled twice, deeply. Each one was a thump in the air, the slam of a heavy door.

A controlled Mirroring walked in, another dark statue. Its feet clacked loudly on the floor. It was the only sound while they both panted with racing hearts, anticipating what was coming next, feeling the sheer rush of it.

The Burning King frowned just a little deeper for a second, pulling their seat closer to the statue. "I told you we cannot wait, the infinite tiny threads have woven in the wind, and it is now time to tie them together. Those people don't realise how much they've let slip, or just how much they've already let me into their lives. There will be peace forever. It is impossible to fight when the idea seems as strange as a unicorn dancing on a wind of fairy-dust."

He winced from his own closed hand, looking down at himself for a second. He was in complete confusion at the claws which had suddenly sprouted from hands which had been dark shadows and wires only the day before. The Mirroring burst into two screens of thin glass, spreading over both their faces as it spun, grabbing at their eyes, seeping into ears and immersing them in the truth.

-

A Mirroring can be trained just like any pet, if it is given enough information, the best it had done before was a tree. It liked the challenge though, and more than that it liked the competition. The Ash Queen and the Burning King both stood behind a muffled glass, forced to stand from the grabbing force, staring at the practising figure of the leader of the GreenView district.

They squeezed into the glass, pushing between the solid structure and through it, a dim burning blackness of their true world glowing in the distance. They knew this place as home, just as they knew of the green fool's nest and its burning grasses.

The Mirroring shook its head, happy to lie in the gap of this false glass instead, happy to keep looking away and keep running, focussing on something else for as long as possible. It learned every tiny gesture, scratching its chin, slowly tilting forward and back while he stroked his tie.

In the divide between worlds, time dragged by as if pushing a hand through syrup. The man that other side of the mirror sneezed, and the Mirroring tried a thousand times to get it just right, any mistake il made, and the Mirroring burned away to nothing. Another Mirroring tried instead, still squinting from the embers of its old brother, and it worked all the harder to copy that man in the real world, not quite looking at his reflection.

So much time went by, every little second was a spider's web of thoughts. There had been a thousand cameras watching along this man's life, and with each moment he slept, a storm of data and quizzes came at the Mirroring. Every memory perfectly remembered, every person in his life mapped against their own minds.

It was only a few days, but it felt like years without blinking, years straining and hurting at the constant information. Then the time came, and without knowing it would come the Mirroring was thrown through the mirror and out into the barely lit bathroom facing that man it had been forced to obsess over all its life.

A power cut broke the light at that time, just the same as it had many times before in these experiments. The cameras had watched traffic flows, the routines of everyone else in the housing estate. Even the air traffic had been watched, some of these take-overs did not go smoothly at all.

They had watched and waited, for so long not knowing why when it became cold, people drank more. They had learned so much since they had started watching. If someone they were working on ended up in prison, or homeless or if anything else had gone wrong, the Mirroring would always try again. It was a position, a place of power in society they were ordered to find, not a specific person.

With the whiplash of the King commanding it to strike, the Mirroring had flapped and fell, almost bumping against a wooden door, and tilting with a twisted body to not make a noise at all, leaning its knee out and punching a hand out to somehow balance. As it tried to stand up, a shower curtain almost clattered to the floor. Right then, the Mirroring used its other talents, those little flickers of weirdness in the corner of your eye. For a second there was a curtain pole about to clatter into toiletries and echo loudly in the bath. The target would come running in, hockey-stick in hand, and in his panic, it wasn't known what might happen next.

That was a chance nobody was going to take. It was much easier to remove the pole altogether, changing any memory to a play of light.

The black exterior of the Mirroring changed to the tanned forearms, the rolled-up sleeves of a blue, checked shirt and the neat trousers. It became the untidy dark quiff of his hear, the piercing brown eyes and tanned face, and the fluffy slippers – the only thing he could find while he wandered in a daze.

"Robert, you are being replaced", the Mirroring repeated over and over. Its voice slowly became his, while the body formed into a reflection of him. Robert slammed through the door and the Mirroring was just in front of him.

Robert paused in a dizzied haze, just awake, it was impossible for him to know if he was still dreaming, and he shook his head slowly in the exhaustion. The Mirroring copied it in an exact replica of the way he pushed his hand through that untidy hair, trailing his little finger for a second, and blinking in a strange shaking vibration as he yawned heavily.

While they tried to figure each other out, Robert started to dance a little. The memory of his dream hadn't disappeared, and he slid both feet across the floor together, flapping his hands and shuffling his arms. They body-popped unsuccessfully, and back to the "Robert

Shuffle". Before long Robert was laughing and dancing along to his favourite song which had just slowly started to play quietly in the background, getting louder and louder.

The Mirroring had been waiting for this moment for a while, with Robert sleepy enough to be convinced this was a dream, just drunk enough not to mind if he was getting a bit slower, that the dancing was now something he was trying to keep up with. It became more complicated, and before long he was clapping and tapping his foot out of time, falling back a little and leaning against the bathroom sink.

The one with the mirror just underneath the little light he kept on, that was enough light for him this late at night. The Mirroring stepped back, and Robert couldn't help it, he stepped back a little too without realising it. It took him a minute to realise he should have been standing in the sink.

That didn't make any sense.

He still stepped back though, and in the darkness when the view of his bathroom shrank away he did just like everyone else and ran toward the mirror. The glass electrified through him, and in a blind panic, just like those young survivors had, he looked for comforting light. He started to run to the brightest light he could see, the glow of the burning world the king and queen had been making together for centuries.

He was lost and exhausted. It would be a long time coming, but soon enough he would be one of those people that would follow the Mirroring ritual. So, the circle of flaming life continued, the circle of life people hadn't heard off, something much different than the green fool's circle of life. It was not survival of the fittest, but the capturing of those in power, and the destruction of your freedom from the inside.

The Mirroring stopped dancing, adopting the clumsy, shuffling walk of Robert, its name from now on. The only problem with a Mirroring was they couldn't quite get things right. You would look them in the eye, and it wouldn't take long before you knew something was wrong. The relationship just wasn't what it had been before, and the Mirroring would be punished at its failure.

The tide of Mirroring would try again. So far, they hadn't had the chance to be victorious, but now they had the power of the distracted man, who trusted more than just what their eyes and gut told them about the people in front.

The Ash Queen squirmed in her seat, she had always been in a fair fight, one where you were given the permission to run away and find a place where you could be whoever you wanted to be. She wanted to be worshipped, but this was something else. This was life without choice. It electrocuted her when she thought that.

No matter how she squirmed, the screen didn't move away from her, it was stuck to her face. She slammed her eyes closed, wincing in pain again, thinking all she'd see was the red light anyone would see if they closed their eyes while they stared at the sun. The picture just continued. She tried to push her fingers into her ears, wincing again. Maybe she could block it out that way. Her arms didn't move, the arms of this sharp grip didn't let them move while they were connected. It was probably to be safe, maybe it was dangerous to disconnect.

She hoped that was why. Her heart rushed at his power, but this time it was easy not to smile. She smiled anyway

-

If two Mirroring meet they don't need to speak, they quietly shake their head in one direction, and then they nod if they are told the other being should also be a Mirroring. As Robert left his room, his wife did just that, already straightening up her side of the bed where there had been a struggle and the real wife had lost, the stain of wine on the bed sheets and a broken lamp. The Mirroring closed her personal mirror Isobel always kept on her bed-side.

The presence of the real people disappeared soon enough, and the Mirroring both sniffed in shock when, in review, no memories flickered or asked to be changed.

No punishment came.

They made a quiet fizzing noise, the smell of burnt toast for just a second while they tried to figure out if something had gone wrong. They were both afraid they'd already done something wrong.

No, the reality was nobody else had been in this room, or even this house. The Burning King had a revelation, it was his first tendril into the world and before long the attack had really begun.

The world flickered forward, going faster past a week of events, small messages and habits of movement spreading from them to the people around them, and with the power of the social network, spreading faster than even they had expected. They had worked through their apartment, tearing down the curtains, kicking down the kitchen units and smashing their television down by working as a team. Both heads snapped up as they caught the signal of a 999-call working its way to the closest police station, and without knowing how to smile properly, they both did the biggest smiles they could at each other, and cracked their faces back to relaxed position quickly like a camera shutter.

They blinked in time and ordered a taxi just on the bridge which looped away from this road and winding down to the town. It had a calm river, and without needing to think about it, Isobel opened her little mirror and they both disappeared through.

Both Mirroring climbed the ramp up, and stepped over the gate to the bridge. They weren't wet, they used the calm water to transport, they came out a little wavy at first, and by the time the taxi parked up in the small layby at this gate, they looked perfectly normal in their suit and dress. Robert was just twitching one hand, frantically making up for something they'd forgotten, leaving a lighter to fall from the boot prints they'd left behind, making sure to hide the jewellery.

"Don't worry about him. We've just walked too far. We're only up the hill, is that OK?" Isobel leaned over the front of the taxi, moving with the slow clumsiness she'd seen Isobel move with whenever she was forced to wear heels. It had been the first engagement with a stranger. The first time while they scooted along the seats of the black Mercedes taxi, he was looking at them both and making sure they were safe and normal.

The radio mumbled quietly, and he turned the engine on, shaking his head and gruffly laughing.

"You think you need to tell a voter and a *fan* where you live? Stay humble man!" He shook his head again, and as they arrived at their house, the police and fire brigade were already there.

There were people in sleepy crowds, the driver tutting and straightening his back to protect them while the fire swelled up.

-

The picture flashed forward again, arguments in a small office and Robert's face posted everywhere. Cheering crowds. Mayor. It had been a billion written words, twelve and a half thousand minutes of videos and air-time and one hundred staff. They had won by a land-slide and everyone couldn't quite explain why they were starting to support him. They'd spent all their time fighting against him, but they couldn't understand where it had come from, they were just happy to have a group they could be a part of.

The information had been carefully played with, words and arguments changed from agreeing to seeking more protection and security in the world and searching for the right solution to their problem. The person that just felt right. A thousand small events continued, made to show that people needed to be looked after. Strange events of spooky shadows and disappearing items.

So many burglaries and small crimes occurred, it was said you might tell people you are going outside. That information shouldn't be given by choice, but should be enforced like any law. They didn't know they were already being watched, their footprints were already in the world of the Burning King.

The Queen felt her hand being grabbed, and with what felt like glass pushing into her hand, she yelled out and was thrown back into the real world. She knew that man's face, and it had been decades ago when he was a leader. It was his son now, and a hundred small questions swirled through her head as to what the world was made up of. "Are there any real people left?" She mumbled, tripping a little over her own foot and wobbling her head slowly while he pulled her forward, still dazed from that strange world that had choked her.

The floor was warmer than it had been, and she felt herself pushing through the humidity, feeling the great thickness of the air and wandering where they were going now. One little thing kicked at her from the very first approach she had, something that felt so long ago though it had only been a week. She had come through from the road, and been thrown up, and then fell through the air.

She hadn't fallen past the ground, but the way their conversation had echoed, this was a huge expanse, and the sound bounced down and slowly came back up, much more than it ever had with any of the huge caves she had walked among. They stood there now, staring down into another deep darkness. The King's hand was not letting go.

He leapt down, and they both descended into the void, a growing red shimmer getting larger and larger as they fell, a sea of black shapes merging and bounding. She had always hidden from the fire in the forests, an ancient fear of what it could do in so many trees. "This is unnatural…" she tried to yell, but the force of their speed stopped any words, knocked under the blows of heavy, leathery wings which had sprouted from the King.

The only other light was the glint of his fangs reflecting the blood red below.

-

"I'm sure it's writing, look!" Jacob pointed, nearly jumping as the little whisper of snow twirled around its own breath and outlined the ends of a word, but the shape had already gone away. He was still getting used to the new powers that were flowing through him, the way that time would slow down if he focussed, and every time the snow swirled like that, he wrote down a word just to see if there was anything coming together. They were just a mad arrangement of letters, there was nothing obvious to it, and he kept staring down at the words on a notepad he always kept with him. He was just thankful it had survived in his pocket.

His mind raced, and he looked up and wrote without looking at his paper, with any letter that glowed in the sky. There were thin trees, shaped almost by hairs, and they all had to walk between these trees carefully. The large, feathered adults would herd them away from the trees, just in case, and it was a lot of focus just to shuffle through the growing grasses and squinting into the blizzard to find those weird trees before you walked into one.

They would wobble if you walked into them, and the other trees nearby would shake their upturned, soft branches too. Little birds would flap away. Every time, the adult sprites pushed them gruffly away from the trees, and each time it got stricter and stricter.

There were all spread out amongst trees, and it was hard with this stronger and stronger wind to know what was a person and what was a tree. Jacob kept pushing forward, the trees were getting thicker, and the ground even more bumpy. He nearly tripped, and pushed softly from the bark, just to try not to knock it over completely.

Ellis yelped in surprise.

They couldn't help but yelp when they were really concentrating. There had been a lot of madness recently, and right now, there was at least a scent and a track to follow, even though they felt to Jacob like they were being pushed and herded by the sprites around them. Now he realised they were all behind Ellis, the only reason Ellis looked so tall was the little light which was just in front of him. It was a ball of ice, seeming to glow from just sheer energy.

"Mum is so helpful, she's helping me track." That kind of dreaming bit at Jacob. Every time Ellis started to talk about their fantasy land. He'd never say anything about it, but he could sense the punch of its wrongness hit into his head, scratching away.

It was an impossible thing, and Jacob couldn't comprehend anything falling outside of the determined rules he'd always seen, however long he looked. For him to understand there were people that imagined and guessed and hoped beyond the world they were presented was another weird itch, a strange, irregular tapping he'd calm down to a steady beat soon enough.

Even given the madness he was surrounded with right now, he made sense of each rule and every step as it progressed, just trying to understand where he was and what kind of morphed real world he was living in. Whenever they stopped still, Jacob tried to look around him, trying to take in anything new in this snowstorm.

It was a maddening kind of storm, but with his internal clock turning, it felt as if days had passed. Maybe it was minutes. He sat down, sighing but quite happy to show his vulnerable side when it came to Ellis. He pushed himself slowly against a snow-drift, feeling it pack tight behind him much quicker than it would have normally.

He didn't mind, everything here wanted to care for him, and make everything safe and warm. It just had a strange way of protecting them with a madness it always seemed a step away from. Ellis was here and smiling brightly, even if their head was drooping while the wind itself seemed to sigh as well. *It's telling me to go to sleep, though the world is buzzing. It is getting darker, and the only thing that seems to have changed is us sitting down.*

Jacob squinted into the distance, staring at the daylight glowed dully in the distance still, but they were both sat underneath a black ceiling, getting darker and lighter and darker in a weird, soft rhythm. Everything seemed blurry just in front of him, darker in the path of those tracks, and it wasn't adding up. Just as he fell asleep, the shadow of trees on a ceiling of the forest shook above him. He stared down the tunnel of the blackness for just a second, forced to think of a monster shark book.

A man stood in his mind's eye, pulling a spear in the air as a shark's huge mouth ran toward him, the constant rows of teeth fading back into an endless black void. Jacob should have felt scared, but the small and sweet scent which whispered at his nose was comfort enough.

-

The words would not stop swimming, and as usual Jacob dreamed in a puzzle. Nobody really believed him when he told them he could control his dreams. Those same people thought you didn't have choice when you were told what to do something by an adult. Ellis understood, they just saw it differently. Ellis would look at the world in wonder and see a thousand different things vying for their focus, and experience whatever looked best to them.

Jacob guessed they were just running, trying to get to the next happy adventure, and Jacob had vowed to protect him. Now, he couldn't keep up with the shadow of Ellis running away, kicking their feet behind them in a sprint to something. It wasn't just snowing in this hazy dream land, it was icy. Every time Jacob got near, he would slip into a door, or just catch his hand on a wooden gate as it slid in his way, or rolled him away on a sliding floor, whichever just to keep him away from the only real friend he had ever known.

He had been told many times just how annoying he could be, and was left wondering sometimes why Ellis put up with him. Most of the time, it felt like the rest of the world was plotting to pull them apart, Ellis's Mother's death had hurt them for a short time, but Ellis had come back soon enough, maybe not smiling as much as before. At least through the tears reaching out a hand to just "hug it out", as they had been fans of saying back then.

In fragile hints, Jacob could just see the faint hint of Ellis's mum, blurry from so many years not seeing her, but still walking with the same flowing dresses she always wore. She never did like sharp shapes. This was a dream, and Jacob focussed on getting ridding of the symbol of that strange water sprite which had been with them for that last few days.

Ellis kept running away from Jacob, giggling in the distance as if he was running toward something, and a bright light started to glow above Ellis, just from Jacob thinking about it. He did enjoy that kind of power when he was asleep, the monsters could never scare him when logic always got rid of them, or he'd just wake up if he had to.

The mother had turned away, getting taller and taller and growing in the strange way the darkness seemed to grant her extra limbs. Then, she was a metal horror, just like the roaring see of silver he had faced, and still growing. He turned around, but knew how pointless that would be.

For once, he didn't let the nightmare continue. That horrible when he runs down the alley as it got narrower and the monster wouldn't get any further away no matter how hard he ran, breathing closer and closer and closer until finally its sharp hands ripped into his shoulder.

No, he wasn't going anywhere this time. He breathed deeply, focussing on the small breaths of wind that flowed around him, but it started to sting. He focussed harder, sure that if he just thought hard enough, the dream would listen and destroy this foe. Just like it had done only hours before.

The winds swelled in the noise of someone snoring, the little trees nearby whistled in anticipation. Jacob had to step back, wincing and flailing at the growing shocks which hit into his arms and lungs. The air was against him, as if the dream had been invaded. Standing over him, the monster that had been Ellis's mother wasn't there anymore.

It was just the shadow of a blackened, huge shadow covered with muscular growths across its back, and with one punch through the air at him, Jacob was flying back, trying to find something to focus on. The rushing air came to his rescue, throwing him in a slingshot around a bent street sign and back toward his old friend.

He crashed to the floor, shaking his head slowly in the groggy slog, trying to push out his exhaustion that clung like a smog.

The scene slowly cleared in front of Jacob, the water sprite and Ellis playing on a beach. Jacob feared the oceans. The unknown out there, where anything could be lurking in the dark waves.

Sure, sharks don't usually skulk and hunt in these cold currents if this was an English beach, but dolphins once went up the Thames, and whales can beach themselves. The water sprite was playing in the water, trying to spell but making mistakes, and without thinking about it, Jacob swapped the letters around. Buaetyfull became beautiful.

Ellis clapped their hands, not even looking at Jacob. As usual in the world of Jacob's dreams when everything turned into what it was supposed to be, the water sprite grew again. Ellis was sat beside another two copies.

The first was green, and coated in the dirt of some strange trail he had been walking down, long hair dangling down with the scraps of branches trailing behind. Another sat with the glasses he was supposed to be wearing, talking quietly to himself and smiling, but looking down at the same time. The third one was their only major argument, the imaginary friend they had both shared for such a long time.

The imaginary friend version was glowing with the light of the stars. That part had been Jacob's idea. She sat in the sand as a little shell, and flipped up to be a little bird for just a second as she flapped in the air, flipping over and diving in the form of a sleek fish, shining in the daylight. They had kept changing that friend, trying to make it both their forms combined into one. It never worked, they couldn't find a middle ground between the two of them, and the more ridiculous it became, the more Jacob let go of imagining. They both made her a woman, they missed their mothers.

Jacob could see just below the waves, the imaginary friend turning into that monster again, and he stepped forward to try and step into the water, to try and stop some of this madness and just get away. He kept trying to tell it to stop in his mind, but it wasn't working, and it came with the same kind of shocks he had before in front of the monster.

There was no way out. It didn't stop him stepping forward, even stepping into the ocean and shaking from the sudden cold of the tide, he didn't step back. Curiosity and protection won. The cold wrapped itself around him, tingling up one leg and up the other. The lapping knock of the tide clattered against little pebbles. That damp smell of the sea rose in front of him, stronger and stronger with each step. His legs moved sluggishly, pushing against the weight of the water, and leaning into the heavy tide, having to kick at the waves as they seemed to nearly grab at his ankles.

Jacob didn't realise it, with the same fluffy cloud around its face, a great monster swelled from the waves with a heavy spine. It grew and grew as its huge tentacles choked the blood supply to his feet and hands. In the water, there was just the hint of small letters fizzing faintly.

It was like when a memory of a bright light burned on

your eyes, even if you were looking at something else. They had the same ochre sickness Jacob had been seeing everywhere since the madness had started. They were random letters, but sometimes they became the right word.

"NO" the monster screamed, every version of Ellis running to try and stop Jacob making sense of everything. He hummed and squeezed everything tightly shut. With the crash of broken glass and a shocking explosion, he was awake, cracking his head slightly on the trunk of a tree which shook from the memory of that shockwave.

14: FOR ONCE, YOU'RE FREE MAKE A MISTAKE

There are animals and worlds you will never see with the naked eye. At night, a crowd of nocturnal animal hordes any food, huge eyes taking in the tiny light and bouncing from branch to branch to catch their food. Some snakes see using scent, their tongues wag in the air, and they chase the movement of prey. It is even believed that pigeons sense the magnetic waves of the earth, and that is why wherever you let them go, they will always find home. Even you can see in the dark if you wait long enough, your eyes adjust like magic. Always be careful though.

They were anagrams. Every word danced again, right in front of him without the need for a notepad. Every little bit of exhaustion faded away in the simple joy of a puzzle glowing nice and bright and clear to understand. His hands fidgeted. The words were hard to catch in this darkness, with the strange trees dangling just above him like an endless set of chandeliers.

He grabbed at the grasses, stepping north where scratches in the ground above him rolled and rolled. He didn't run in one long duration. It was starts and stops, kicking at the thick snow trail as it still twirled from that magic fox. All that snow and cold disappeared again, and there was the light and warmth of this swampy strangeness.

Now he was kicking from tree to tree, chasing those

words as frantically as possible, just as he grabbed at the scrap of another word, he was gone. Onto the next one. It was a run which had him looking up and down and all around, and as he jumped at a hovering word in the space between two leaning trees, he had something.

In his mad running, he hadn't paid attention to the fact the trees were moving, not just bending back and forth under some hidden wind, but rolling along as if he was in a twisted hose. Through the small cracks in the trees at this densest point away from any light, he could see it was not two surfaces that were rolling together, but one huge tube.

The words had been found, and Jacob tried not to feel like running and running. "From the body, you will have risen and ran in all the madness. I cannot see you yet while you do not see where I think." Jacob added in some of the words, just for a little cold thought to try and escape this feeling he was standing right on the edge of a cliff.

Every instinct shouted at him to take a step back, but the world and its servants said the best thing to do was to jump. The mouse in a maze would keep running. Booming and clattering filled the room, crashing the mossy soil and leaves rolled across his nostrils and he tried to back into something, but the assault was coming from everywhere.

The sprites broke through first, and with a bright glow, the fox seeming to fall from above and then in front of him. Ellis was there, standing next to the huge fox, smiling and knowing – somehow – Jacob had found the right place. A purple mist he had barely noticed on the edge of his eyes started to swirl and strengthen.

"Eden swoops and hopes, watching every aura. Now, finally, her tracks have grabbed and tempted. Only those who've earned it will see the blessed nest." The fox whispered, the soft hushing of snow. While it scratched away in the deepening blackness of the trees which grew back much faster as they had under the attacks of these sprites, it caught on something with its huge paws and shook its head in the air. A thick beam of liquid purple exploded.

The light whirled in a way they were starting to recognise, wailing at the dark trees and deforming the world in front of them. It grabbed at them, pulling their faces in long stretches as weird funhouse mirrors of how they usually looked. The ground started to fade away from them, no air left to breathe in.

-

Is the house as nervous as I am? Ellis's dad couldn't help but think, seeing what looked like Ellis flickering by in their mirror. Or even in the spoon as he tried to stir the tea and calm his shaking hands.

There was no way he could know it was a hungry Mirroring.

Ellis wasn't hiding anywhere, he couldn't have been listening while the doctor had explained just what was going on, just how important it was to keep trying with those pills for once. He must have stayed away, distracted as always.

It wouldn't be easy to explain those bruises and

scratches the doctor had not let go off. The way Ellis ran away whenever they wanted. The way they didn't think they were one person, and didn't talk to anyone. Well, anyone except the one boy, but Ellis's Dad couldn't get used to him either. He kept trying to convince himself everything was OK, that without Ellis it might be easier, at least that way everyone would keep eye focus, and he might be able to work his way out of it.

Lord, that Doctor was sharp though.

Frede, and this time he'd pronounce it right, he'd have to be just as delicate as if he was walking a tightrope or standing in front of those staring parents, someone had reported him, and he wished he knew who had, just to give him some advantage against their preying eyes. He chuckled to himself, choked on the toothpaste while he brushed his teeth, as Docker Frede knocked on the door, that same rhythm played out he always clattered "*de di-di-dah dum-dum di-d-d-d-di-di*".

It was his ringtone too, and the speed at which the Dad ran down the stairs showed just how much he knew Frede took time seriously. Dad was famous not just for being hours late, but days late before, this time he wouldn't let it be more than a minute. He smiled, pulling that clip-on tie onto his shirt and with a tight-fisted swing opening the door and keeping that smile as the slight hunch of Dr Frede was there in the little light outside the house.

Ok, Ellis is right this time he thought, that long nose, and the deep-set eyes with an almost black line underneath them, the long trench coat. *No other word for it, vulture.* Rather than chuckling to Dr Frede's face, he turned and mumbled "Tea?" knowing it was just what the Dr wanted, the calmness of routine and a normal, lovely time with a family friend.

He turned the scoff at that into a quick cough, and mumbled out of the situation. Dr Frede was weird about being watched while he took his coat off and organised his things. Dad kept checking in his mind's eye everything had been organised properly, with that armchair clear, and the bedside table he never used, and the "casual" circle of cheeses there, as they obviously always were of an evening.

He kicked the rubbish pile back up behind the door, and shook his head as a half-built metal model Ellis had been playing with on the front room floor clattered and bent against the shelving. He swore, still balancing the cups with their tea from spilling. With a little spin, he caught himself in the kitchen window.

He saw Ellis again, just for a second, the Mirroring tilting its head just the same way as he did, and with a twitch, it was his face again. *I'm just going to keep going. I closed the curtains in there at least* he thought, and cleared his throat at Dr Frede, smiling again more from the joy of that exact same picture he'd seen so many times before.

Dr Frede sat cross-legged, laptop tilted away from Ellis's Dad, and a neat arrangement of a notebook, a folder, his phone, and the little pens. It was all arranged like a cityscape. It was the same sharp black suit, the black with thin pinstripes that shone in the lamp light. Dr

Frede always turned that lamp on even if the light-switches were on, just so that he could see everything clearly.

There was a slight tap of the pen in Dr Frede's hand going back and forth like a monochrome, placed calmly on top of a thin black notebook. The hand-writing was impossible to read, but you wouldn't look away from the piercing eyes anyway.

"Where is Ellis, Mr Sharp? He should be here while we're deciding his future." Every word almost crept out, seeming to sneak with the taste of some predatory need to find weakness. Dr Frede had been throwing so many terms at him, there was nothing he could do while he was told all kinds of definitions and ideas about care and management and thoughts of "fair conditions" and "hands-free coupled assessments".

There were far too many words to make sense of, but it felt like two things were very true; he was under threat somehow, and whatever he tried to do seemed to be the wrong thing. He tried not to think about his own dad when he did something a bit harsh or uncaring, but it was impossible to just be kind and replace his wife as the loving part of the family.

Lord, how he loved the kid, the hours he'd spent reading and trying to understand about gender assignment and trying to make the doctor understand it's perfectly OK for the child to think he has a different gender than he might be born with. Sure, non-sexual wasn't something they covered, but it wasn't his fault, it wasn't his late wife's fault either. The inner fury and confusion was covered by an open smile, and he looked at Dr Frede happily, nodding for him to go on.

"We have had reports of Ellis's condition. He has made a friend but there is a problem there as well in that child's violence and his very unsteady home. Ellis' scratches and bruises are not going away, and they are getting worse than ever. We can't ignore he runs away without reason, and though you might be able to find him, he does not seem willing to come home.

"I am sorry to say it, but I hope that if you read this you will understand." He was starting to get tried, all that reading and trying to contain that information when he was just used to using his hands. The sick feeling sank around him, and it felt like a tunnel was closing around him and here was no way out, it just kept getting smaller and smaller, pushing you away into a horrible future.

He couldn't tell if Dr Frede was smiling with joy, or just looking to make sure he understood, to try and reach across the void of all this administration and make any kind of relationship. He couldn't step past the fact this Dr didn't even try and understand Ellis, that he looked at them like they were just a broken machine to be analysed and ripped apart into its separate pieces.

Dr Frede never listened to the words they used, or ever thought they might be telling the truth. You can't just correct Ellis and think their mind will change because you tell them it was supposed to. He could only cough, it wasn't worth getting into an argument about who Ellis was anymore, Dr Frede would just frown and tap his pen before making a scratchy note. He hated that noise, he knew what it meant. Another black mark against his name, as if he'd listened to a wild animal and chosen to take Ellis out into the mountains without a care for his safety.

He'd tried to say how school was for Ellis, how horrible it was for them to be in a world that didn't and wouldn't try to understand them, but keep fighting anyway. Then they'd just about found a friend across the barbed world of insults.

Even that had been wrong.

He shook his head and looked down instead. "Putting you first" was the overly designed title, a little smiling face to both sides of the bubbly text, and he could tell this was supposed to be for Ellis. Dr Frede couldn't see the difference maybe, or just didn't care.

Being safe is just what we want for you. We want you to smile and play and know you're in a safe place. It isn't fun to get hurt. If it's something that makes you say "ow", or something that makes you feel bad inside, we want it to stop as soon as we can.

Holidays are the most relaxing places you can go to, and we think it is nice to be free and go on holiday with us. Your doctor friend will be there, there will lots to talk about each day with all the fun you will be having, and anything which might make you sad. Don't worry about anything, you're in a safe place and it's lots of fun, with so many new friends to meet.

We only ask one thing, and it's the easiest thing of all. Just be honest and remember you can tell us anything you need to. You might have been told it is best to keep things quiet and not tell anyone when you're not happy. This time away is the perfect chance to do just that. I hope you can come to join the party soon? Just hear from some of our other friends what a great time they've had.

He had been trying to run away from the truth, trying to keep fighting and explaining everything to Ellis, even if they didn't care or know just how important it was to do as they were told. Those pills were horrible, and he just couldn't understand why they thought you were one way or there was a problem. They'd made his wife cover her hair when she was so ill, and that had been enough of a twisting knife.

This, this was just a sharp stab in his back, and he panted just a little at the sheer force to hold back his temper and voice under all this pressure.

"We are assessing everything right now, and child services will be in touch shortly. I'm sure you have questions?" Dr Frede was ready to answer a flurry of questions, ready to make him feel small against the red queries, but Dad just shook his head, not caring about the problem with the friend, and feeling like something out there in the world was breaking everyone down into strange little puppets of people.

He hadn't heard of any fights in the pubs for months, he'd seen people with their shopping smashing to the floor, and just walking past it, not even frowning or screaming at the injustice, just walking past it. He hadn't heard a police alarm for such a long time, and people seemed to be weird, blank mirrors, whenever he tried to speak about those things which had riled them up, they barely had a twitch on their face.

He was convinced they were all moving slower, and he noticed just how long it took Dr Frede to stand up, slowly tidying up his things. He stared down at the mass of smiling children's faces, saying just how amazing the holiday had been, and not able to escape the inner scream that told him everything about this was wrong.

Dr Frede's eyes were caught in the lamp as he stood up, glowing in the ochre gaze he had seen in that strange thing in the mirror, and that uncontrollable, sick fear forced him to sit down. "I'll see myself out" Dr Frede said, seeming to slip in a strange gargle on one of those words. Dr Frede kept shuffling out though, knocking his head against the corner of a wall and just walking on without a care.

Ellis's Dad stood up quickly, ignoring the rush to his head, and leaned against the cold door to the garden. He kicked off the lamp light, and pulled away at the curtain, hoping to see that delicate little robin. He was just trying to find some comfort, but instead he forced himself to find his reflection in the darkness.

He shook his head and shuffled off to bed, marking it all off as tiredness and stress, listening to the quiet whispering that worked its way through the air conditioning and any static between radio stations. The Ash Queen chuckled to herself from Dr Frede's Mirroring, surprised just how easily the humans let that authority figure of a Dr get away with so much wrong.

-

"Eden is a nickname, a lot of different words came and went, before and after this one. I liked the ring to it. She did most of all. You've spent enough time playing with the little tricks and found the secrets, so you won't be surprised to hear she's a huge fan of music. She had a son a long time ago, Jacobel-Lisaelanon... yes I know names were longer back then, but we had more time then." The fox said simply, every word a sweetened note so thick it seemed you could have almost eaten it.

Jacob chuckled nervously at the name, wandering if there was anyone called "Aelanon" out there, or if she was just happy with the spare room. The sound was nice at least. Jacob was just about holding onto things. It was impossible to find any message in the whirling purple madness all around them, and anyway, it was hard enough to just breathe and stand up, let alone anything else.

Ellis was lost in wander, leaning back and staring around at the shimmering, thick brightness they were nearly swimming in. Ellis looked down from some little indication in his body. Neither friend had quite realised their feet were not touching the floor. The feet had been planted in the moist surface, but now around them the gravity had given up. It was just like standing in water, treading it at first and then feeling buoyancy take you over.

Jacob was in the centre, and just felt the huge hand covering his shoulder almost down to his elbow. The sprites weren't floating for some reason, small feathers just keeping them on the floor, even if the force was still playing against their strong bodies.

Jacob hadn't noticed, still trying to understand what everything meant, and where they were supposed to be going. Ellis was used to going on adventures, and every part of these worlds stayed lit up, so it was just like a walk in the forest on the longest day of all. So, Ellis was much happier to stare at everything around them, grinning while they floated.

The forest sprites frowned at Jacob, and he could pick up their nervous energy, they were fidgeting like birds might when they jumped down for a feed, knowing somewhere close enough there might have been a cat just skulking in the shadows. The air was getting lighter and lighter, small flecks of leaves and soil floating around. In one clump, a tiny little insect flapped fragile, gold wings, clawing its legs at the land which was there just a second ago.

Ellis put their hand out to the creature, always feeling a sympathy with anything. It was only ever humans or the scared animals that didn't like help. They might snap and bite, but this thing heated up on Ellis's hand. It glowed as Ellis closed his hand, and while their ears popped under the dropping pressure.

Ellis's eyes dripped a little from the strain, just like when they might cry, while the bright light of just where they were going. The tear softly bent over itself in a glowing ball, it rolled back up Ellis's cheek and floated away. He kicked and twisted over it, grabbing the water and turning, always with the sprite following them. The clothes were billowing, and Ellis couldn't help but feel a little embarrassed at the waving shirt, and the shoes that fought to stay on.

It gave them some time to look down, and check what they were wearing. There was a special audience coming, and the raggedy mess of muddy and misshapen tears of clothes really didn't feel good enough. Neither friend cared about the latest fashions of course, but right now Ellis felt like here was a need for even a hint of natural strength, the defences from so much madness tingled the nerves in their neck.

If they had been a dog, their hackles would have been raised and the tail hung between their legs. The fear was a strange thing, but both Jacob and Ellis couldn't help but feel excited and curious, hearts running faster and faster as their whole world lost all gravity and glowed as only light.

"Beware, children, she has not had guests for a long time. This time, it could not be truer the animal is much more afraid of you than you could ever be of her." They were soft, glistening words which echoed in the sounds of twinkling bells. The fox swam forward, and into a thin tunnel, its fur a thick ball of fluff.

The sprites pushed the only humans ever to be in this world, and a sharp tang of grassy breath hit each of them. A thousand eyes blinked on, lighting the way. "We have to rush, she has been waiting for the cursed enemy for so long." Even the fox was whispering now.

-

The buzzing was a cacophony of taps and ticking, the sounds of millions of tiny eyes opening and closing, watching every little sight before them and taking in this new arrival. Little roots wafted in the airlessness, never quite getting a place to stay still. The group pushed off the tunnel and worked their way forwards, blinded in the huge light they were swimming through.

Before too long, they were out, standing and struggling in the swampy splodge of this next world. "So, those tubes are an elevator, I always preferred it when you get the little 'ding' on a new floor." Jacob joked, he was never too far from a joke, and having worked something else out, and being surrounded by no one that wished him harm, he was finally relaxing.

Unlike Ellis, he was never very good at picking up the energy of the people and situation around him. Right now, he was stood at the front of the group, just behind the starry glow of the fox. The rest were in a circle, trying to protect the group and hoping they might find some clue to tell them the way forward.

There had been two sprites at first, but by the subtle, purple lines they spoke along, this was a swelling group, and now twenty-four sat around them. There were different marks on them, and though the first two with their red marks were six-feet tall, brown and white ones stood beyond 10 feet, glowing with the pale white light of the moon, and bending down to whisper at the other figures.

They were surrounded by blinking eyes, and a misty silhouette that suggested huge beastly muscle, or a spindly insect. It was impossible to know quite what was out there, and the trees didn't help.

They tangled and bounded across the path, hopping and doubling over themselves, as if a toddler had been let loose with their crayons on a pad of paper. There were no flowers or leaves, like the level below, just dark lengths of timber, bending and warping and warping and bending.

In the smoky atmosphere, it was impossible to see any detail past the shine of the Fox which bloomed larger in the darkness. The fox stared back at the crowd, sniffling its black nose and squinting just like Jacob was doing into this new environment.

Half the figures changed and unfolded, what had been a set of robes or feathers folded and wafted under a conjured air. The breathy fog grasped that purple light, and small golden sparks flickered off it. In a well-practised gesture, twelve hands grabbed at the banners which wobbled and sloshed in the trodden mud of the floor. They grabbed at the symbols, shuffled slowly behind their friends, and before long they were in single file.

Ellis softly pushed at Jacob's back. *First is worst*, they whispered, far too nervous to laugh at the line they always spoke at school whenever someone had to volunteer for something and stand in a silly line.

"The path is strange and shifting, follow me and keep to the light. We will be there soon. Do not take a step in the swamps' waters, they are made for someone who isn't of Eden's purity. There are traps here to grab at your weakness. Care is key, and never speed. This is not a journey for those who want to rest though. You must make the choice when to stop and when to rush, far too many have run and disappeared for me to say you must. Believe in your magic, and nothing can stop you." Already the voice was growing faint, and Jacob didn't need another push to his back to be told to start moving.

He ran for just a second, tripping on a grasping string of wood which grew and pulsed, flicking at his rushing leg. He pushed his hand against another branch, and that moved just the same, groaning and spilling just a little piece of soil. He coughed it up, the wet spittle filling his mouth, and without thinking he stretched a leg forward, pulled on.

The smog was deep and hungry, it stole your breath and forced your eyes to focus, every tiny gesture minutely perfected while you balanced on the thin length of wood the fox was skipping along. It had just the memory of its pure white light, and that was enough to let you keep stepping, on both sides for everyone, all they could see was that cotton, bright glow.

Jacob kept going though, no matter how many times he paused, nobody bumped behind him, and even when he leapt between two high branches, nobody came any closer either. Every panting breath threw the smoke in front of him, and the longer he balanced and poised and clasped, the more he panted and the harder it was to see.

Any small fragment of wood you knocked made the world scream, and the noise was a wave you had to almost ride, it knocked you forward. So many times, hands which were scratched, grabbed and he kept balance just about, unsteadily feeling balance try to tip them over, but sitting if they needed to.

Anything to stop stepping in that water again. There were spots where the lengths of bark were stuck together in the tightness of a nest, only leaving a tight little hole to squeeze through, but that was enough. Then you would have to crawl and scrape through the gap, climbing nearly vertically and grasping onto the next hand-hold. It didn't matter how high you grabbed and climbed, the water was always just there, running after you

One tunnel ended, and there was nothing else out there, the only sound was the slow tide of that thick water, that flickering noise now just a dull drumming in the background. It was so dark in this growing maze. The only sign of any water down there was just the tiny line of white which bounced off the end of that water as it lapped against the trees.

Jacob was stood on a tiny, long path, nearly just a point in its skinniness. Ellis could just see that fox leaping through the little gap and just jumping up. Ellis tried to work out how to make it across that space. The water was not in a tide in one direction, everything was still without gravity, and that is why you had to hold on so hard, grabbing while always feeling like the whole world wanted to pull on you and make you fly.

Jacob frowned at the gap, a whip-crack in their head making them realise the light was running away from them now, and that must have been why the fox was calling on the magic, and not the speed. The way those branches, or trunks, worked, you could quickly run after a light which was just reflecting off those strange pools.

Twice it had stopped Jacob as it twirled, but now the tempting warmth of rest was whispering. A hand leaned out between the two branches, the little scratch of blood dripping into the shifting pool below it. After a few seconds, the pool was getting closer and closer, seeing a dangling hand to grab onto, and taking their chance.

Jacob forced their eyes back open, feeling something pulling on their hand, and for a moment thinking that gasping face was Ellis, making him reach out and make another joke while they ran together onto the next wander. It cleared, and was their own face, staring back.

Both eyes grew, and though Jacob could feel it happen, it was still hard to believe, as the hand tugged further and further away, disappearing into that dark pool. With a huge effort, he pulled the crunching bones out from the water, stood, leaned and jumped without thinking.

The chattering noise around them died into a silence as another, blue light joined them. *That sprite*, they thought, seeing the ice crystal just across the gap, standing on the edge of a different branch, one somehow Jacob hadn't noticed. Pushing their back just a little against the flexible wood, he leapt across the gap, grabbing for the branch.

The picture disappeared, and Jacob remembered they weren't supposed to stray from the light, breaking at the branches and barely able to even form a scream. The last fragments of light disappeared.

-

Even if the gravity was dead, Ellis still screamed and grabbed at the maddening branches, and when they approached a thick branch, they thought they were going to just slide down and crash against the sharper points at the bottom. Ellis covered his face, groaning before they would start screaming. Then the speed took over, and how they had fallen stopped.

Ellis was whispering the scream and it held their body perfectly in balance, perfectly aligned with the light of the path again, and in the panicking rush of their heart, in the bleakness, it was only possible to barely keep following the glow.

The scratch of a growing root tore into his hand, and there was just one left now, just one path to crawl forward. They pulled their legs up while they pushed through the tangles, gawping around but feeling dragged by the tiny warmth in the shimmer. He saw just enough of a massive outline, some colossal worm over eighteen feet tall rumbling and pushing away at the word around it, chewing and biting with a gross hunger at some massive branch, and still squirming in the weightless air.

The blood blocked his path, and he spat at it, wincing as the branches punctured through Ellis's leg, rolling as it tried to push against a rib. The branches were everywhere, entangling and biting and darkening the world even more. Ellis pushed their unsteady hand forward and braced against the black of a thick branch. The scratches of thorns snipped and fed, but Ellis just had enough space to stay still for a second and stare around.

Imagining can work if you are in the cold, you can think of a beautiful beach and the hot sand nearly burning your feet. The sun baking down on you, the sweat dripping of your forehead just while you squint in the sunlight. Then the cold would go away, the harsh wind was gone, and you could walk for much further than you needed to.

No matter how much Ellis strained though, they couldn't imagine any light, couldn't see a comfortable path forward. The bedsheets and soft pillows as they imagined them kept fading away in the deep darkness Ellis could feel. The dank stench of soil wafting past again. There was one gesture that always comforted them though, one little thing Daddy had been using for a long time now, and it was something Ellis couldn't help but cling to in these times of need.

If you're lost, the one thing you know you do have is you. There isn't anything that can separate you from yourself, and so long as you don't give up, you can do it. Ellis was starting to feel exhausted, the dragging on their eyes was getting stronger and stronger, but they would try anyway. The simplest way to tell yourself it's ok is to just grab your hands together and make a shield around yourself.

You know then that no one can get past that shield without you letting them in. Ellis dragged at one hand, and left it hanging there uselessly by leaning in with his head, the soft hushing of sound was a comfort. He pushed his other hand against the first, trying this time not to just scream as the hands just wouldn't move any closer.

It was like there was something in the way, and it grew colder still. Ellis couldn't tell if they were sinking or not, it was impossible, but it was so much colder, the little chills on their arm told the story, and an odd shiver tickled up the spine. It was darker too, just the impressions of an outline remained now, but Ellis could feel just where their arms were without having to think about it. As they pushed together, they stopped again, just as if they were pushing against a solid wall.

Ellis hadn't realised this whole time he had been screaming quietly, and as they let in a quiet breath again, panting hard, the hands slapped together.

The fox was right.

In that moment, a shock pounded away from the colliding hands, knocking away at the weightless roots and leaving just a slit of bright light in front. Ellis held back, just about holding on against the shockwave and feeling all their breath disappear. The wave passed, and a great shrill echoed and bounced against the bark, the monstrous worm running scared from the force.

Without thinking about it, Ellis swam as hard as possible, kicking their feet behind them, and quickly enough reaching a point of light and pushing right to the top. It would not be long before Ellis wished those times would come back, but for now they were just happy to make it out of the darkness.

15: THE MOTHER OF ALL THINGS, TO THE AIR YOU BREATHE

Kangaroo mothers have a pouch which gives their babies, called Joeys, a perfect home wherever they are. Many types of spiders and primates let their young lay and hold onto them for years while they grow up. Birds spend months perfecting nests for their young, Hornbills even sealing themselves in while their babies grow up. Thank your mum, even if it isn't Mother's Day.

"A thousand years of tiny scratches, nudges in a distant sky. Now you come tumbling and burning into the most sacred world, and ask me to wait? Any delicacy or prayer is lost in the chaos you have brought me. The realm just below me is burning with their hellish touch. You brought them here, you did not deserve my patience."

The great tree stood before them. It was a colossal length of wood, and though the seven survivors stood in front of it, the width of that massive tree still went beyond their sight. The voice boomed in the soft tones of an owl hooting quietly in the background, just floating by and scooting for a mouse. It was still heavy though, and the exhausted gang buckled under the sheer power of the tone, wobbling at the heavy voice which swelled with the boom of a thousand growling beasts, just in the background.

They were shaking, scratched and panting, bending over themselves and trying to stand up as straight as they could in this audience. Jacob and Ellis sat down though, exhausted and staring at each other, and shuffling as close to each other as they could. They held each other's hands, and with one other sprite stood behind them, the burning sprite Jacob could just about recognise, forced them to stand. They tied to stand and let go of each other's hands, but trying to stand at the same time, trying to balance. They were just like silly school children, trying not to giggle and trying not to be too loud, and shushing themselves while they laughed.

The nervous energy was overwhelming. All their eyes were closed, and they were trying just for a moment to get some rest. It was impossible to know how long they'd been down in the darkness and running through that wintry endlessness.

The fluffy cloud they had munched was a long time ago. It was like stretching and stretching dough, you do it for too long, and the dough will snap. They were wavering, but with a soft hand, a strange wooden sprite softly helped them up. "It has been an age, I have forgotten manners and the ways of humans. Please, rest and do not stress blessed ones. The madness and the fear are over." The voice boomed from the wood sprites, and they seemed to stretch from the tones depth.

A ramming noise filled the space, rolling thunder and a warmth forced the straining eyes of every guest to squeeze shut. They breathed in time, and the immense tree went to work. Eden hadn't moved for centuries, and the noise was the sound of her long braids struggling to support the little form of her body. They might have thought they were standing beside a huge tree.

The reality was far stranger though, and Eden was a calm figure, descending from the cover of the leaves high up in the sky. Small fruits followed her, the wood of this immeasurable tree groaned and shifted from the maze of roots below, forming a table and laying the fruits out into a beautiful rainbow platter. "The cruel fates have picked two such young people, I can sense the coming pain, but the world will only be flames without their blessed power. I will teach them everything I can, but I can feel the sickness on them both, Ashes breath has reached this high." She couldn't help the strained tear that trickled out her ridged, old facade.

-

"I need your hands and your minds, so you may be within the very first time of this terrible battle. Please do not fear a thing, just like you always could Jacob, you can escape this memory whenever you wish. All of nature runs through me, all you need to do is hold the table." The few survivors fed hungrily, shipping from ornate, carved cups at a thick syrupy juice, not chuckling but calmly leaning toward one another while they chewed and grabbed to another treat.

While Eden spoke, they all bowed their head, acting in a shared instinct they were protected and in the presence of real power. The small lamps that glowed phosphorus silver bounced off their faces, and the light, the clarity and the thick smell of leaves was a great comfort. Each time they leaned against the table, they sank a little further into their cushioned chairs, ruffling the browned leaves, and feeling the sweet call of a dream.

At the head of the table, shaking her head each time she passed an empty seat as she felt the loss of everyone that had gone. Eden sat, algae stretching down her sleek, long back, curls of beautiful hair. Vines worked around her arms and down, in one great flowing dress. Her deep green face was a tally of wrinkles so deep, they were river valleys, folding over themselves. When she blinked, the coiled runes of her cheeks were a little clearer for just a moment. The skin flickered over where her eyes were hidden.

She bent down into a comfortable and ornate seat with all the others, smiling at the knowledge of just where she was going, and with a deep breath she took them back centuries to the first time she could call a human "friend".

-

They didn't lie, I guess that's good. If this is a demon's curse, I am coming to prey to you, God's. *I pray to the guardians of the world's spirit, to the unchanging winds and every drop within the rains. Hold me close*. The ash is running after me still. It rose from a river, catching and feeding away at prey without pause.

The story tellers came and danced and died in their plays, but labour and hunger pulled us forward. We bring them back to the fire, feeling that same safeness, we always did in the darkness. Those wolves hunt and do not blink. Now I run from the chaos of that rising ash. Small feet seemed to flow out of it for just a second, I felt some burning gaze hungering for something.

Many of us felt stuck by that gaze, instincts from the wolves' stare, the other tribesmen holding their spears. Every second must be held back and tensed, made to judge whether they might strike, whether they might lean away too far and die under my blade. This thing didn't wait, it moved slowly, spreading along the surface of the hours, squelching in the mud.

The second it saw one of our brothers, everyone else had ran. I can only thank these Gods who must hear me soon enough. The forest is calling, I can always feel its power even if I am not a shaman, I am here now. *Please in your guidance and all those gifts of life, please see me.* The darkness of the forest could have anything in it, and it was impossible not to tense, not to throw my spear high up to creep in these green shadows. To strike at the slightest hint of this enemy coming closer to strike at us. We were the prey.

There was the totem, and as the storytellers had said, they had run from us. There were mountains to the north, holy lands where even the ones talk to you in the echoes of the gods. Down here it is hard to see if they are hearing me. A branch has snapped. The ash must have taken someone, just like they said it could. I had watched it wobble and wander in the air, shadowing people and striking at them, but the darkness fought it off.

The clack of wood on my back should have been warning enough, the sharp point of wood kicking over my shoulder, and creeping forward with hungry eyes.

The heartbeat tries to rise, tries to blur my sight and fight all my focus in the hunt. The sun always seemed brighter when the panic comes up, the colours became brighter and every movement slithered across the wooden gaps. This was the hunters pose. Every breath had to be slowed.

You feel the heart ramming and kicking, but every breath comes out of your nose slowly, as it whistles through these leaves. Those leaves were brown far too early, and the smokiness in the air was stinging at my eyes, but I had to force my breath to stay steady, keep the muscles strained and prepared for the coming enemy. There were a few accidents in this time, the creeping hunters finding each other when they are young, laughing when they see a familiar face in front of them, blinking and working together as a spiked nest of wrath for our prey.

This was something else though, I had seen shadows in the town while I ran jumping into the height of the trees, leaping over a river without thinking. I just hoped they were shamans, or some great rabbits I had never experienced. The darkness was growing stronger, it was not the shadows of the forests, that was a warm dullness.

This was the blackness of what remained from any flames. Shadows passed in front of me, the creaking of some huge tree grumbling and clicking. Tight snaps broke through the air, making me jump back, each remnant of those heavy branches booming on the ground, and smouldering.

I hate fire.

I hate the burning, and the brightness and I cannot abide being displayed so terribly next to so much wood. I have seen the catastrophes of burning, running people, panicking at the site of everything falling apart. The sharp, kicking stench in a forest was a horrible thing. I stare back out, and the darkness keeps rising from that burning town, cracking at the huts and breaking their lovely, squat buildings down.

The burning mud sent a great plume of smoke, and while it seemed to form a leering face, I had to skulk under the trees, bend a little more in the darkness, stepping back and leaning against any trunk I could. It was an old method, just enough to keep the darkness behind if you were on your own, always making sure the hostile world was in front of you. Your foot creeps out, drag it along the floor and feel for any grabbing plant.

Make sure you don't trip to raise any alarm.

As slow as a field grows and spreads, you keep your balance, roll your back against the tree and look for cover again. Always sense the smallest gap, the tiniest shift of light. Move like lightning to the next cover, following a path you know from the glow of the aching sun. Through this smoke, it seemed to be bleeding, crying out for some care, some hopeful need to hold it together.

I knew I needed to keep running, but life is given to those who practise and tame all within them. My heart will not stop panicking through, my legs will not stop shaking no matter how slowly I move, or how much I practise my breathing.

Please, guardian of the forest and protector of life, hold me in your holy hands. Keep me close as you push my soul forward, along my lighted path. In this time of thorns and blades, protect me from their wrath. I have not killed, and I will not force my blade or hate onto anyone. Please hold this purity in your golden eyes and do not let me go.

My eyes were open again after this prayer, for it was a calmness no enemy could assault. No predator would growl when I am in touch with those blessed Gods. I had seen tribe members at war, stopping for the prayer of the Moon's rising. The world though, does not remain calm, it does not beat with that peaceful harmony forever, and so you must stab the spear into any darkness in front of you. Do not take any space for granted, not even a shimmer of belief you are protected, there are traps and death everywhere.

That heavy tree had blocked my path up to follow the river, and down underneath the scalded hill, hidden from the nearest tribes. It was shattered right across that opening, and any kind of familiar path. East? That was a mystery to me.

The nearest tribesmen's screams popped, just off in the background, only the smallest twinkle of a sound, but enough for me to tense. They were now mad things, unblinking and dancing without any loss of energy, rolling and flipping from some strange possession. It was said there was something in the sands the other tribes collected, or maybe it was the shiny clumps they

200

grabbed and added to their strange outfits, more bright lights to the strange collection already. I don't think any of us were pure enough to escape this judgement, but perhaps powerful enough to beat it.

I stabbed the spear into the soft mush of the floor, always leaning back on my haunches, just in case something reacted. I was pulled forward, caught on some strange, sparkling twine, shooting up out of whatever kind of tangle they had made. I dove to the right, kicking out with a leg like some deformed spasm. Just in case. It had been enough to stop capture before, once, clacking just between some huge, grasping hands with a sharp click. I didn't look back. The groaning noise had been enough to know I had made an impact.

This time, the snap of my old spear was a horrible noise, I would have rather wounded a hand, and I squeezed my eyes shut for just a second, clasping my now empty hands closed too. The rough nails felt good. Now it was time to run and climb. I pushed up against the nearest tree. It rolls away, shaking itself and then just stopping before it rolled own a short valley.

"You should learn to welcome your Gods better, child. Please." The tree said something else, but I was already yelling at it, grabbing at the shrubbery of the ruined tree, coughing through the cinders and trying to beat away at the flames. Smoke and fire and demons. That feeling of a grave curse rolling over this world was impossible to escape.

My panic ceased as the flames themselves calmed and disappeared, the tree slowly unfolding and crackling in front of me, standing back up and snatching each root back into the moist ground. Even a bird roosted in its nest again. "There is no curse here, child, only a blessing. You have to follow me, and we can save everything you hold so dear."

The distant screaming continued, the smoke kept spreading, somehow the world was still alive, and this tree stood before me and smiled. It had unrolled from some tree plumage, unravelled now into a fully formed woman and lengths of leaves that cascaded away from her long hair. With the twinkle of stars, two spherical eyes glowed back at me. She had a calm dress, coiled around her in the tangle of vines, small fruits glowing brighter than even the green shimmer all around me.

She stood taller than me, and a calm spread along me, just enough to slow my heart, just enough to pause the world. "You... snapped the branches? To scare that thing away…" It was so hard to trust anyone, to look at anything new and only witness the wild biting world. The grasses grew faster than I'd seen it all around me, straining for the half-seen sun, but I buckled under the growing smoke, knowing the enemy was always watching.

It was something you would only notice with time, like the wearing down of a valley, of the swell of a pregnant stomach. The smoke was everywhere, clinging to the surface of the world and seeping through it. It burned at the skin, biting and squirming through my rags, trying to find more skin. The tree woman started to run, coming straight for me and not slowing down.

Before too long the bright glow had shot through me, and without thinking I ran after her, clinging onto the only weapon, the only tiny sign of hope I had left. What has been a maze of traps and ugly shadows exploded into a single, lit path of purple glitter. Before long, the space between the forest and our huts had disappeared, and there we stood, squinting in the smog.

Shadows collected around us. Those dark and smoking figures coughed and bit at the air, snapping and dragging themselves forward. The darkness was spreading, but somehow, everything was moving far slower. I felt the cool touch of her hand, wriggling and clinging onto mine, with the roughness of bark. It slowed the world down, and there was time to take in everything. Her hand was behind my head, and I could feel its weak pulse.

She tilted my skull back, making sure I saw the sun, it's small roundness so strange in the midday light, when it should have been a huge, blinding sphere. All of me focused on that ball of life giving. I could feel that power, the small flickering strength growing into great lashings of power, like some immense tide. It was hard not to fall under the wrath of this assault, but I just breathed hard and tried to hold back everything else. A sweet song faintly grew, over the groan of all those bodies. They writhed while the sun tried to sing and call to me.

The air itself slowed down, I could see each breath, every small stream of atmosphere swirling and fighting for space. The darkness of the ash and feeding smog was only part of it, the pure living wind of the world was still there, holding on hopefully. Every time I breathed now, I only allowed the living air in. I stood taller, but still she pushed at my head, forcing me to stare into the sun.

Her other hand slipped, I felt some shock kick at the enclosing bodies, and they kept coming, not slowed down so much now, one almost laughing through a strange gargle. What was she trying to say? I pulled my eyes back to when I had seen her first, she had been standing in a break in the forest, gasping up at the light, even if she was buckling under the smoke. I remembered the prayer.

Lord of light, may you pull me from the shadows of my enemies, may you grab me into the purest glow of your life, so I must grow eternally, and not either under the shadow of another. May we all find our space under the gift of your life.

The air was swirling around me, heavier and heavier than before. It was still into parts though, and in one fell push I three all that poisonous gas right into the beastly things around me, feeling great that bright glow in the open air. The song rose, a sweet wordless melody just like the ones we would utter in our meditations, and in the quieting moments, I could see the very light as a whispering, golden sea. There were just the fragments of strange buildings stretching up out of the light, and then they were gone.

"Every gift of life is a gift to you. We need a saviour, and as the only one to save my kind and not burn me in fear, I have blessed you to hear the world. A creature has destroyed these men, brought them down to the place of beasts. You must kill, only to save them from their suffering."

Those figures were scratching at the ground now, yelling and biting at the light I glowed in, gnashing at it, and chuckling that same dark gurgle of a laugh. They seemed to notice I had no way out but a path of destruction. There was no blade nearby, nothing was here to protect me or hide behind. I grabbed at the small scraps of wood still left in the fire, grasped at the horrid remnants of wood and tribesmen, and winced from the burns.

They broke in my hand, and my heart did not rush with the focus I might have by hunting. They are men, no matter how much they are cursed, though it seemed impossible, I would not let go of hope. Another piece of wood broke in my frail fist, and I was almost going to bend down and look for something else, just for the shine of a tiny blade, or a trap to launch. Just something else to ward them off, something to guard against the coming enemies.

A cackle snatched in the air while one of those things snapped just above my head. It cackled again while I tumbled to the ground, holding my hands up in the hope there might be some protection. The pulse of light slammed me into the ash, and as I coughed, the air escaped me, throwing me high up into the air.

The tree woman was back, and with calmness, she turned my head softly to one side, forcing it to follow the river. I flicked my eyes down quickly though, watching her silver light slam through the burning bodies, reaching into each of them and lifting them high up. As the gold pushed through them, a human faced glowed and smiled out of the force. The small smoke sizzled, and a luscious scent of flowers grew.

My breath had hit into the burning ground, and as it hit our small river it bloomed, cascading lengths of grass and flowers with it, breathing life back into the world.

She carefully squeezed my hand, swelling my heart in a way I hadn't felt since my father embraced me. Before all this chaos. I followed the river, and with it, the soft blue shimmer darkened and thickened. "Life is with you, and my gift is yours to give. They must pray to me, or all will be lost. Here, you can see it." I looked up just a little, following her guiding.

Even if she didn't have to say anything, I knew to keep looking down the river, further forward where it was thicker and stronger, but it squelched like a black slime now. The darkness stuck to the surface of the earth, growing in dark veins. I kept looking, gliding through the air to get closer, and pushing those flowers with me.

It was tiring, and I faltered to the floor, but with one smash of a fist, the light rammed right into my heart. It is a booming light, an overwhelming warmth which beat with my pulse, throbbing out of me, slamming along every hair and with that light, a sea of gold began to spread around me. Every flitting heart began to purr. They rose and pleaded, running to me as they sprinted to hope.

I could feel it all, but while my heart rose. There in the distance, it was not just ash and smoke which flew along the wind, but huge flames riding the wind. The hill was burning, seeping darkness from it. That screaming from the horrid tribe had not been them, it had been something far worse.

Every muscle tensed, and sickness rose slowly up my throat at the sight of a hunching man, large enough to grapple with the roof of the great hill, and grind away at the rocks with his great hands. Whatever it was writhed and grew, smashing down at their temple's wooden structure, the deer antlers falling to the ground from the huge body they had built.

It grew taller than the statue, that thing I had seen people burning from. Once I had crept up to it, believing the legend of giants, and though it stood higher than ten men, it was just made from blanks of wood. They took, and they ate without care, and now the first giant was bending over the ugly, heavy mound.

It grew immense in the distance, heavy wings flapping against the slime. Flames sprinted from every little movement. With one push, it threw that slime below it and disappeared into a storm cloud, moving south to the beauty of the sea. Something called with high notes of song, and as I settled to the ground. I could only weep at the pain around me, the wonder of the brightness in the distance, echoing in the voice of that vine-coated beauty.

"You can cry. We will find a way to save the Burning King's victims, and for that we must head to the healing seas. You are the first of the Hearing, and thousands will follow behind you. They will be walking before a shadow they cannot understand. You will know why soon when you meet her, the Ash Queen. I find her devilish ways far worse than the stupid violence of that beast.

"Hold the light steady, and free all his victims. With me." Her slight body glowed with mine, and all of us crafted the shimmering tendrils into those fearful souls to save them all. Battering away at a babbling madness I could not even touch without a terrible shock whipping at my spine.

"I will tell you again, son, we must leave her for now. A war is coming." Like standing in a lightning strike, the world clapped away, exploding before the dreamers in one bright smash.

-

Eden would not show them the terror and survival that came next, she could feel the frailty in the children's hearts, and she would never hurt anyone again. This was a place made only for love and care. The pain of where they had been run over them and gurgled in dark tones. She winced back in her chair, in this old age unable to hold back the tears at the scars the Ash Queen bled.

There had been a thousand disasters before this latest assault, but that was always a moving battlefield, a distant thought and then explosions and then a distant thought once again. This was something different. Eden held her breath, feeling the brooding power on this table and feeling it was worth waiting for someone with the Hearing, when someone else had made sure to have two come along at once.

She didn't like how much they matched the cursed Queen and King. While she sat and thought and wondered about the best way to tell them this was not the end, a deep stab wracked through her heart. She faltered in the seat, her oldest servant – that scalded sprite – was right next to her without a thought.

They were attacking. So soon!

"I can feel your fear, your strength, your racing hearts. There is a huge weight of pain on both of your hearts. A running which has led you right here. Right to the hidden soul of all this, the very place they are dreaming of. You humans have come up with many sayings for it. A picture says a thousand words.

"I am sorry for this, another journey so soon when there is so little energy, but it is the only way I can convince you it is not time to run and hide. If you must leave this dream, do so carefully." She felt that seeping call hit her again, this time felt the snap of that electric warning. It was a risk to dive this much into the stormy hell of the Ash Queen. The flaming tongue of her hate was here now too, something was out there dripping with it. Her neck cracked under the pressure of lashing up. It was fighting against every defence she had built. A few leaves in her braid darkened as she let more of her power seep out, but it would be worth it.

She caught the connection, her hands snapping the wood at her side of the table. With her claws clasped closed she pushed the rotting through into their heads and fell back. The burning sprite stood straight, armoured now with his metal conjuring, ready to hunt once more for that most cursed prey.

Jacob stood up, shaking his head from the exhaustion, feeling that same call to protect against some oncoming pain. He was so used to standing up for Ellis and destroying anything that might hurt them, and there he was beside the burning sprite, and running a little, trying to keep up with the sprite's huge strides.

They reached where a long branch had bound together and grown up into a long tangle, sparkling as if it was made of little jewels. The burning sprite pushed his hand toward the trunk of the glowing growth, just as it morphed into a blade. The sap didn't come out, it just shed the outer layer of bark and glowed a rusty grey. It stank of oil, and a long length of black started to spill out of the wound, crawling round the tiny gap.

The sprite moved back, scraping at the black as it bit away at his arm, crawling up and leaving bloody metal scraps behind it. The sprite moved back, swearing under his breath and trying through some strange words to summon back the flames, striking at the metal with sharp cracks but getting nothing back. He still looked up at the branches, standing back a little more to try and get a better angle at whatever was clinging to his attention up there.

That recognisable ochre gas started to burst out of his hands, and he tried to push it away, falling back again and smacking into Jacob who had been trying to help but couldn't find it in his fuzzy head to summon strength he was sure had been there so recently. Everything was hazy, and the floor shook below him, crackling into his nerves, knocking him down to his knees so quickly.

"Rusting, you should let us protect you. Please." He spoke through haggard breaths, trying to stand up straight again but finding his legs wouldn't quite let him. Not even questioning how he knew that sprite's name. Jacob had landed face down, and right away the world became a far brighter place. The grass was rich and minty, a green which was glowing all on its own. He ate without thinking, still feeling his arm weakening under that horrible ochre smoke, and knowing something was wrong.

Something which had been waiting for a long time, but Jacob knew, something which had just been waiting for an old woman to fall upon it by accident. In one forceful push into the ground, the grass's fumes blew into the air. Jacob grabbed a clump of grass, chewing on it and showing his strength by standing over Rusting with what little power he could muster.

He could feel the tingling of something else staring at him, and it was easy to see the silver thing looking down, a long thing, grabbing and leaking into every tree around it. Long pipes streamed from its body, that dark ochre a thick sea up there, still falling slowly down the way snow drifts. Without thinking, they were both climbing.

They had planned, chewing on a strand of grass as they climbed just to find as much of its electric power as possible, just as the blackness seeped down, they leapt to another length of wood. They seemed suspended in the air, and for just a moment the picture scratched, fizzing and disappearing before it was back again. The trees reached the floor this time, and before long Rusty and Jacob were either side of the beastly Mirroring.

Rusty held one hand up, just about balancing on the tree without the grip. Three fingers were visible in the sick light. Though the picture shook, Jacob's heart raced with the little energy there was left this high up. Two fingers. He tensed his legs, leaned forward, just estimating the distance, and grabbing at his Swiss Army knife.

That's at home he thought, just as he leapt through the distance. Eden just saw their two heads crash against the wooden table. They had disappeared, and with it, this pretend picture of their bodies at piece disappeared too.

-

Back in Greenview, a homeless man with yellow in his beard and eyes, and tattoos covering his face with heavy teardrops, jumped awake, raising his hand to the dog. Of course, it was barking at nothing. Then he snapped fully awake as a boy and a burning man fell from the floor, rolled up to the wall, fell backward and seemed to roll into an awkward stillness. They snapped awake quickly, staring at the homeless man.

He looked down at the alcohol by his knee, shook his head and went back to sleep. The only other sound was a statue clicking into place, catching its pyramid head a little as it almost lost balance, focusing its beam on them for just a second.

"Rusting, we have to run." Jacob whispered, running

across the road in a flash, crossing the whole distance without passing any time, and even though a car went by as he ran, not even a horn blared. Rusting was stood on the other side with him, and took one step away from Jacob.

"Did you do that, just by feeling it? With the urgency rushing through your heart?" Jacob just nodded, looking behind him, and flexing his hands, letting just a little purple light fall off his shoulders.

The world was rushing in front of him, and even if Jacob had watched all the star trek there had ever been, understanding what teleporting is and doing it were very different. It felt just like they walked out of something, fallen right through and into the real world again.

A short scream cracked and stopped almost instantly, just where the huge statue had snapped into place. They looked at each other, both moving closer to the glass of the skyscraper they were stood next to, squinting through the gap to see a group of people.

Every one of them was facing another person of just the same height. "Is it even possible?" Rusting whispered, shaking a little at the chill from the office as he stood on the other side of the building in the same breath. He didn't have time to do anything but open his mouth to say how dangerous that had been. The shock stopped him saying anything else.

Glass twinkled to the floor softly, from the office nearby, rolls of paper rustling, and they both struggled to stand. Rusting leaned forward to walk along the path, to step into the only lights in the city, bending forward but a sharp hand cracked against his shoulder. "Have you never seen a road?" Jacob snapped, looking from left to right, but realising Rusting didn't care. He felt the same calling, that rising in his hackles, but there was far too much madness for him to just let the rules go.

Things needed to make sense after all.

"Wait, does any of this make sense to you? Please." Rusting stopped, sighing visibly through his burnt armour, seeming to chew on the words to try and find the right meaning.

"Ash is the memory of pain, its soft footfalls upon the ground, after the fire has burned and everyone has fled. Over time in the first wars, she took that name to be the coughing disease after battle. The small rages and the biting madness of surviving. Her horrid master is war incarnate, but she is everything that could summon pain. She is the Ash Queen.

Before, in the most chaotic war, she started to do this trick to innocent people, and found a way to almost send the world mad. The rest of the world destroyed the creatures though, so she must have planned something more this time. The only way to end her reign is to free people and take them back to the wonders of Eden."

Jacob scoffed, "I don't know if that's possible anymore." He mumbled, knowing what the world was like now. For the first time in his life, he didn't want to know any more information. They ran across the road together. A huge crowd were stood under a glass sphere, every one of them reflected in the mirror. They didn't need the mirror now though, as they were all standing in front of another version of themselves. A version with ochre eyes. "The Mirroring has made their move. It is time for us to work." Rusting mumbled, trying to summon the old war spirit back against such odds.

16: FOLLOWING TRACKS, AFTER THE HERD HAS RAN

Humans have been following tracks for centuries, now we know predators spend a lot of time thinking about their prey and learning. There are animals like crocodiles and baboons who time their own movements with their prey migrating. Lions, wolves and chimps can surround and herd their prey into any corner they want. Never judge anything as less than you.

Eden felt Jacob and Rusting disappear, but she was sure they were leaving this dream. She knew why Rusting had left the world, they were just about to go and find Ishmael down in this darkened dream, and Rusting liked to forget those memories. It was a wound she couldn't fix, or he'd lose his discipline, and the rage he was keeping in check might explode out without control. Jacob was like a swooping eagle, protecting Ellis and running to keep the predators away.

Jacob liked reality, to keep his feet rooted in the floor, and she could feel the pain from Jacob, not being able to fight them away, but finding more and more enemies were coming and he just couldn't do enough to stop them. He hadn't like the first dream, the lack of control. She was glad Rusting would be in his company and teaching him the ways of the sprites.

They were all sat in a haze of murky grey, the swirling mass before the dream activated and they were taken somewhere else. Eden was taking a deep breath, a harsher one than usual. She knew many of the sprites were not the cold, driving blade Rusting was, they were learning the different ways of the natural world. Each of her talents was being perfected by them, and even though they didn't talk about it, everyone had felt her weakening.

She sighed, knowing she would have to fall into her own dream, and show Ellis the world that terror "The Burning King" wished to bring on everyone. She shivered, reaching out to find his flaming aura, chasing after the wounded souls he left behind. The trees in her hair withered and small embers of fire fluttered in the air.

In an ancient tunnel, she had built to that monster of a man, from a time when he had lied weakened in the mud. With it, the embers grew, and as everyone groaned, the smoky scene shifted to a dark surface on the floor. As she searched through his acidic mind, she scraped at the edges, and found her way through the old tunnel. With a snap, every one of them slammed onto a dark surface, each of them on all fours with bent legs and panting breaths, coughing as the ash bit in their throats, squinting through the angry ochre gas of the world.

Eden stood up from her own strength, this time in her youthful form, and she couldn't help but look down and smile where she could see her little, shiny feet, fidgeting in their bareness. Even around the storm clouds, and the gargling thunder, she couldn't help but giggle at her little toes. Her belly had swelled in real life, and it was lovely to see this version of herself again.

Her hair was just thin lengths of roots, luscious and flowing. She was turning on the cold floor, tasting the kick of tar in the air and trying to look for the fumes she knew would be close.

She stepped forward, feeling the rough floor of molten waste crack a little below the weight of her will. These dream worlds throbbed with the power of your presence, and she nearly fell to the side as Ellis stood up. Ellis had the smell of candy-floss, and they stood closer than Eden did to the towers and smoke in the distance. As Ellis tried to stand up, they tried to lean against a nearby winter tree.

The fizzing image of the tree broke away like a TV turning off, and Ellis nearly fell to the floor again, but their talents put them standing up again. "This is what we're fighting against!" She shouted, hearing the rumble of a furious volcano build again, realising they couldn't see the towers because they were on the volcano.

The Ash Queen put me here, she must be nearby she knew, tasting the rising sickness, and with a sharp gesture in the air, forcing the other sprites up with her, running with a false air right behind her. The hill screamed, a sweltering heat pounding and beating at the floor. A heavy roar echoed along with it, a heavy whoosh whipping at their backs and nearly flipping them over the steep hill.

"Run, and don't look back to me" she yelled, but most of them had already gone down the hill, trusting her power. Ellis was right next to her, and with a soft smile they shook their head. A small bird landed on their shoulder, and the volcano calmed. The slime slowly rolled down the hill, gurgling quietly from the small magma it had pushed out.

The thunderclouds crackled and formed strange words in the sky, lightning cracks in the shapes of circuitry popped and scrambled over them. Eden stood before a churned square of farmed soil, emitting two notes at once and clapping at the tunnel that opened. She had a plan first, show them hope and then show them the coming plan of these evil overseers. They had to see all this pain coming, but see it with the weaknesses it had. She just hoped they would last against the toll.

They ducked under the tunnel together, the sprites of life, light, earth and the shadow bowing to her as they entered. If she had planned this, lord of the water sprites would be waiting. She just hoped the other grandfather oak had survived.

-

She shuffled when she walked, just about lifting her feet and slowly wandering through the strange tunnels. Ellis was jumpy, remembering the collapse of the other tunnel and listening out to any sound but the rustle of her soft dress across the hard floor. She was being careful, pushing with her will away at the angry world around her. She knew this was a cursed and terrible place, but this was a safe path she had walked through many times.

It was the only path with any purple glow, but she paused for a long time in front of every tunnel. The three sprites were ordered and sticking behind her, calmly standing to attention as she stopped. Most of them hadn't made it this far, there was an exhaustion which came from stepping anywhere near the world that Eden hadn't touched. They were trying to protect her, hoping somehow, they might hold out against the beasts they knew were waiting.

The five of them paused, drained just by walking. It wasn't the tiredness which forced you to pant or for your heart to rush any faster. Instead, it drained you with hunger and tiredness, something was feeding on them and they couldn't see it. Even in their calm order, and in all of Ellis's nervous energy, they couldn't help but feel their hope take a hit when they noticed Eden checking the floor to find a comfortable seat.

Small roots grabbed down from the blacked ground above them, the slop of slime sploshing to the hard floor and squelching through the veins, the roots shrivelling up before she could turn them into a seat. Steps clapped behind them, running and racing and echoing in the strange, bouncy sound all around them. Ellis stepped slowly forward, but felt the flick of something behind them, somehow already slamming their head into the nearby wall, falling forward and nearly through the picture as the picture fizzed and bit away at her.

It all faded for just a second, and the wall corrected for the fall, making the blur fade away. Ellis might have winced back and even yelled out, but there wasn't any pain. It was impossible when you're in a dream to feel pain. "Don't move Eden, they know we're here." Someone panted in the distance, then they were there without thinking about it, a huge bulky cloud of a man, dwarfing everyone around him.

He glowed just a little, like lightning rolls in the background of a cloud, two misty eyes staring down at Ellis and Eden, grabbing at one hand at a time. To his side, a smaller man shivered like a leaf in a harsh breeze, almost not there. The other sprites sprinted through the tunnel and down the entryway, one of them sneezing, another harrumphing like a horse while he trampled down with heavy feet.

They nearly crashed into the two men, but they faced a wall of swirling air. They didn't frown or punch it, they all seemed to understand. Even Ellis could feel where the force was coming from, the faint man wobbling as a huge torrent of force. He was stretched thinly across nearly thirty feet, as if he had sprinted faster than sound, the sonic boom crashing in solid fist-blows.

Ellis looked down, smiling and quickly feeling a horrible pang of sad sickness, their hands were clasped together. It was hard to see where one hand ended and the other didn't. The huge shoulders of the cloudy man turned to look at Ellis, barely holding back the sheer torment of that force himself, anchoring his puffed-up arms against the wall of the tunnel. His arm moved a little, the gesture shuddering down the other man's arm, and soon enough they were both laughing. The huge man had a hearty, drunk chuckle, fitted out with the knock of his huge fist against Ellis's shoulder.

It was the softest thing in the world, the air banging just over his head at the force he must have held back. "I am

Whisper, old friend, don't worry about him. He's Misty, but you won't hear his voice outside your head." He chuckled again, nearly falling over at some huge charge of energy, "You'll grow used to it kid."

An egg-sits by the entrance. They exist while they're ex hits at the walls. Everything here is His. Don't hope there's a way out, there's no need, I just told you all about the exit.

Ellis stood up and ran from the sheer force of the air that ran around the tunnel, there wasn't to take in the fact that noise was their voice, just singing and rhyming with a cheeky rhythm. Its laugh echoed while their panting and mumbling voices came out. *Something else too. It's a quick tune. This is like a little toon. We're all in our true forms down here. Don't worry, there won't be wounds. Just don't get lost, we'll take all the shots we need to get out of here.*

The air blew harder, and without realising, they were all running, stamping and kicking at the rising waves which lapped at them, trampling through it. The wind just rolled off the solid water. Running drained their energy. Roots scrambled, and Ellis looked around them, not questioning a tunnel that suddenly widened as they looked to the side.

It was impossible for anything to be behind them, the ground was exploding and burning. Spits of dark flame spat past. They fell against strange shadows, hit into tumbles of aggressive wind. Or the sheer force disappeared without any reason. Ellis learned quickly to take a breath when that happened, the oxygen literally escaped in a gulp of one breath any other time you tried.

The water grew deeper and deeper, and wouldn't move out of their way. Small leaves fluttered in the water, growing to oversized lilies. *If you wait, they'll take your weight.* That one didn't sing, and it was impossible to know if Ellis had thought that, or it had come from Misty herself.

They grew quickly, and Ellis scrambled onto one moist length, feeling it push underneath him. A pulse of light ran past them, walking a trail behind them, and that was the first time Ellis realised how dark it really was in here. Everything had been lost to just staying alive. Other than the burning behind them, there wasn't anything else lighting them up. The sharp and hungry echoes of smouldering flames licked at all the other paths they could have taken.

The small light disappeared quickly under rumbling earth, and with that two small brothers jumped and crawled past, clinging onto the roof of the caves with roof arms that seemed made from the cliff itself. Ellis jumped again, the thoughts of that crumbling cave crackling at the back of their mind.

The cave rumbled.

The whole scene shook, and there Ellis was, sat in the water, scrambling for air, tiny hands flicking at the space above them and finding nothing but a slick, thick liquid, drowning further down into a huge blackness. The shadow moved and tried to become something solid, but the water was fighting their attempts. The silhouettes of all those powerful sprites dashed past, chasing the thickening waters up to breathe and taste the light again.

Somehow Eden was keeping up. Ellis couldn't get the picture of her quietly fearful face staring into the void of the tunnel just a few minutes ago. She had been shouting then, but now she wasn't.

That picture in Ellis's mind was suddenly very real, the face covered in bubbles and yelling out. She was patting her hands in the air and trying to say anything. Even the bubbles were solid though, and Ellis couldn't see a thing. *If you can't see, that's fishy when we're in the clearest water. It's an iffy sea, that's something you ought to know. There's a fish, she's just there, doing just what mother taught her.*

The water echoed with that sweet sound, and the scales glowed bright silver, huge beautiful eyes absorbing Ellis, and they did nothing while webbed fingers reached around their chest and pulled them out with one little gesture, leaping over the water.

In the splashing spin he escaped the waters, Eden landed with calmness and a tall, slight figure coated in long cloths clattered to the ground. They both rose from the softened ground without thinking about it, trying to run a little more.

Even in the panic, Ellis didn't keep running, with their whole body exploding in a huge scream, every tendon pushed out as their mouth unfolded and just the slit of those bright blue eyes remained. The blonde air flashed back like a crack of lightning. Their whole body was bent forward, legs pushing down into the soil and still Ellis was held up there, silently exploding with that horrible fear let go, all the madness and that terrible beast still chasing them. This screaming power was working against them now.

The water was slammed up against the burning tunnel. The flames swam and smoked to nothing on the other side of the scream. The earth itself had moved, and they stood with a huge shadow against the water, looking like some great monster with the tangle of hair behind them. The water shot back once, twice and exploded for just a second. Ellis took a frail breath and started to shake with the sheer power of what they needed to scream. Both hands were stars of strain, every hair was standing on end from an even bigger force Ellis was starting to conjure now, learning the threads of the sprites near them and picking up on Misty, who felt so close to them now.

Their hands met, and Misty took everything in one hand, shaking bodily at the power of it, Whisper grabbing onto that hand and holding on still. Whisper stood in the way of Ellis's force, taking the air through him and letting the sheer pressure leave Ellis in one great boom. They could just catch the sound of the others starting to run as the water thrashed against the roof. With all that power behind it, Ellis had destroyed the cave wall, the tide already starting to build.

Whisper and Misty shared a quiet gaze at each other, feeling just how much Ellis was still holding back under their own fear, knowing the last Sprite Lord would know just how to stop that fear. They ran past the Earth sprites, not hearing the small fizzing sounds over the boom of falling earth and roaring water.

A torrent of water fell through, overwhelming them. Even the earth sprites in their usual coldness turned and ran, sensing the crackling force of the earth all around them. The whole world was shattering. As they ran, the floor kept changing and they nearly rolled as they got away, tumbling onto each other as they tried to keep up with each other, running and trying to keep away from the wall of wrathful water which nearly crushed them in its force.

It went faster and faster as they ran, the tunnel twisting and tightening, the earth sprites rolling and smashing through the earth as it stood in their way. A chaotic net of wires and sensors filled the space in front of them, and one of those sprites leapt without thinking, and the electric force captured her, coiling her spine in the electric force of it. A screen untangled itself from small extensions of silver. A roaring, inflamed face started to appear, a large grin spread on his face, small ochre fangs butted up through the heavy-set jaw.

They stood in front of it, surging tide to one side, growing maze of machinery to the other. *My roar is small. It's not all there is. A Taurus wouldn't give up. I can see the other side of the mirrors. The place where no one can scare us. An old man, but Ishmael is the toughest one. Smile!*

Whisper clapped his hand with Misty's other hand, they both met each other without having to think about it. The waves had stopped, and Ellis's hand clapped too, long hair fluttering in the strange liquid. Golden lines stroked through the water, and in something that felt as close to a hug as it could have been, as the water embraced them all.

The electricity crumbled, but the monster had been awoken. They were still dreaming, and it didn't matter where they went, they were still in the dream-world of the Burning King. The King tightened his fist as he slept, and every flame begun to roar and grunt at one another.

-

"Fire is chaos and pain. I was born to control it and hold back the pain. We must back away and try something else. There must be some answer. Fire may burn, but these machines have done something worse." Rusting was panting and haggard, looking strange and ashen in the stark dawn light. Jacob had realised something very quickly.

As they had stood under the darkness off the near lightless night, it had been completely still. The only real sound was all those people breathing. There weren't even streetlights left on, none of the bedrooms glowed, and the only cars had been in the distance. Jacob had tried to run forward, but one stare of bright fear, and he'd been clasped to the wall. Forced to stand and watch as the day started, and those without ochre eyes slowly walked down into some strange tunnel, the other beings walking away as if they were filled with lead.

The Serpentine turned its head slowly, and every piece of glass shook with the reflection of someone, a picture still trying to keep up with their victim. Jacob didn't look at another mirror. "It's not war he wants this time, he's talking to that rotten women and plotting and hunting for more torture and desecration. It's slavery they want this time. Please, take me to your safe place."

Rusting hadn't stopped panting, just as with Eden he was another sensitive being that felt everything a thousand times more powerfully than just a moral might. Now he had nearly collapsed onto his arms on all fours, surrounded by the huge, driving exhaustion that destroyed the fibres of the world around him. Jacob looked up sharply, following Rusting's gaze as he gawped at a rooftop. Jacob couldn't see anything but the distant twirling of a birds' shadow, far higher up and then turning away. Rusting pulled on his arm, gesturing with a gruff and shivering grumble. Forcing himself to stand up.

They had shouted out at the people around them at first, seeing if that would be enough, but it was like shouting into a wall, like screaming right into the very soul of a waterfall and hoping somehow it might hear your voice and change its ways. None of them had stopped, they had tried to walk through them both, flinching out with their hands in a dreamy daze to push them out the way. Jacob had tried to push back, tried to make them see, but the reaction was even harder than it had been when he had looked at the glass.

Jacob had smelt his own hand burning, wincing back from the pain of that, and letting the unblinking man pass. They'd ran alone, flitting from person to person, trying different things to wake the people. They weren't in a dream, they spoke and sang and worked and seemed completely normal.

Rusting marched, forcing more strength, while the fires of his body dulled again. Jacob pointed his hand at the path they needed to take, and again they were both bending just a little under an immense pressure. Rusting pushed some of his pain all around him, and it grasped right onto the nearest person it could. He tried just enough to push a tiny piece at a time into Jacob. They both reached the bridge by that lake much longer than it would have taken normally. Jacob always feeling the map around him while he stepped, but as they reached the graceful white bridge, Rusting had to stop him, his shallow breaths coming out in sharp crunches which seemed to bite at his lungs.

"The floor seeps a hunger I know too well. Be afraid and be thrilled. Are you still with me? The Burning King is." He coughed hard then, gesturing at a soft twinkle with the edge of his hands twirling, flames bit away at an ochre splatter that stretched from his mouth. He stretched up straight, clacking both feet together like a soldier.

"He feeds and crawls at everything, look." Rusting sat down then, closing his eyes but not relaxing with a straight back or two clenched fists, resting against the corners of his knees in a meditative stillness. Rusting was always ready, and he'd never truly rested since Eden had found him so long ago.

The grasses on one side of the lake were darkened, as if it hadn't rained for weeks, and even Jacob thought the sun was a little brighter today, that something was pushing every little whiplash of light toward each other far more than it might have before. Like the Golden sun, or something that was shimmering up there was trying to say something. The water didn't move in a straight, sparkling line, it seemed to almost roll toward the other bank, and twirl back on itself, constant whirlpools shadowed even in the new daylight.

Jacob saw the small carcass of a small deer as it decayed must faster than it should have. He turned away, for the first time wanting to get back home before anything had changed.

17: YOU CAN RUN, BUT THEY'LL FIND YOU WHILE YOU SLEEP

Everything has instincts in them. You too. They are the inbuilt actions to something without thinking. There is one that is different, the decision whether you should run or fight something which is scary. It is the fight or flight instinct. What scientists have found is there are levels we are born with that will demand how much you compete, or whether you would give up in the face of someone you think is stronger. All of that is lost though, if you have someone you need to protect, then mothers can lift a car without thinking to save their baby.

The day started just like normal, there wasn't any shouting, there wasn't any fear on anyone's face. They didn't pause to stare at one burned man, and another covered in small scratches with half a trouser leg missing. One jogged past, straight in front of a car which didn't beep its horn or even react. They were perfectly in time with each other. The care swooped past each other in some distorted, graceful dance.

It made Jacob feel sick. Everything had its rules, and this world moving with a strange new layer of rule, too much of it, and that was wrong. It felt exactly like when he'd moved here, the traveller family finally trying to live in a house that didn't have wheels. He had hated that for so long, moving along as if he had been on wheels against his control, just like being told he should have another go on a rollercoaster, this time it would be fun, honest.

Well, this was the seventh or eighth time life had felt like this, just being pulled along by a rope and told to keep going no matter what would happen next. When Ellis's Mum had died, the world had just kept turning and pushing you forward, asking for more work, and the tests couldn't wait for you to stop being sad, there was homework to do. Now, it was the opposite, and that was even worse. The world had gone mad, and Jacob felt like the only sane person left watching it all happen.

Jacob was always thinking, always trying to understand just what was going wrong. He could see the little mechanisms of people now, walking about with meaning as the morning really started. He'd fixed a car once, just by looking at it, but this time nothing was wrong. That what was eating at him, scratching at the back of his head and telling him to stop. It was like his stomach falling off the edge of a cliff.

They were just walking up the small alley that would welcome them to Jacob's squat, simple house he still hadn't called home. Jacob stopped, suddenly and completely with a small spasm in his neck from all the tension which had been growing since the first moment they had skipped from that other world back to reality.

"What are we fighting?" Jacob croaked, recognising they had been running around for a long time without thinking of why. Rusting seemed to work in rage and felt like fire when Jacob looked too hard into his eyes. Sudden and impossible to ignore. Jacob felt the floor disappear from his feet, only looking down for half a second at the lack of shoes at his own feet. Rusting had Jacob's shirt scuffed in one hand, the other pushed with the inside of Rusting's knuckle pressing against his skull.

Screaming and a swirling darkness rammed itself over the picture of that calm, new day. The image the Ash Queen wanted them to see. Shadowy silhouettes bit and growled through the madness, attaching themselves to the running people. The ash in the skies circled, swiping and catapulting others into the air, dripping ochre waste. Jacob grabbed onto that striking hand. "Enough", he grunted and in one tight twist, Rusting's wrist was twisted down and away, dispelling the picture. In a fraction of a second, Jacob had seen the perfect way to push down and hold his hand there, and he copied it.

Jacob might not have been a warrior, but these new powers levelled any physical weakness he might have had. Rusting let him go, sighing and placing him back on the ground. Jacob scuffed the ground as he stood on his own, he was just about to kick down. For a second, they stared across what felt like a huge chasm, and neither could ignore the wounds.

"There's no time left, this madness is growing, when it starts to rot through the land and the air. The sickness is flowing, and I know that rage you're feeling and the same one swelling at me is it's suffering. It will make you weaker and buckle your knees. The last time, all I could do was watch others fall around me, that cursed Queen leaving me with even pain, just enough to watch their pain.

"This time will not be the same."

Jacob felt small again after that assault, new to this where everyone else seemed to know every step the enemy would take. Without thinking, he followed Rusting and wandered just how Rusting knew which house to go to. The heavy click of the door echoed sharply in the silence, and without thinking Jacob was right there and standing in the little entrance of the house. The light passed through beautifully, and Jacob followed Rusting through the flowery furniture of their front room that swept to the right.

Jacob's head snapped up to the steep stairs, as he closed the door behind him, that familiar floorboard creaked. His uncle must have been waiting all night for him. They walked smoothly round to the kitchen, Jacob copying Rusting and looking around him to try and see if something was hiding, always making sure the walls were to the back of him, feeling afraid without thinking.

For just a second, something was off about the room. Jacob hadn't noticed all the silver had been thrown to the floor, he'd just stepped over them. The big, sparkling gold mirror had been knocked down behind the unit. Rusting's foot crunched on glass, and from his hand, he summoned a short and curved blade of stone. Rusting bent over, waiting for something else to happen and flinching at the smallest sound.

Jacob moved in front of him, feeling the hairs rise on his back, and heavy instincts weigh down on his shoulders, and he puffed his chest without thinking about it. Now his heart was racing, but while he reached out to find the same special, strange sense of slowness and raw force, something in his skull twisted.

Jacob couldn't question it, his uncle was coughing, pushing on the banister as it squeaked, groaned and then clicked as it always did when his uncle struggled down the last part of the stairs, always huffing against the steepness. His uncle sighed as he came near the door to the living room with that same sharp cough he always had, along with the same chuffing cough he always had. Nobody would make him go to the doctors, and as he shuffled forward into the room, it was impossible to ignore the sickness anymore.

The dark twist of another smack shot along Jacob's neck, and one leg shook under the force of its wrath. The light outside had gone. His hard uncle, that unsmiling man with a pot-belly and a large red face from far too much drinking wobbled in and smashed his hand straight through the glass of that door.

This time, he wasn't shaking because he was drunk, his body was smoking with the fumes of that black disease smacking its way through his veins. "This shows you… nothing good comes… from fighting back… stare down… look at the glass and… surrender." With the gargling sound of those beasts they'd met in the forest, his uncle was a melting body. Every part of his body had been blurred and rubbed into irregular madness. Ochre seeped at the bottom of his feet and in clumps across his destroyed hair.

"The smashed mirror…cursed me… freed us all… father, to devour… the last Hearing… defeated!" He lunged, splurging black mess as he crackled with a slop against the nearest wall, crashing through the sofa and throwing the waste of its destroyed remains against that wall, clearing an open path. Jacob couldn't summon any of his strength, that knocking spasm shattered into his leg and he buckled. The walls wobbled and started to sweat from the horrible infection.

They didn't speak to each other, they ran right out the garden and over a fence, feeling the sheer weight of that monster behind them. Jacob could taste it on his tongue and spat while he ran, a biting cough rising as a thick smog blocked his way. Rusting smashed through the fence without a care. The evening had rolled back, and under the beam of a watching statue Jacob couldn't help but feel like an ant running under a magnifying glass.

-

The water had risen to a burning spring, kicking them off to a sparkling plane of silver. Far away, a deep purple waterfall and lake glistened powerfully. The long emptiness of silver was filled with small statues, and strange skulking figures in the distance tried to keep away from them in the bleak darkness.

Those strange figures were each staring at the lights in their hands, shuffling their feet along the floor, and held in a forward hunch with the long wires pulling them into the same steel floor. Massive shadows pushed away at the floor, and it rolled in long waves. Each time it passed a person by, they writhed, and the light glowed through them, black fluid splattering in a heavy slap.

Ellis, Eden and the other sprites were marching to the

waters, and as they grew closer to another one of those figures, Ellis couldn't take it anymore. They had to try and save these poor people. The Burning King had been waiting, building this world to show his dream of what might come. As Ellis stepped closer, the true form of the person became more real under the glow of that screen they never looked away from.

The rest of the emptiness was dank, and Ellis winced from the light. Ugly red eyes didn't blink and gawped at the glowing screen. Ellis locked into feeling just what the other person could, and as the hellish madness dragged at them, Ellis didn't notice the floor writhing toward him, built off the back of some ugly monstrosity coming fast.

"Hello?" Ellis whispered, trying to find something in these strange figures, hoping to take their eyes into theirs and just like they had a few times with wild animals, they tried to reach into the soul of the beast and find some beauty or peace. This was a dream, and the normal swooping twinkle of that connection wasn't there. Even though it was a dream, Ellis could still see something, and the whole world started to shake right in front of them, struggling against their will to tear away at this link.

The burning king was pretending, smirking in his throne so deep underground in that tower. He decided it was his time to play his hand, already having pushed his play in the real world, this was the time to punish Eden for so much hiding and betrayal.

The sprites were matching forward, Ellis still leaning, staring into this figures eyes. The figure groaned as Ellis stuck their face in the way of the sick ochre light that swept from the thing's burnt hands. The hands moved slowly, stuck together, and Ellis couldn't help but move his hands back a little, confused and scared at the strange scaly sensation its hands gave them. They were long, stick thin extensions of bone, shaking and barely able to hold up the glowing screen, but holding it as well as it could.

Ellis could see the pain coming from it, in just the few small seconds Ellis had been near that light, a pulling need to see it again slithered up their mind, and without thinking they were stepping closer to the frail person, a pang of need like wanting to have another bite of cake. It tore into their legs, forcing every step and pulling them forward like a puppet on a string. Eden was shuffling strangely in the mid distance, a sign language the sprites knew from darker times when they would walk through the terror not to be seen.

Where is the treasure, the youngest of us? She asked, shivering tightly in the stillness, feeling an illness roll over her as she turned back. The sprites of animals always led from the front. Right now, another sprite, a bright eyed old man was sniffing in the distance. He had wisps of white hair along the usual grey fur. It was a thick mess of hair, wrapped into an old fur tunic, in this form of heavy-set muscles it was impossible to tell where the clothes began. He was stamping one leg on the floor, the callused feet slamming down again and again, scraping the floor a little with his hoof as he counted.

238

He whined and turned his head to one side. He whinnied, growled in a bubbling noise with small barks, and ran backward. He easily fell onto four legs, running in his wolf form toward the scent he could feel in the air. He bounded across the expanse, kicking the paws softly down as he slowed and howled while he was still a short distance away. It came out as a very long note, echoing down the expanse as he ran again and forcing Ellis to stop staring. The ground shook, the dent from that monstrous form pushing at the surface.

Within a couple more seconds, the silver ground began to swelter and warp in a huge heat, melting under the growing hand which pushed at the metal above it. The frail figures flicked a stare behind them, and shuffled out the way. They had looked like a strange kind of horrible lamp, but now as they moved and severed the screens from their faces, it was obvious they were really people. One of them looked right at Ellis, gasping.

It shook, talking to itself, but the light from that screen glowed bright red and burned at them. The frail thing winced away, battering its tiny hands at the light, but finding nothing but its sunken face seeping further into the blood-red light as it choked and whipped along its spine.

The figure waved at the air, as if it was drowning, and with a simple nod of the head, it seemed it had agreed to something. The other figures cracked and shuffled, the screens from those lights forcing them to run forward and straight at them. The leering faces faded away to a dark and shattered picture, a face stretched and stretched until in a simple explosion the massive light bloomed from where their faces had been, rampaging through the crackling eyes and out of their mouths as one.

A long humming note dragged over behind their snapping forms, the wolf figure whistling a tune Ellis almost recognised, jumping and skipping through the zombie shapes, the wolf's own glow falling to a darkening grey. Even with the energy being played against him, the tune didn't stop.

A huge smile was glowing from the animal's face, the deep eyes and a sniffing snout on the beaming expression. He stood in front of Ellis, pretending to pout and sulk in the chaos, playing with Ellis. "You liked the fox more, didn't you?" he shook his head, ruffling snow from the thick cloudy hide. A high yawn pierced out, and he was still smiling, squeaking as he shook his head and sitting down.

The glow around Ellis was a warm feeling, like being held by a star. "I'm beast-shadow, there's no time. Climb aboard." He jumped onto all fours again, snuffling at the arriving people, growing just a little more and standing up as a huge wolf-man, great shoulders and a plume of fur behind a bright white coat, flickering with purple.

The ground rumbled and cracked, snapping under the force of that huge hand coming toward them, and as it closed like a mountain, a small growl crackled out of beast-shadow in the sheer urgency. Ellis didn't think about it again, they were onboard, and with it, a huge leap took them over the zombies. Ellis looked back as they slowly turned around, and the ground itself began to react.

Purple paw prints shimmered against the dead metal of the floor, and beast-shadow started to splatter against the floor as the metal melted and gripped to his feet. It was turning to smouldered black segments. He jumped from it, and sprinted from one boulder to another, gripping at the strange heights which bubbled from an immense wrath that was growing against them, all.

The whistling wasn't stopping though, and it was obvious beast-shadow could keep running and running. As he leapt from one black piece of magma to another, he clapped his paws together in the bass beat of the tune, bending his head back a little to try and find some answer about what that tune was.

Ellis couldn't help but clap along, trying to sing the tune with him, but giggling as they got it wrong, and beast-shadow tried again to whistle and sing the tune, singing louder and louder over the bubbling madness of this land. They were still running to the purple fountain in the distance, and Ellis could just about see the shimmering shapes of those pale sprites against the dark floor.

Their heart rose as the tall Sprite Lord of the air could be seen past the mad surface. The black sky seemed to swoop in the way, just glowing by the light of the burning floor. Beast-shadow stopped, jumping from one stone to another, and not being able to understand the motion, as the air shifted further down from him.

Ellis felt that sicky flip of their stomach as the wave of magma. The dark of the evening took form, and a gurgling laugh so many beastly things had echoed rocked along the world, and with it an immense hand of flame pushed itself around the two of them. The fingers were great columns of burning. Ellis looked through the space of that fire, and while they pushed their face back and squinted heavily under the colossal heat, trying to find that purple symbol, there was only black and those strange zombie figures.

They were caught by the fire, as they rolled over the heat they kept looking down at their hands and staring at the screen, trying to grab something more. They watched as one of them pawed at the screen while the waves of fire blew away at the light from that display that all seemed to need.

The air itself seemed to shake and boom, and the small rock they were on disappeared even more under the biting flames. Beast-shadow whimpered and shook, Ellis patted his thick back, nearly losing their hand in the packed fur. He tried to jump up while the waves spread, and the hand closed, the hand closing into a tight fist, and Ellis trying to find some scrap of a scream in the sweltering warmth.

Under the biting magma, it was impossible to breathe, and Ellis fell against the shoulders of beast-shadow, trying to maybe whisper something against this sheer heat before the nightmare took them somewhere worse, hoping in some way the golden shimmering world from the air above might come and save them.

Beast-shadow grumbled, and Ellis could feel he was going to do something to save them. "I almost have that tune sometimes, de di-di-dah dum-dum di-d-d-d-di-di. Then it goes weird and full of bass, and I've got no idea what's happening. The wincing ferocity of the lava cursed any flicker he might have had to see that purple glow once more. Then he thought he had it, a bubble of thick purple surrounded them, and Ellis had to laugh under the taste of candy floss.

"Mum hasn't left you, she's a sprite-splice and I love her. I hope you're not thinking of letting go while you lay down and relax. Yahoo!" he screamed and laughed, still somehow keeping the tune in step with a click this time, just trying to work out what it was.

The jumping hadn't been panicking or fear, or anything from the heat of the surface. He was trying to get enough momentum to leap into the air. As he did that, long wings fluffed out from the lines of fur and a great eagle's beak opened out from his great face. With one hoot in the air, they pushed sideways through the closing hands, flapping a great wing and pushing at the hot air, flying straight through the space and shooting up from the thermal path.

Ellis had dreamed about flight for so long, but now his head flashed back to the ugly, long head of a monstrous enemy they were sprinting away from. A purple flare shot up like a flash of biting lightning, every person doing the one thing they knew how to in an emergency. Please for help.

The metal floor had all but disappeared, and the troop of Sprite Lords were trying to calm down the flames around them, just about pushing at the embers of magma, kicking their feet, flailing with small sprinkles of water and gusts of air. The air was boiling, and they could hardly breathe, but they pushed on. Eden pushed the sweet air she could, and they gulped at it while the heat clawed away at them.

Beast-shadow swept down to try and catch them, zooming through the spumes of fire. He tried to push through the punching flames, running from the panicking hands which scraped at the air in front of them. The air was filled with the scent of burning feathers, and Ellis gasped while they ducked through another narrow avenue of whipping heat.

The immense waves of force rolled across the space between them and the monstrous giant. He leered over them, both hands combined closing like an overlapping tent. Beast-shadow circled close to the Sprite Lords, Ellis tried to reach through, and the talons scraped at the short spaces, but they couldn't get through the rolling thermal wrath.

The air tried to push away at the huge fingers, and as his arms rose like an ugly tsunami, they were all pushed back and into the cupped hands, finding nothing but that immense face of laughter still chuckling with joy at having caught his prey. "This is the future of the humans. They are staring into their screens, and they will not see anything around them while we feed on their world. I am the eternal hunger, and I have your home, green fool. While you are alive, you will be trapped here. Jacob is running for his life, and you sleep it off while the world burns. Ha!" The great volcano squelched those words, his huge mile thick arms lifting them up.

The slop and roll of those immense words was chews and spewed in huge washes of burning heat, and Ellis kept trying and trying but he just couldn't escape the picture of hell and caged horror. The hands choked down and the shadows collapsed over them in sheer exhaustion, a rampant rushing heart from the colossal sweltering chaos pressing down on everything. Only the sound of the groaning lava was left while they couldn't even pant.

The world went dark while just the red explosion of light was left while Ellis closed his eyes in his overwhelmed state. Ellis felt beast-shadow shrink underneath, the tense muscle failing and descending with a crash to the lava, but flapping to keep up just a little more. Ellis tried to tap out the rhythm, trying to play at that tune and stick to the fun they had. The embers flickered around them, and they felt pressed and strained by this overwhelming force.

It all went dark.

Ellis spluttered at a deep pool of salt water, spitting away at the horrible taste and wiping at their mouth, splashing in the pool and trying to float. He paddled and splattered into the clear light of the day, "Jacob" they yelped out, a high note lost in all the laughter.

The hell of the Burning King had disappeared in the bright daylight, and a long sparkling tunnel of clear water glowed in the new day. "Ishmael", Eden trilled, her soft, large hands reaching down to Ellis and grabbing them up to the soft shore. They looked up at a long tunnel of a swirling ocean just in front of them. Already Sprite Lords were stepping through it, disappearing away from the purple dancing falls of rain.

The sound of bubbles blubbered in that same tune, and Ellis just stepped forward in complete exhaustion, looking up at a whale which flapped through the waters at Ellis, pointing one flipper onto his back and waiting for Ellis to follow. Ellis just kept thinking about Jacob, just remembering the flicker of Jacob's hair as he ran away to protect them, still recalling the squeeze of his hand.

Their heart rushed even while they struggled to keep their eyes open. As they stepped into the swirling pool of water, just like those long tunnels in the cloud world, they were pulled along the immense tunnel. Great purple swirls of strange runes echoed on the outside of the tunnel, but there were no people there anymore, just a beautiful purple sea. Whirlpools swirled, and Ellis slept as the name of "Ishmael" whispered through the torrent of sheer speed.

Don't worry, this voice can't fail. Whatever the distance, once we've met you I will always sense. My life is now part of your tail. If you believe in legends, this is the first male. The legend from luck and circumstance. Rising out of the chaos as the king of the oceans. He was caged in dreams, and now it seems, we will have him free again. Just this once, we can save you, Ishmael!

-

Jacob had pushed the fence back together, witnessing their exact make-up and pulling the tendons of wood right back together. The ochre eyed were swarming closer, and Rusting with Jacob huddled by the entrance of the forest.

Jacob couldn't avoid Ellis here.

Every piece of grass was a day of fun, a moment of laughter. Some tiny glimmer of escape perhaps where they'd tried to escape from the real world, and now for the first time in all the time Jacob could remember, normal sounded just about right. Then he would check himself, would remember the pain of that electric whiplash in the dream world, and the thought of all those people lost and captured, but acting as if they hadn't seen anything strange happen last night at all.

Rusting sat beside him, cross-legged on the grassy floor and smiling a little, though only his mouth showed any sign of cheer. "I played on this hill centuries ago, the trees are still here, every part of their spirit still plays around it." He mumbled, talking to himself as he did on these strange missions, but finding someone else sitting right next to him, staring at the trees just like he did.

They were both looking at them, and Jacob could see the whisper of something in the air, just the smallest golden memory from the calm breath of wind. They had run across the town to this safe place, as the darkness had rolled in a third time, and the groan of those statues had started to grow, Rusting had moved without thinking about it.

He had stood and prayed at any full-sized tree he could find, each time kneeling and mumbling something quickly, clacking his hand against the armour in his chest, and while the armour still rattled, running on.

They got used to the people avoiding them, to them running right into a crowd and that crowd just stopping where they stood, some of them pausing in the middle of the road.

Jacob's uncle was still coming though, that was impossible to ignore. The stench in the air would grow and they would feel the presence of that beast come closer again. They were both sniffing, both picking up a fragment of that ochre rot. The ground started to shake, that ancient tunnel tore apart and seeping, and there the uncle stood. Both arms were connected simply by the play of shadow, but in this bright light, the sheer strain of being seemed to play on the body.

He still growled and spat every word, "You think you are safe, well now you have no choice but to face me, not skulk and hide away in the green. Don't forget, trees can burn." He was talking faster, and for just a moment something flickered past. Rusting didn't need a second look.

He grunted, as if he had been struck, and even though he winced at the sight of something else, he didn't stop running. Jacob turned to follow him, already trying to run but flinching. Rusting was pushing his hand up to say "no", but Jacob didn't see it, a gross length of a hand grabbing him by the shoulder and throwing him bodily into the valley of those trees Ellis and he had fallen into, what felt like months ago.

Even as the heavy hand had pierced through a wound in his shoulder, Jacob couldn't feel fear this time. *That is not my uncle* he thought, bracing for the impact. *There is no time to be a coward, no escape, it's time to stand straight and fight the great ape* something thought, he wasn't sure where that voice was coming from. The great rhymer, Misty had reached through him by Jacob.

The Burning King was violent, and his servants couldn't help slapping their chests when he thought they were winning, and that with just the name mentioned in the dream world, it was a powerful link. Every thought rolling along the winds and used as any kind of potential weapon.

"They may have called us cowards, but they will learn we were only being kind." The forest echoed in a deep voice, as one. The trees rumbled and fluttered in their darkness, and with a heaving groan, the trees tried to push their roots out of their resting places, groaning on old and aching muscles. Jacob was trying to make the branches move, or to get some support wrenched out of those wooden lengths.

Before he could even see into the ditch, the trees had reached up with their branches on their own, suddenly fast, and with a soft grip, they pushed Jacob back up onto a shelf of grass. His uncle had to step back in disgust at the survivor frowning at him. They walked forward as a group, the trees trying to stand in front, to protect Jacob even with the bright searchlight of those Serpentine swooping closer again, the eyes of hunters.

Jacob stared up, craning his neck at the sheer size of the largest towering Serpentine. It must have been more than five times bigger than him, an immense machine with one sharp eye piercing the searchlight down.

A siren clattered out of its speaker for just a second, and some answering rumbles marked the approach of another Serpentine coming closer. The trees bristled and slammed their thickest branches together in a strange battle cry. Jacob couldn't see Rusting, just the burnt embers of where he had been, and from the sheer held breath of the air all around him, he felt like they were waiting for something.

That familiar, rampant rush in his heart came again, thrashing and then slowing down time itself. His twisted both feet in the ground, rather than falling back to that L shape, his legs twisted in a writhe of sick nerves as he stood alone against such an enemy. He looked hopefully around himself.

The crackled remains of soil and rock pushed itself up his feet, rolling along his legs and thickening skin with a dark exterior. Jacob was locked onto his uncle though, and the hardened skin rose, unnoticed.

His uncle squelched and wobbled before him, one fist crashing through its body, clattering against the sludge of darkness in its middle, and the body disappeared for just a second, squelching back in the waste that fell from Jacob's hand. Legs stretched back where they had been, and through the decaying body a thousand roots tied the spasming figure to the ground. Jacob closed his hand without thinking, forming a tight fist and seeing the ochre light fade in an ugly fog from the half-form under the aggressive assault.

Huge black blades struck into the ground, branches thrown up at the figures, growling faces etched into the ancient wood glowing in that purple mist Jacob knew meant real power. He didn't look at his own hands while they shimmered, too blinded by the charge of staring down that giant.

It struck down lengths of electric wiring, and though the material stretched away from his hand with Jacob's thinking, the Serpentine body just grabbed at the blades, pulling them back. Jacob wasn't strong enough to stop it, and he rolled away before the onslaught of another strike.

The trees assaulted the Serpentine's legs which slowly lumbered around, throwing waves of leaves up at the oncoming attack to hide themselves, and shooting their own weapons back, little branches clattering against the solid body of that huge mass. Jacob was caught by a hand, dodging to one side and to another, trying to get close to those kicking legs, grunting every time he saw a tree flail back to the ground. The storm of roots struck through the material and seeped away from its immense legs. Still it boomed that ugly horn, defiant and in total control.

Jacob couldn't do anything but run and dodge and hope a gap might present itself to try something. A hand slammed down in one place, and Jacob rolled to try and bring his own attack, but just as soon even more blades and wires descended from another attack. The thing seemed capable of turning one arm into twelve, slamming the black lengths on their own, or grouping the attacks together.

For the second time, Jacob spluttered as he slammed

into a tree, stepping on the footfalls it made while the earth burped and ruptured, leaping over the crushing assault. The whip-crack of the wood as it snapped was a harrowing sound. Then with a swipe, the trees were thrown aside, so attached were the Serpentine's legs they didn't think it could rotate the arms around and swap its weakness of those rooted legs into a horrible weapon.

The trees swung helplessly, Jacob looked around for Rusting and could see the smoke from him running nearby, but the shadow of another attack was far too big now for him to keep looking. Fear cracked his neck up. The metal blades pushed down in one collected attack, Jacob took one huge breath and turned into the air itself with a thrust of pressurised gas, only able to hold it just long enough for the blades to pass through where he had been.

They were long lengths of sparkling wire, and with the spread hand of that status still opened, Jacob could reach up to the outer shell. He grasped the solid weight of that strength from the earthy hands, with a roar he punched heavily through the arm of the beastly Serpentine and tumbled straight through the space, panicking eyes flashing from side to side, just in case another enemy would strike down again.

Rusting was only heard shouting "Ash Qu- ", before his voice disappeared in the crushing darkness. Small lights glowed in the tunnel of the moving beast, and Jacob had to push out his hand to stay balanced, as he rolled again, grabbing at the wall away from all those crawling wires. The lights hopped closer, blinking and rabid, screeching and hungry ochre eyes happy to finally have some prey to play with. Jacob squinted, exhausted in the dark, just catching the sound of clacking machines.

18: MAKING A MONSTER ILL

There are a lot of animals that work just like viruses, they make animals ill or take over their children. There are birds which take over the nests of others' young. Even more powerfully than that, there are ants which can get into brains and take them over, just like zombies. Those zombies become more aggressive and spread those ants even further. The world is dangerous, always stay careful.

The world rumbled, shook and cracked around Jacob. He punched out with the toughened fists as the arm crunched down and tried to destroy him. The whole statue was nearly collapsing around him, sharp flecks of that black material falling all around, and he kicked and shoved himself away from it all, the tunnel getting tighter and tighter.

His shoeless feet formed with the black material, gravity pulling at his back while the arm rotated and nearly snapped off to the ground. For just the smallest moment, the space which had been in front of him became the sky instead. The sound of its crashing was everywhere, shaking the air and rattling Jacob's bones.

The pinched, aggressive stub of its arm bit away at his back, and he climbed as the arm started to spin, seeing the day rising again, then the ground and back again, dizzying him while it crushed him. Rusting couldn't be seen, just the squelching mess of his uncle trying to find him still, pushing away at the trees which stood in his way, punching at the bark of one tree.

He didn't catch the rest of that fight, as the mass of branches rose and exploded in fury and a heavy clatter echoed through the spinning sickness. All the spinning stopped, and he was left dangling just above the combat, watching as the thick trunk of one tree buckled under the strain of black pain from the ugly mess of his uncle grappling with it.

The Serpentine started to build itself back together, the trails of its black form bridging thin tendrils together, tiny lengths of the dark illness twining back together with a web work that spat down the same acidic burning at the touch. As the tendrils combined, they solidified back to a wall. The arm reached up as the statue bent down, and rose back to its full strength, booming that same signal again at its coming victory.

Ash Queen groaned through Jacob's mind, and the little lights were watching him again. The blackness had thin, pulsing lights in lengths of bright glows, some baubles twinkling with the strange rhythm of its thinking. Signals must have pulsed along there, maybe the remnants of a language, or the figures from its power consumption. Jacob didn't have the energy to analyse any of it, no matter how he tried. The time slowed shakily, and he tried to grip to the minute messages just below that burning skin layer of the Serpentine's innards, but it was a biting madness, and he flinched backward, finding a storm of biting blades lashing out from the sharp pricks of light which had been gawping at him in the bleakness.

He had to roll away from the attempt, exhausted and clasping at the sharp floor, just about staying up. The creatures purred with an electric fan hum, they jumped forward and hopped, snapping in the darkness like any playful puppy. Or like the hungers of a predatory wolf-pack ready and confident to feed on their weakened prey. Jacob stood up, and they stood up with him, copying the way his wasted body shook itself to stand up one more time, leaning heavily against the wall, toughened earthy skin smoking just a little from the aggressive defences of that surface.

He leaned back, and they did, glowing as if they were made of stars in their strange smoky forms, just about making up the remains of Jacobs ashen form as the smoky glittering lights worked to make Jacob's reflection. The dull, brown eyes, or the scratches along one, ever-so-slightly hairy arm. The faces blurred but the hair stayed together. Jacob's heart was sprinting, the eyes were expanding in the dark, just about catching the fragments of those creature's real edges.

He leapt forward at them with abandon, falling straight through them, and smashing at the wall behind where they had been. He nearly tipped out of the huge statue, spinning and balancing on the tip of it, punching back through the wall, as he tipped, and panting to meet them again.

They panted too, deep ochre eyes blooming like rotten flowers at him, the strange memory of his own face nearly staring back, but still just behind and fading. He knew they weren't him, he had seen enough of the horror of those lost people not to get caught in this picture of a strange reflection. It was a dizzy feeling whenever they flocked in his way, and he tried to turn and run.

In his mind's eye, he could just about see where the neck of this beast worked its way up, and with that, he had enough of an image to start climbing. He was stood in the thick chest of it, just about seeing the faded cracks of a surface to grip onto, and without thinking he tried to jump and grab onto a length, tried to keep going and find some way of taking this enemy down.

Trying not to think about how many of them there really were, just surviving and doing anything he could.

The booming slap of an immense hand clattering against the translucent plastic Jacob had ran past and over, trying to climb. The sound echoed in the strange darkness, and he couldn't help climbing down to see where this sound was coming from. The muscles in his arms screamed against his efforts, yelling as he reached down and stretched those legs down along the figure, just about holding on as it shook along the surface of the wall. He wobbled and felt his balance go, but he was fused without question to the wall now.

He climbed down just a little more, coughing from the overwhelming ash around him.

A person was splitting into two pictures, fizzing and bubbling as a weird shaking shadow rolling and biting around itself, but losing in the bright light. Jacob squinted at the blinding light, nearly falling as he lost his grip, thinking he'd bounce off the plastic screen, but his head pushed through the sweaty visage and he grabbed onto its spongy matter. The man was sweating and shaking his head angrily, trying to escape from the shadow just behind him.

Jacob pushed away at the screen, opening a space and slamming his feet through the shadow and bouncing from the thick slime of the damp wall on the inside. The heavy ochre light faded away, and the shadows stopped, the man stood still, unflinching for once. He could hear other people struggling and yelling out too.

The darkness in the chest opened, and the Ash Queen stood on a blackened tree, its length stretched up and paused over a pile of the ruined trees. "You've found seven people, freed one, what a miracle you are. These ones are immune, and they're in more danger than they knew. Jacob the brave. Jacob the stupid. Jacob the far-too-easy-to-trap." She hiccupped a cackle "We've got them both now, so soon!" The laugh exploded again, and she rolled back a little, laughing loudly into the air. "This one was even easier than the last. One person might have liked you, we had to take your uncle first! Dumb. Dumb. Dumb. My lovely King was right. This will be over before the silent war has really begun. The world will be deaf to its destruction."

The Ash Queen cackled in loud clacks of her sharp tongue. She pushed the ash all around her, shadowing Jacob in a tomb of darkness while the blooming flames of the Burning King coated the forest. He pushed the strength of his flames from those tunnels his beasts had been working on for so long. He had known Rusting had been there, knew there would be someone perfect to blame. The roll of fire wasn't under any control, the Burning King was fighting a battle of his own, and with this small fragment of freedom, he let loose the tide of burning wrath without reproach.

Jacob lied in exhaustion under the assault of all that smoke, Rusting pushed at the flames with the new commands he couldn't let go off, possessed now by the darkness of the Ash Queen's whispering, scarring the grasses with his ochre eyes, breathing flames in great breaths. He buckled under the ferocity of Eden's protection to her blessed trees.

Eden could feel the suffering of her oldest servant, but she was overjoyed by the calm sea of Ishmael still holding back a dam of strength he knew the world needed to see again. The Ash Queen worked away at her attention, forcing it to stay away from this destruction, and gawp forward instead.

-

He had a lisp, and even though it was a little subtler, that didn't stop Ellis's beaming smile from erupting when Ismael the huge finally stopped laughing. It was a warm bellow that echoed of the solid ice of his crafted building. It was throbbing with purple sparkles in a display of his raw strength. He knew everyone as children. Little fireworks flowed behind the giant shoulders, and the capes of water which fell from his back sparked little points of light too.

There were little glows of fish swimming through the cape that danced to the little gestures of his hands.

Some flickered back to one of the many pools he had in the small sculpture of a house he'd scratched together. The only sanity in the madness he should have had under a toll of centuries imprisoned in this cursed land of dream.

Ishmael didn't seem to have any wounds from it though, there was ice cream cooling, swirling in an icy pool, and he crafted delicate cups around his gesturing hands to give everyone a little piece of it. Nobody asked how long he had been waiting.

The others were panting and burned, most of them felt like they needed to sleep even if they were in a dream. They didn't disappear, even though the edges of their body misted while something tried to take them away.

Ellis was just hearing the echo of beastly laughter in the strange evening light. Ellis didn't trust any of the dream, it all glowed just a little off, like it was being viewed through a plastic bottle, almost right, but not quite true.

Ishmael glowed with a purple and blue echo, two thin lines rolling over one another in a strange light of his own. Ellis was still just about following the trail of a simple sparkle he left behind, walking through the hut and tracing their hands along the little steps and that graceful swirling pattern of his home. It spiralled up, and Ellis followed, watching the mist that came off the sleeping bodies.

Eden slept calmly in a hammock of her own making, and the mist spat at Ellis while he walked past it, and they almost slipped on the melting ice, floating just a little whenever it became too treacherous. They leaned out a hand to try and get some comfort from Eden, but winced away from the heat. The barely held back panic started to rise again then, waves of it hitting up at them with those Sprite Lords who hadn't made it and the idea of losing Jacob. It was all getting too much.

Ellis stopped and leaned against a wall, feeling faint and drawn, and sweating under the sheer pressure of these attacks, the monsters to come. They leaned against the balcony, and held themselves for a second before following this trail. They had felt the sadness and loss, but more than this the sheer drive to keep moving, knowing that's just what Jacob would do, and for whatever reason really wanting to just hold Jacob's hand again. It had been a long time without him now it felt like, and Ellis wasn't feeling amazed by the dream world, far too much in need of Jacob's strength even more than that.

They kept walking up the high tower, and then soon enough, as they approached the roof, stared out at the mass of purple lakes and strange blue creatures that came and went in a single breath. An amazing calm from the pain that had been there before. "You know, she used to rhyme and scheme, and that's when I knew something was wrong. It's a dangerous thing if you stare into her eyes for too long…"

Ellis could feel the win of him shaking himself from rhyming himself, still trying to keep his own mountain of a mind resistant to her whispering temptation.

His heavy shoulders loomed as he leaned over the

fragile balcony, grabbing at the water and reforming it back to a heavy bar he could lean against. It glowed faintly and started to melt again, with a sigh the back of his shoulders glowed and one whiplash of purple the whole structure twinkled brightly and vibrated under his sheer power.

Ishmael's hair was shaking in the wind, shivering a little under the onslaught of his power. Ellis cold feel it, and they walked through this raw strength, leaning against the balcony themselves and breathless. They both stood and watched the twirling little runes, and the dancing small shapes, twinkling in the fake moonlight, and most of all Ellis wandered why it was darkening again, and what was going wrong

The flashes of old Sprite Lords danced and shimmered away to thin silhouettes, little buildings fluttered and fell away. A thousand constellations fizzled, vibrating against the pretend air, one aurora exploding against the next, but with each explosion, the picture only grew weaker and collapsed while he grunted at himself, trying to find the next best word, and seeming to scramble with so many different possibilities before stopping.

Unprovoked, he leapt through the small space between the two of them and yelled out, "Are you staring into her eyes right now?! Do you dream of her burning hands?! What demon brought you here?! Show. Me. Your hands!!" His regal robes disappeared into a shabby, hunched and weak figure with a long great beard tinged with yellow. The tattoos of tears draped down his face, and along his muscled but scarred chest.

Sharp nails dug into the side of Ellis's face, just to either side of his eyes, and the deep purple, bloodshot gaze of Ishmael glowed heavily against Ellis, there wasn't much for them to do but try and scream. With one dirty hand, Ishmael stopped his voice, knowing the wrath that was coming. He smiled then, that warm hug of a sound echoing again, and hugged Ellis, as they watched his scars disappear underneath their touch.

"The beastly Mirroring always run and hide then, telling me they've got the blessed Hearing and I need to save them. The theatre of that explosion is new, but it's been too long to know to believe any hope can be true. Now I know. It must be. Yes HA!" his aurora screamed in one great glow of light, and the tower struggled to stay upright, spots of mist rolling around them both, the heat swelling and Ishmael buckling for just a second.

"Thish ishn't real, the world ish shick and we have to get out. Pleashe shave me." Ellis pleaded, unbalancing from the collapsing building and feeling their own powers swell up, just to keep that monument standing. The ground started to growl and rumble. Ishmael leapt from the building, disappearing before he hit the ground, and Ellis couldn't think of anything but madness and scratching nails.

The growling swelled, and Eden was right there beside them, Whisper floated with her hands tied together, not quite able to fit her fingers together on her own, and looking for some companionship leaned against Beast-Shadow. Beast-Shadow's body faded away in a blood-curdling yelp, and with it all the air rushed out of the tower, tumbling at any parts of that structure. It left them to fly up high into the airless sky with unkempt speed.

The assault smashed hot whips of breath into them, Misty having been found out as a Mirroring, unleashed as a torrent of mad breath. Whisper struck her hands together, storm clouds floating down and appearing just above them. Ellis could easily float up, and Beast-Shadow grew wings and sang the tune as he rose.

"There is no need to call me now, my friends, I am here with you. That hot-head won't know what's hurt him. With me." He yelled, the deep voice sound like a heavy echo, and up from a spring of his own making, there was Ishmael, yellow beard glowing bright as his deep-set eyes. Shots of geysers spat out from around him, clattering down the tower. Driven by instinct and knowing Ishmael had to be trusted, they leapt onto boats of floating purple liquid. They all felt a shock, and for just the shimmer of a second, the trees of the real world exploded in front of them, then they were back in the chaos.

The clattering noise and whispering came back, two sounds rolling over each other, one of the noises deep in their heads, and with that, Beast-Shadow just sang ever louder. Ishmael lifted them all down to the lake, and toward the whirlpool the placid water had become.

"Ellis, you have freed me just by your touch. Now it is time we freed all other victims. With me!" He commanded the seas, and the tower collapsed in one great splash, the tide pushing them all in just the right direction. In a flicker that great white fox was back and in a leap, disappeared in the tides as a hundred penguins, chattering and running from the sudden blasts of sheer energy that shocked their way across the water.

Each blast of violent air exploded, but was quickly surrounded by a white, foamy wave of Ishmael's own attack, silencing the assault. Ellis was thrown down onto one of the boats, still looking back over a sky that hadn't stopped erupting with Purple, sharp runes. They bumped on the heavy onslaught of waves, feeling that sick spill of their stomach as the bumps grew bigger and bigger, and what seemed like a massive whirlpool opened in front of them, scattering the sections of memories.

All this madness echoed across the watery chaos, Jacob's thoughts intermixed. Ellis's hands slammed into the void without realising, feeling the warped signals and trying to pull back. There were two paths in front of him, and Ishmael stood in front of them all, directing the growing ocean's swell, forcing the water to rise and wipe out the chattering of the ochre eyes behind them. His roaring face was planted in the white waves battering away at the coming enemy, that sea of silver in this dream growing far too late.

With one last laugh, he leapt onto their ship, and Ellis looked up at the huge figure, feeling a lurch as the ship tipped to the right, and hardening his face as he wielded the ship on the edge of touching the burning waters, whispering the name "Rusting..." as they fell into some other realm of the dream world the Ash Queen had created, just catching the shadow of her slight wings in the whirlpool before they disappeared.

-

Ellis shook his head slowly, wiped out and hazy. The whole world blurred into place, the corridor of their school with the bright posters and the angry headteacher at the end making sure everyone was in good order. Ellis was staring at his locker, fused to the reflection of Jacob. He was here, and he wasn't hurt, he was smiling at Ellis's back, holding in his breath with the sheer joy it gave him knowing Ellis might get caught and jump when he caught him.

Ellis turned faster than should have been possible, and hugged him instead. Then the picture of Jacob was in the background, waving one figure toward him as he did whenever something else had fascinated him. There was only one person he was going to share that with. Crystal was staring down at her phone, giggling at some comment someone else was probably making about Jacob. Sharing it with all her friends, naturally.

She looked at him and laughed as loudly as she could, tutting and lashing out with her nails as Ellis knocked the phone from her hand, screaming without quite realising why. Ellis stamped at the screen, and something shocked him further forward.

They were both sat in front of the forest, though this time it screamed and burned, ugly straight-lined statues slowly walking on both sides like some angry earrings, hooting and scorching the ground before them with ochre lightning. The people didn't even run, they reached one hand up like puppets and grabbed at the shock of it.

"They're not real, you know?" Jacob mumbled, his mouth stretching against every word, and Ellis knew this was the real Jacob somehow. No, it was obvious when he looked at it, that eyebrow raise could never quite be copied with the smirk of knowing something you hadn't quite realised yet. Ellis looked again, knowing the whole thing wasn't true or real, but that someone had made a mistake, and let them stay close for just a second to each other. It felt like Jacob had forced them to.

The Ash Queen was almost there, things almost burned and choked them like it had in those dirty cages. Quickly in answer though, it started to rain, the clouds forming slowly, and the memories falling firmly back to that quiet moment on the hill when the gap between reality and dream had broken down and disappeared.

Ellis still didn't know what he meant, and they tasted the rain to get the energy from it, both glowing and holding the picture where it had really been, a horrible looking forest of darkness, even in the daylight, writhing with the possibility of all that whispering.

"The whispering and rhyming was another Ash Queen game." Ellis strained to say, and Jacob chewed the inside of his mouth at that, almost fizzling out. Ellis reached out a hand just as he almost faded. Ellis could not lose him again. The rest of the world disappeared, the gaping opening of a tunnel was the pitch black against the stark white of everything that surrounded them.

"She's gone now," Jacob winced and writhed, shaking

his head, barely able to hold onto the world around him, but squeezing on Ellis's hand. Looking down at the hand and back up with a smirk that never failed to make Ellis smile.

"You did this when I was blind without Mum, I'm here even if you can't see me." Ellis whispered, forcing Jacob to come a little closer, closing the white space around them to a tight space. Ellis didn't mind. Being this close to Jacob again showed how much being apart hurt. The shimmer of the new Mum glowed on their shoulder, and Jacob frowned, biting firmly down on his lips just like he always did whenever he was trying to lie or hide something.

Ellis had never seen him do that when it was just the two of them. "Tell me whatever it is, there's too much lost for you to go anywhere. I won't let you." Ellis quivered, just about holding onto everything, and even with the small tinkle of a tear caress their face, they hoped Ishmael must have been watching at least.

They had both falling into here together, but Ellis didn't have time to think. They were staring into each other's eyes, just like they had whenever the worst moments had taken over. "Nothing is real but the Queen and King we have to save everyone from. The silent war is scaring me. They're mad and they're taking everyone from us. My uncle had gone crazy, and half the town is destroyed." Jacob gulped deeply, writhing again from something hitting him, and his own tear fell from his face.

Mum pushed her little hands against the tear and

smiled, trying to comfort both. He waved a hand out like he was trying to swat a fly, and his hand stayed just there, just held in the air and prevented from moving any more. For the first time in their life, they weren't on the same side.

Jacob sighed, just about pulling himself away from Ellis's gaze, he had to hold onto that. "None of this is real but the people we're losing. You need to get out of the forest and wake up. There are ochre eyes everywhere, and they've got me captured. You're Mum can't come back, and we're not magic. They've infected the air, and everyone is being taken over. If the disease doesn't work, everyone else is left in a cage. That's why they captured us, and that's why they keep letting us hide in our imaginary worlds.

"You aren't magic, you're just the weak Mum's boy you always were." Ellis didn't have time to see the hurt in Jacob's eyes, the way he kept trying to shake his head but couldn't. The way his eyes glowed yellow. Ellis was trying too hard not to cry. The Ash Queen had been playing about with their relationship, and pushing at the gaps between their closeness as much as she could. Waiting and preparing for the perfect moment

Jacob had been taken, and now he'd been forced to say the one thing that would sever them apart, the first thing that had ever brought the two of them together in the first place. Mum.

Ellis didn't have the time to be nervous about their fist this time, didn't have the time to wander if the punch would be effective or not. They'd faced far too much to be told they were wrong anymore. They'd stood up to bullies, and now it looked like Jacob was just a bully that waited for the perfect time. They'd never punched anyone this time, but their hand was backed up by a huge power they had slowly been summoning.

Light glowed on the edge of their fist, and the air didn't move away from their hand, but pushed in front of it. Jacob didn't flinch from the blow, he slammed to the ground, quickly reaching up to where the blow started to bleed. It bled a deep ochre, and the sick scent of it rose like the whisper of a thousand flies. The tunnel swirled and grew, the darkness grasping and screaming.

Roots clamoured to grab at Ellis's legs while he stepped forward. They bounced off the pure wrath, and just before the Ash Queen could grab the second bounty she so desired, Ishmael exploded through his messenger, leaving Mum behind and filling the gap behind him. With a heavy waterfall of purple, Ellis could open his eyes for the first time to the truth, gulping in the splashes. The body of Jacob faded into a flailing, messy Mirroring but Ellis couldn't see anything through their shocked tears.

Ishmael took them back to reality, pouring all his energy into not burning from the power that seeped from Ellis. Rolls of liquid rolling in the way of the furious force. "We will all be home soon." He mumbled, barely able to speak as he tore apart this false world, slamming a wall of ice in the way of those great beasts that had fed away at the tunnels and were just as real and huge here. His laughter was the last thing the Ash Queen sensed, her rising claw the last thing Jacob would see for some time.

Even the Burning King had been a lie, his real form was still waiting in the madness of the city to the west. They had a ritual, and that needed a first meal, a first sacrifice to bring in the new age of power and victory. The Ash Queen couldn't face it, but no matter how hard she looked there was no way to live without doing just what her King, her owner, said. Jacob's tears had not been his, and even while he faded into unconsciousness, he chewed his lips slowly, thinking as hard and fast as he ever had.

19: TIME IS RUNNING OUT

Though it might be true that you can only teach a dog a trick by giving it a treat, it will always try to save you if you're drowning. They have an instinct to save the people they love without thinking about themselves. You should treat those you know the same too.

Ellis collapsed into the table, clattering the spears which had been gathered and prepared for their retreat away from the attacking anti-sprites by a crowd of busy tree sprites. They had been watching them rest and fight with their nightmare, kicking out once and smashing down the trees around them. It was only Ishmael, beast-shadow, whisper and Eden left now, and the flutter of other sprites ran amongst them, collecting the spears and bows, praying to Eden in thanks for her gifts with every moment.

She snapped awake sharply, snipping the scent of pain while it faded. She held one delicate link of a root along her wrist, letting it fuse to Ellis's hair and stepping into the madness around his nightmare, coughing as the corruption of the Ash-Queen racked her, and she buckled under its assault, squeezing the hands of Ishmael while he wielded the onslaught of all this corruption, sensing it all around him. With that, he pulled at the snow underneath, summoning it, and Beast-Shadow rustled in the blizzard.

His thick fur swelled, muscles grew as the hackles strained and his voice growled at the ochre gas which rolled across the air. The corruption died as the snow blew in aggressive breaths. The two Sprite Lords were working together, air and water assaulting everything that crept through the darkness.

The air screamed with a high and horrible yelp, long streams of roaring black which tried to grab them and pull their bodies away to the real world again, and the sprites leapt as they could in the way of these harsh roars. The trees started to burn from same attack, slamming back at the purifying breaths, and it punched away at the branches, crackling the stinging snap of fire along those ancient trees.

Eden buckled again, trying to hold onto Ellis as the Ash Queen tried to pull them back from the brink. Ishmael was a new figure, still shimmering in purple as he reformed in the real world, and the whole of his body barely visible in the dulling daylight, swirling in dense pools of sparkling liquid. He pulled one hand away from Eden, grabbing as he did at both their minds, and launching them both up out of the madness the Ash Queen had been creating.

"The scent of something I have never seen is closing in!" Beast-Shadow bellowed, bouncing off a tree as he knocked it down onto the beasts which were still coming out of the dark screams. Their black forms were barely visible in the dying light, and their ochre eyes became the only glow as an enemy many of them had tried to forget came back to the world through a most cursed memory.

The snap of a whip cracked, waking Ellis in a sharp

convulsion. Eden sprang on her haunches and summoned the guardian trees awake to try and buy some time. Their gold shimmer swelled as the guardians pushed at the roots and all of them were summoned together in the fight against the Tamer they had thought disappeared a long time ago. Where everything else sent a disease which could be cured, this man was the Burning King's executioner. The disease defined.

Nobody saw his face, there was just a hood of warping shadows flopping and writhing in the way of any clear sight. Beast-Shadow howled out, wincing from the sharp lash of the whip, just from the sound. He knew the hurt it could bring and all the young he'd lost from those blows, without being able to leave the animal side of himself, he cowered and tried to sustain his growl. A heavy spear slammed into the earth and exploded in a collection of electric roots across the beasts which cowered and bit, and Beast-Shadow hated the memory of those beasts being his once, of their tiny whimpering faces staring up at him in the moonlight.

The blizzard was grasped and flew through the beasts, pulling them up and against a sharp net of those thorny branches. They shattered in the light, and it was impossible to forget this was real now, the shock that slammed against the snow and made it burn was a heavy sting, a paint so dead and whispering in the dream. You could feel the earth shake, and with it, the trees stood on one side, just as those ugly tunnel-devourers exploded from underground.

Ishmael had seen enough, he could sense the flow of

this assault, and was chilled to see the holy place crumbling. Eden rose both hands up, pushing on a walking stick she had to summon, but with it, the golden spears of those guarding trees flocked around her as they grouped together to make their own spears of raw power, just to find a way out of this darkened maze this holy forest had become.

Ellis didn't have time to ask what was happening, they were busy throwing starlight at the front of the snow drifts, blinding those skulking beasts and knocking their warbling bodies down to the ground where the roots were waiting to find them. For the shortest time, the heavy hood of this wrathful Tamer appeared on the back of a grotesque, roaring tunneller as it ate away at the earth and the trees, snapping the great wooden table in two as the Tamer force it up in a wave of biting destruction. As they tumbled down, a gross gargling laugh flopped out of the Tamer again, and it echoed with the sound of a language filled with terrible words. Each syllable clacked like horrible strikes of their own. Everything the Tamer brought was fear and wrath. It cackled and with a single whip, impaled the very trunk from a tree guardian as it exploded in a firework of gold.

As they fell, Ishmael and Eden summoned the old runes to try and save them, stroking and writing in the wings of Beast-Shadow as they descended, buffeted from Whisper's cushions, as they descended from the falling forest. They were lost in the swirling mania of Whisper's wrath conjured up and brought to see them through one tiny passageway hidden for just such a time.

The Tamer crashed down amongst them, a storm of wood falling to either side of his troop and they charged again. Whisper didn't even stop as he landed, bringing tornadoes up with a twist of both his legs right into the snow, and with it coursed the blades of wind right into the immense creature. It snapped into smaller parts, swelling and biting out with its endless fangs.

Ellis fell into the snow, and the great explosions of war tumbled around them while the remaining guardian tree strode over his small form. He leapt between the legs, and winced while another beast exploded, grasping the light of their death. They could feel the electric force of its demise roll along their nerves, and feel the strange jangling ramble at them.

The noise of it was too much, the incessant light pounding from every little figure, every brush of glowing snow-dust, and Ellis let it scream out, shattering the light through their nerves, and shackling each of them to the ground. Ishmael threw himself further back, following the trail down again, and closer to the world they needed to save.

They tried to pull the assaulting wave back, screaming and glowing, and even burning Ishmael's webbed hands with the sheer static force, but he only chuckled at the onslaught of this attack, feeling another old memory come sailing past. The air itself crackled and shattered, fragments of ice driving through the sprites which woke up from the simple presence of Eden communing with the surface she made holy. The storm clouds disappeared, and a single torrent of earth fell like the talons of an eagle, and with that, Beast-Shadow swept over them all, and drove them through another purple, whirling transport pool Ellis could barely remember.

The Serpentine scratched in the tunnel of nearly unbearable, unbalancing force, bending their body and sending them over one side or nearly through their own bones. Liquifying them for just a second. Then even the air was solid, crackling with barely hidden lava behind it, with the cursed cackle of Tamer following them even further.

Ellis could still see the imprints of the conflict above, while it faded, a sea of abominable strange shapes leapt and darted through a beast only to find the animal disappear behind a darkened, warped cage. The Tamer lashed at them with light and dazzling, pushing them forward on a leash of pain they almost welcomed.

Ellis crouched, breathing haggardly, still glowing with that healing power. Ishmael squeezed his hand to try and tell him to stop. They slapped his hand away, wincing and forming a tight fist in confusion, but running on none the less. For the briefest moment, they both shared the thought of what living in that tower had been like in the acidic prison for such a long time, weeping as the hunched figures stared more and more into their screens, as hopeful saviours and victims were paraded and disappeared down darkened tunnels, never to be seen again.

Those memories of the brave heroes came and went, too many children biting at him and crazily driving away at the fabric of Ishmael's hope. Ellis hugged his arm, stretching across its muscular form in their slightness, and that was all the truth they grasped onto as they writhed through the powerful light, the only real thing in all that light.

Endless pictures of different figures, and seeping runes which stank or dripped, spun and danced around them, the memories of so many other times; the laughter of that first time with the flowers in Eden's hair as they learned to talk, something gold and giant descending from the sky to stop the growing darkness, purple dancing along the arms of small children as they chuckled against the snow's breath.

Before long, they collapsed down in the shrine's ruins where the cloudy sprite had been flying such as short time ago, the purple gems sparkling in the dying sunlight. A dying light in a land with no night-time, just clouds and silver all the way down.

Ellis panted, grabbing at the tepid light and throwing every part of their energy right into everyone around them. Doing all they could. Ishmael reached up at the tendrils of brightness, grasping tightly with a smile on his face, winking as Mum came back with the rush of energy they all needed.

Without stopping, they ran across the cloudy walkway, sprinting on the silver steps, and bouncing of the light airiness. Ellis pushed themselves to follow behind as fast as possible, heckled by something that grabbed at them from the strange stone of the shrine itself. Two hands clasped at their face, stretching their eyes open.

Ishmael was even larger here, crushing rocks beneath his feet as he anchored himself up, beard rustling in the wind.

"Look away from anything that captures your focus. The Tamer is writhing in the dust and smoke. Run and don't look back at this cleansing!" he screeched, and Ellis was taken by the water sprite Mum, riding up in the cloud as some ugly, great worm formed right out of the rocks themselves, coated in the blessed jewels and dazzling in the new day's light. Ellis steered the sprite down and crashed among the others, none of them looking at the way back, knowing the Tamer for the curse it was.

Ellis knew it had followed them through the worlds, growing stronger just as Ishmael had, and they ran all the faster.

A wave of driving icy points pushed them back, every bead of sweat pulled toward the standing form of Ishmael. In huge lengths of whirling pools, the sea bridges exploded and lashed down to the monster. The water didn't drown it, it bounced straight off. Angered, Ishmael summoned the weight of every cloud descending, the whole world disappearing except for their tiny ledge at the very end. They held their breath, sudden thirst grasping them as every part of the water in the world was taken without remorse.

The onslaught of pressure pushed them up against the side of this tiny world. It was a land built in memory of Ishmael, dreaming of his return. All turned to a weapon. Ellis's hand was forced against the space in between.

With just a thought and a hopeful memory, they danced light across the void, and grabbed onto every friend's hand. Their last sight was the ocean following behind their fall, and with it, the tide of black beasts coming for them like a volcano's ash stopped in a line of spittle, as all the water rushed, and this group left that world behind.

They turned in the air, feeling the rush of the void disappear as a green dot in the ground below them turned to flames before their very eyes. The darkness seeped back in, and Ellis stared as Greenview sheltered under the darkest evening it had ever faced. Nobody looked up at the falling sea, not even wincing at the whale-song as dark creatures appeared from the sea.

The Burning King smouldered and screamed, turning back to the town, but making sure to show Jacob's uncle following him in smoky chains. Ellis could see that as they crashed into the burning great forest, before their vision was blinded by the sea of sound from the screaming. Ellis reached out to the decaying uncle, feeling his pain, and reaching further into the recesses of his strength. The ochre infection faded for a moment, and the Burning King saw his chance to lay a trap from Ellis wanting to heal everything on their own. His claw hid all the corruption and cackling as he disappeared into the town, knowing the pieces were shuffling slowly to the world's doom even while the last lord-sprites were freed. He was hungry, but he could wait just a little longer.

-

They coughed and ran in a rush, pushing away at the smoke without thinking about it, and pushing hard for Ellis's home. They ran there without thinking, picking up the energy of the town around them, and noticing somehow it was perfectly OK to be walking through this place surrounded by magic. A giant talking bear, a talking cloud and a teardrop which wouldn't stop singing, the walking tree, and finally Ishmael who took the form of a tamed waterfall. People should have been running in fear. They walked by without a care.

The glowing group stood on the fence behind Ellis's home, and Ellis could feel something was wrong. There was a coldness and a hunger coming from the house, and that was enough for them to sense this wasn't the right place to be. Just creeping over that fence, there was no sign of the tree or any sign of the chaos Ellis had left it in. "Is it true, we're back to the real world?" Ellis whispered, pressed down and nearly crouching under the pressure of all the strange presences around them, untrusting this was not just another dream. Another trap.

Ishmael shook his head, pushing his hand through the mist that kept growing even in the new day. "This place only grows sicker. He said simply, barely holding his form together with such a long time as just a figment of a cruel and sharp imagination. Only the thin fume of a purple glow surrounded him, and Ellis felt the other half of him draining way to the strange other realm, repairing itself and growing stronger.

Whisper was disappearing into the mist, and Ellis continued to flick fearful looks behind themselves, wary of eyes staring and hungry, feeling the scratch of claws in the faintest recesses of their mind. "Those birds are gone from me now, any could be her spies. We must step carefully now, child" Eden whispered, and they skulked away, every one of them feeling like a rabbit scrambling across a field just as an eagle called out to swoop down on them.

At the same time, the Ash Queen was remembering something, and she had made the slightest mumble of an excuse to get away from the Burning King while he stared and growled. Anything to get out of that cold nightmare. To be back out amongst the trees and running in the sweet breeze. Those dead ochre eyes had stared right into her and nodded his heads in hungry humour. Every time she felt sick, and she tried to convince herself it was just something wrong in her aching head, it would go away soon enough.

The sickness which forcefully told her; anything natural was wrong, any conversation with anything the green fool had made was an atrocity. If all these feelings could have been forced off a cliff, that would have been a victory, but here she was still following the figure of Ellis again. No need to follow him, the King had a trap, and every step she took against him was a corruption of this idea, a ruination on everything of the hunting, harsh past she could remember.

Well, everything she was supposed to remember. Something else was wrong though, there was another figure in her mind that crept in the background in fear, just like she did here. They were walking back down the alley, the sheer weight of all this confusion was plaguing her skills, and she would be lucky to survive. It was fine, it was a bright midday and in a scream of nervous energy, Sally came out to make sure her cats got some time outside.

The Queen stood behind Sally's silhouette, watching with a smile that had no hunger in it, just enjoying the moment of those two most blessed figures in this world again, catching the shimmer of the sea falling and knowing exactly who it would be that was coming. They were meant to be the creators of everything, just after the Golden City and its Eternal beings had allowed the light to leave their holy-land, the waters flowed, and nature's roots reached to make life exist outside their raving hearts.

That memory should have been impossible, but she pushed through the pain which told her to ignore it, shaking against its attack. She giggled without control anyway, this time not minding the high flick of her laugh. Without thinking bowing a little at the nearest tree. She slapped her right hand as it tried to form a prayer, and was thankful Sally was ochre-eyed, staring straight past her and shuffling back into her house, ignoring the open dressing gown and leaving the gate swinging in the wind.

The glowing, slightly mad crowd of Sprite Lords kept walking, past the forest, and each time they hid the Queen hid. She was made to plot and think, not destroy. To silence people in other ways that violence, for those statues were something forged from the King's harshness. His cruelty seeped out of them. The troop in front of her stopped as they walked past a huge Serpentine which loomed over the school, the echo of screaming the only sound when there should have been so much play and chatter in the daylight.

Ellis moved in front of the Queen a short distance away, and the trees stepped sharply to block her way. Her heart stopped as she wandered whether a sprite would attack her, and everything would fall apart. Two tiny sprites sat on each side of the school gate, one to each tree. One riding each long branch like a horse. Both frowned down at her, whispering to each other, and one yelling at the other while he shook his head. It was impossible to just believe the Ash Queen didn't have a plot that would hurt them somehow.

They spoke in the first language, the ancient tree-speak, all whistles and groans, and before long the gate parted to let her in. The darkened side of her fought back again, wiping away the small bust of happiness she had. She went to kick one of the trunks, slipping as it moved just a little out of her way.

Then she was running to hide in the bushes at the other side of the playground, out of the sight of those sprites. Out of danger, she hoped. She scratched her nails down an old, hidden knife, one of many. The other mind winning for a moment, wishing Ellis's window had been open, and the whispering right at the start had worked in the thick mists to trap him.

It was misty again, but she was far weaker, and each piece of dew she touched, every step she took was sensed by Whisper. She held her breath as the mist grouped around her not knowing if it would help hide her or not. She was grabbing at something, but it moved straight past her. She didn't let her breath out though, Ellis was face to face with a Mirroring and it had focussed all her attention, and she was transported as if she stood right amongst them all. She ached for that keenly.

The hackles on Beast-Shadow's neck rose, and the Queen backed away further, wincing from the yells which told her this was the time to strike and silence Ellis. End the Hearing with Jacob captured. She could only feel pity she wasn't there right alongside them. Quickly the pain struck her again to tell her off, and she had to breathe out. Everyone was focussed on both these people staring deeply into each other's eyes. Both in their own way trying to feed at the essence of the others' powers, and save them from their fate.

Flames rolled in the Queen's head, and she fell to the floor under the wrath of the King's whipping. She felt the waves of Whisper roll past her to try and calm her suffering. For just a second, no part of her was filled with the burns of the King. It wasn't too long though until she was walking back without thinking it was time to finally deal with Jacob, knowing just how to do it.

Ellis walked slowly toward Crystal, taking the last few steps delicately as if through oil. Everyone had disappeared behind the trees, from Ellis feeling every sensation. All the Mirroring children turned as one toward Ellis, no longer kicking a ball slowly between them, they had no information on this face at all. They were all built to absorb information, but the glow and swirling mist was making it hard for them to focus.

The boy they were facing now didn't look the same as the usual Ellis they might have been expecting, the pale skin was usually one sign, the long blonde hair was another. Now Ellis was tanned, and the hair had been caught more than once in a snatch of a branch. The way they stood was different too, straight up like their Dad. Just like the last time they had met, but every bully had pretended that hadn't happen. Forgetting it had meant the Mirroring didn't know a thing about this confident figure.

They had remembered the young eyes and the frail body of Ellis, maybe the lisp or that odd laugh, but it was a different person standing before them. Someone aged by tragedy and without fear now. The ochre in the Mirroring's eyes glowed in the midday sun, and the stillness didn't stop. Whisper formed quickly out of the mists, shimmering powerfully right in front of them, waiting the assault that cursed King might bring when he finally noticed who had returned.

The rest of the children rotated, weirdly mechanical and only turning their top half. There was a pause as the metal joints forced the bottom half to keep up, the statue nearest rumbling a little to command them to keep moving. The trees rustled without thinking, a charge of energy travelling from person to person.

The statue quietly hooted, the air caught in the middle of its second breath in, and Whisper began to summon clouds close to her, knowing just what was coming next, and disappearing into a mist of her namesake, lashing out small shocks as she went. Ellis felt the sickness they had first felt when they saw a rabbit limping across the road.

The unbidden instinct to do something, that right now you had to act, or the world would just continue to be a worse and worse place. The mouth of one of the students opened and opened, cracking far more than it should have, glowing that same ochre. Trying to strike first as it sensed the coming assault. The statue hooted loudly again, the noise leaving a mechanical twang after it, like a spring falling back into place.

Something was wrong, two of the figures were sweating and shaking. It was Crystal and Sandra. Ellis stepped forward, and the air cracked, sunlight coiling around and snapping across the void. Ishmael stepped back twice, fizzling water falling from his hands. He was still in awe at the raw power. Every pair of eyes was locked on them and they stepped forward without thinking about it, while the mist tried to collect and stop them, they floated slightly in the air.

Ellis stared and tried to grasp anything they could from the staring faces in front of them, as the crowd began to slowly copy every movement Ellis made, not just one Mirroring being enough to stand against the glowing power of their improved mind, every child began to fizzle and copy their face.

"These people have been taken, Ellis. I'm so sorry." Beast-Shadow half-growled, half-spoke on their shoulder. He was an oversized bear with the purple crystals still stuck in his fur. The snout struggled to move to form any words, and Ellis wouldn't let him move forward any further. Beast-Shadow yelped at the burning line Ellis made, frowning at Ellis. That creeping darkness of the Ash Queen's whispering struck him. Force him to think the enemy was anyone in the way of destroying everything the Burning King had made.

"I can hear the pain in their soul." Ellis answered, shaking on that last word as Beast-Shadow grew even taller as all the Mirroring turned to face him instead. Their second calling, to destroy when stealth had lost. Ellis pushed him further back, making him wince behind a fence of that burning, stepping directly to the focus of every Mirroring again. Black exploded around Crystal for a second, a poisonous explosion, but Ellis held one hand up and all that wrath turned silent.

-

There were a hundred lost voices swimming and thrashing at the water, nearly drowning and yelping out for some aid. Ellis could hear that above all the rage. The Serpentine sat back, waiting for the small Mirroring to report anything strange, then it would be unleashed.

They had to wait though. It was supposed to be a quiet invasion after all. Ellis had never been this close to Crystal before. It was hard to ignore the badly drawn eyebrows this close, or the point where the blonde hair became brown again. The lipstick was just a little irregular, a shaky line, and Ellis could see she was wearing socks again. Something hadn't been keeping up with the latest fashion fads.

Something had to be wrong for Ellis to be this close, but most of those wounds were coming from much further back. It would never cross Ellis's mind to hurt anyone, but as they raised their dominant right hand, the memory of hitting Jacob in a dream surfaced for just a second.

The pleading eyes of the Mirroring were enough to force him on. Mum was sat on their shoulder and Ellis hadn't even noticed until this second when she moved away a little from the energy seeping out of Ellis now. It was like staring directly into the sun, but these Mirroring had eyes made in a burning factory, and they didn't wince away. The sprites squinted and pushed their eyes through the cracks in a leaf, smiling as the healing warmth touch them just a little.

Ellis's hand landed on Crystal's left cheek, covering a small bruise where she must have walked into a door and not even thought about it. The veins of the bruise disappeared, and the black flickering came back with the ferocity of a firework. Ellis's other hand rose, and small Golden lengths reached into the blackness and wiped it out cleanly. Crystal leaned forward in her weakness, and Ellis with their eyes closed travelled through its mind and into the terror of its inner workings.

Without realising it, Ellis was right in their mind, running through it on the front of a tide of light. The maze glowed against the bright light, the walls breaking apart from the onslaught of their strength, and soon enough all the blackness and biting ochre turned into a gross and gargling lake. Ash was flopping softly on a frail body which kept flailing to stay afloat from the biting waves, just about keeping afloat.

Ellis reached both hands together, slamming a beam of gold at the darkness, Mum rushing from their shoulder and taking all the liquid away from the fidgeting beasts. There was the real Crystal, hair wildly twirling in the air like she had fallen through a hedge. The picture fading but under Ellis's wrath it became stronger and stronger, the real person forming and being pulled back into reality against any of all the rules the Burning King had created to keep her away. She shrugged her shoulders as she shook from weeping, long lines of mascara tracing down from both eyes before Ellis wiped it away with calmness.

-

In a dizzying flash, the real world was back. "I'm sorry," she whispered, holding her breath without the ability to cry anymore. Already under the Ash Queen's whispering forgetting the darkness and pain of where she had been.

She pushed Ellis away playfully, with just one hand. A small smirk bounced on her face, and it was almost like she was flirting to them. "You always, like, scared me in some way, you know? Something different, I don't know…" They were both standing on the playground again, a dancing twirl of ash which faded to little pops of purple fireworks popping around her. The flashes whistled and clacked against each other, curving sparks bouncing off the golden rays which still beamed out of Ellis's gleaming face.

"Thank you, was I dreaming or something else…?" Crystal mumbled, her eyes heavy baubles glimmering in the new day. It was the ramming of all that whispering. She buckled under the pressure of simply standing. Ellis could feel she would be fine now, every hit of gold making her stronger and stronger. They had walked on, pushing the waves of golden light into every Mirroring. The light lashed and played like the tails of so many fish. Without needing to think, they slowly walked amongst the group, pushing the energy through every one of them without fear, and smiling each time one gasped back to the real world, striking away at the oncoming pain of harsh whispers.

-

Just a fraction of glass peeped out from the edge of a bicycle mirror, just leaning enough to see this healing taking place. Sandra was in spasm, and Ellis snapped quickly back to help. They placed one glowing hand through her brunette bun, brushing the fringe away and trying to get into their mind, not thinking about themselves at all.

Ellis had never seen themselves as a single person, and now the twinkling memory of each one they'd saved follow Ellis along, making them even stronger, lifting their feet off the floor without an effort.

Ishmael was pushed back into the trees as a pulse rocked along the ground, leaving a slight crack, and it tried to clasp around his legs, the gnawing growl of those horrible devourers the only sound for just a second. Eden had her eyes closed, straining hard to keep the connection between these last two blessed members of the Hearing together.

The sickness in the atmosphere continued to grow, and she clasped her old, chipped nails into Ishmael's callused hands, but he didn't wince. Everything for Ishmael was still amazing in this new world, and that was just another sensation, a memory of beating back the Burning King, or running too hard in a field, catching himself on a thorn bush. He took her suffering, and felt the heavy stare of those huge Serpentine pushing him into the ground, and a swipe of acidic light crashed along where he had just stood.

Somehow a memory of the Tamer had crashed along with them, crawling and yelping with joy out of the tunnel that mirror had created, squelching to try and reach out to one of the wandering students while the memory of the Mirroring remained. it was just the black shadow of a person, not enough of a Mirroring made together with tendrils of sweaty distended mass. It was the beginning of the Burning King losing control of his servants as his ferocity beat away at any reason.

The Serpentine hooted again, and the fizzling screen of white Ellis had just about seen before forced everyone to squint their eyes. Ellis was still trying to heal everyone, trying to find some calm in all this madness, but that figure falling and struggling was pulling everyone's focus. In the sharp movements, Crystal's blond hair caught on her tightening hands, and she knocked to the ground, not even groaning.

It was an allergic reaction, kicking out again at the

illness which didn't take her over but bit into her mind instead. Ellis stepped past the biting black whips that flew at them. They tried to fly into their back, but anchored themselves hungrily with sharp strikes under wild freedom, forcing the waves of ochre pain to wave over the whole crowd. The wrath disappeared quickly though, yelping in the wind and defeated.

It was a horrible hiccup of noise, and Ishmael punched his sheer weight against Eden, seeping through the hand as he turned to liquid for just a moment, dazzling in the sunlight. As he stepped out into the light, the reason for Eden holding Beast-Shadow and Whisper behind her became obvious.

Sprites shot out in a wave of leaves, opening like a great claw. Something had to absorb the blows of ochre terror, darts of anger knocking at them and burning at the flesh. Beast-Shadow winced and pulled back without thinking, ears puckered to his fur, eyes huge and shivering. Tamer's effect just the same as every other time before. The sprites which remained kept throwing themselves in the way of the white beam which slammed down so much stronger than the daylight itself could.

The screen of silver webbing that had descended around them all was just the same as was thrown over Jacob and Ellis running from the ugly beast. It was an immeasurable, thin screen, pulling a picture of calm in the place of any pain. It reflected and bent everything behind the screen, silently moving over whatever space it needed to control.

It shed the memory of what had been there, the sharp light clear and every Mirroring looking up for a moment as the screen glowed and covered over the slowly swelling madness. The outside world must never know what was coming for them until the screen would rise just as the enemy was assaulting them.

Ellis could feel their hopes and need, the beaming but confused joy of Crystal, suddenly turning maternal and protective with her newly found friend. They felt this strength coming around them, and the great looming hate and hunger above.

There were people there among the scarring flames. They'd been running from that infernal whispering for so long, and somehow, they had still survived the change. By now, like a blooming flower the golden lights swirled and slapped around Ishmael as he pushed at the trees in his way, bounding past two broken remains of the Mirroring, and leaping as hard as he could to wrench that Serpentine to the ground.

The liquid from the cages seeped from the Serpentine's innards, and in a moment where Ellis's hair shimmered, they pulled the light from the Serpentine. Every part of their skin was aflame with white, everything stood still. A voice echoed out of the light, crackling and high like lightning, it danced across the rays of sun, and everyone gasped except for Ellis, burning in the light just a little, and floating where they stood.

The whole of Ellis's body was electrified, pulses of static rolling across their eyebrows and along their arms, kicking out in short bursts. With one final and exhausted pull, each survivor sank and was absorbed by a splattering of the Serpentine's beam. The light turned inward, uncontrolled energy surging and overwhelming the cages that still held people in their comas. Even though the Serpentines hooted shrilly, trying urgently to summon its brothers, the sound rattled and turned feeble. The mechanism of its chest slowly closed with a groan, as it tried to protect itself from the fall, always attempting to rebuild with those ugly, black lances. It was too late, and from were now remains, exhausted bodies fell. In a glowing, kind touch, Ellis caught each one, healing them powerfully, and buffeting the speed of their doomed descent without thinking.

"Please. Help them." Ellis pleaded, feeling their pain. As they struggled to walk, Ishmael filled their cupped hands with silvery purple water, filled with the fuel of a hundred missed meals. Ellis stared into the distance, feeling the same hits of pain now that Eden had. They mumbled *Jacob* to themselves while the frail bodies came back to strength.

It wasn't that which hurt them though, the fluid Ishmael could summon was turning patchy, ochre and black blotches rolling across it. Even though Ellis could taste the burning of Jacob's hair somewhere in the winds of thought around them, there was nothing they could do but keep following this path, seeking as many people as they could to heal, while still following obediently behind Ishmael.

Eden pinched one hand hard in front of her, forcing

Beast-shadow to run without pause and find the scent of Jacob, feeling the world around them shatter if something was changed now. She coughed into a rag she tore from her own robes, ignoring the small splatter of blood, there were people to save. She flinched with a shudder as the shadow of the Ash Queen flickered behind another tree.

If the Ash Queen saw her enemies, they would know. There was no flicker of a blade or the small cackle of someone that has found their weakness this time though, just her pleading eyes. Eden could not think on it longer; Ellis's glow was already fading in front of them. With a grinding rhythm, the huge Serpentine was slowly rebuilding itself, breaking out it's huge tendons with the sounds of snapping bones, and hydraulic whining.

She could sense the growing madness of the Burning King, he had lost all sense of honour in this last battle. All sense of caring for those that might pray to him, turning them into food. She could see already, everything he saw became his enemy, growing only the more possessed and hungry.

Eden caught see the needy eyes of the Ash Queen again, shimmering faintly amongst the elbows of four old branches. Though she winced while she looked at them, the sight of Ellis commanding the last Sprite Lords and not stopping for themselves was all the hope they might need. No need to think on her plotting, the malice which fed on the smallest hope the Queen might have been healed, and return to whichever fate she had ran from, and into the beastly claws of the Burning King.

A shot of gold popped from Ellis's bedraggled hair, an echo of the light caught in a city's shimmer in the sky. Ellis was hope.

-

"If you speak again, you'll taste our muzzle, and my whip." Something spat through the shortest moment of consciousness. When Jacob had finally woken up, he knew they hadn't been lying. The strange metal things laughed and joked like it was sport, throwing scraps of meat at his feet while they dragged him on their back. He tried to shout back, the muzzle stopped him with a gross and oily taste.

Two strange lengths of black metal grabbed at him, stabbing his nerves to echo each spasm, each movement. The pain always made him kick again, even if he was asleep. It was impossible to say where one vine started and the other ended, they both spun in knots and dove into the ground. Jacob groaned and tried to hide the sound, but quickly enough a black beast was staring at him, with a snarl, shoving Jacob's scarred knees down against the metal floor of his cage.

Encouraged by something, and nodding along, the beast grabbed the cage, crushed it just a little under his strength, picking the whole cage up under one rotten-stinking armpit. It trooped forward, and Jacob collapsed again. The next memory was the sliding and heavy squeak as Jacob slid across the silver floor and realised anything he'd felt before could not have been fear with the shaking sweatiness that beat at him.

"It is a lovely morning for it, isn't it Jacob?" the Burning

King jovially announced, with a theatrical wave of one huge hand, the sharp lights wrapped around every statue the Burning King had built. The sheer hate and predatory hunger was a bloody taste in the back of Jacob's throat. Of course, he couldn't cough, the muzzle stuck right into his teeth and tongue. On the stand of another one, a heavy metal pole stuck out of the stonework, and the Burning King smirked at him.

"No?! I'm surprised you don't know the answer." He chuckled, staring at the bruised face and the broken nose, unable to hide his growing smile. It was a deadly pause, the freezing hurt in the front of your head, all along every muscle when a predator was staring you down with slobbering lips. "A good day for an execution? I thought you knew. My wife has been whispering about your doom for so long... Oh…Wow, you really are disappointing." With a smash, it all turned dark for him again.

21: A HIDDEN SAVIOUR AT THE VERY END

Mother animals are happy to raise anything, their instincts are so strong. It is used against them sometimes, when predators use it for themselves. There are children that are found sometimes which have been raised by wolves, a gorilla has adopted a kitten before and many other strange relationships. If someone cares for you, it doesn't matter who they are, the care is the most important part.

The moment Jacob woke up, he wished he hadn't. The exhaustion faded away, and the world slowly clarified itself, but it was none the better for it. In the sharp light of the city, it was impossible to tell the time of day anymore. Jacob's mind worked and grabbed onto any of the strange mechanisms around him it could, but it was impossible to find any answers. There seemed to be faces screaming every surface, and it was impossible to think.

He opened his mouth to start talking himself through it, to give himself any kind of encouragement. The exhaustion made him forget the nightmare. A muzzle bit at his jaw, stabbing into his cheeks and just a little shock rode up one hand and tangle in the snapping pain as the hand was strained open and pushed into the harsh concrete of a road under the sheer weight of all that electricity.

The little scraps of black from the road stung and bit into the calluses of his hand. He tried to roll them away from the floor and stand up, groaning heavily and feeling the sound in his throat instead of hearing it. A sea of laughter and cackling was all around him. It echoed horribly against the high sky scrapers which surrounded him, as if the creatures were right in his ears.

"CAW!" a great big high note slapped against his ear, and he fell to the side again, snapping his back under the shackles as he tried to stand tall. He regretted the silly act of defiance, but couldn't control it.

The laughter grew louder, and he was squinting up at a false sun, flanked by two huge Serpentine which boomed and trilled in laughter too.

He coughed away at the muzzle, swiping at his hands where the remains of ugly poisoned feathers rode through his veins. He tried to scream, but nearly choked on the rag instead, biting down at the stringy lengths at the top of the rope, and nearly choking.

He was picked up by the chest, tipped upside down which stopped his choking, thrown right onto the back of the ugly, winged beast and it squawked with a hacking cough as it cackled while it rose into the acidic air. The harsh sound shot through Jacob, but he held onto the slimy back of the beast while it swirled about, dancing for the audience.

A statue playfully swiped at him with a hand that was far bigger than his whole form, but it threw the hand out the way just before Jacob crashes into it, hooting again with a shaking chuckle. Jacob blinked repeatedly, trying to get focus, and latched eye contact with someone else who wandered through an office high up in one of the glass skyscrapers of the city.

He hadn't noticed the people on every floor just going about their work, stepping around the remains of a crashed helicopter as it burned. A pilot hadn't reacted well to seeing his reflection roar back at him and strike. This was the Burning King's home, the first world he had taken over, and every person that was still allowed to wander in the capital Carletonville all gawped back with ochre eyes. He had captured this world, and the nightmare Ellis had walked through was now a cruel reality.

The day was never-ending. Jacob rolled about on the ugly bird's back, trying to reach with some little slippery balance and gesture at someone nearby. Hoping they might save him. It had always been a struggle for him to understand people rather than machines. As sharp feathers dug into his scarred legs, fear rose like bubbles filling a bottle, more and more feeling like it needed release, he yearned for freedom in a panic increasingly with every second. His breathing sped up, and the flying beast sang a gurgling song in the same rhythm along with him, mocking the rampant breath as the bird rolled in a tight spin. Jacob couldn't hold on, tumbling back down to the aggressive bite of the ground. He gasped to catch a breath, staring right at a strange apparatus of huge gears and long cables reaching down to a crowd of gross, waiting figures.

The air itself pulsed thickly, and even Jacob could sense the power which smashed into the city. For a flash as he was thrown, Jacob noticed every building was the same, all the colour had left the people who still wandered about, every little piece of the road was just the same, repeated over and over. He was falling down the long road as it just kept rolling. Every surface and piece of shin glowed with a metal light.

He was picked up by his ankles and thrown again, hard through the air. Toward the skeleton of new towers built from the remains of a fairground. He crashed through what was once a big wheel, tumbling and crashing through the struts. They collapsed away from him, brushing an already bullied body. With a raging focus, he started to sprint away through the grass, catching himself off small bumps and speeding along, just hoping all those ochre eyes might miss him at this speed.

His hair was wrenched back by a huge, ugly claw he had seen in his nightmares. In a slam of sick light, he laid right where he had started, just outside his cage. His arms and legs shook violently, recovering from their stunted run, and Jacob felt the force rack through him, but he controlled it, watching tufts of his hair tumble past him his crumpled form, as he fought not to collapse to the floor.

He pushed his fears and weakness right into the ground, kicking one worn leg back and finding a fragile grip on the floor. The black road grasped his feet, crawled up his hand, and with that he slowed everything down as well as he could, one more effort to fight back. He focused on just standing up and trying to grasp one second without those hungry eyes as they focused squeezing at the little sanity he had left. Though Jacob couldn't sense it, they were filled with the same power the Ash Queen had, it fed at innocence and sanity to break you down into a victim weak enough to be taken by the glowing eyes of your own Mirroring.

Beasts were sprouting out of the ash pools that lied around this strange contraption, as they appeared thy bowed. Delicately craning their necks forward, flicking the yellow glow of their desperate eyes up to make sure the lord was watching them. The people in the buildings were pressed against the glass, or scattered on all fours, head bent hard down to the ground. There was no need to pretend they had any humanity left.

Jacob fought the force commanding him to prey, a slicing storm of overwhelming thought that stabbed and bit to take all thinking away, seeming to know just where he was strongest. Just what needed to die for him to surrender to this greater calling. He fought to keep time slow, to feel some tiny sense of strength. He pushed with everything he had to stand, struggling as he did so, straining against something else that struck out with a stench he had known for a long time. Everything around him was gross and sweating, or biting and swiping through the air with wild abandon, as if driven hysterical by the presence of this beastly monster.

Jacob rose, straight-backed, buckling under the pressure of that massive presence's weight knocking into him. It came as a heavy, sweaty blow to the back of his head, the tapping and scraping of nails in a playful rhythm over a constant whispering, commanding he stop. Still, he stood defiantly, haggard breaths wrecking his lungs in this sick air. Without faltering, Jacob straightened his back under the pressure and shadow of all those flying beasts approaching. The black waves of the dark illness throbbed in thick strobes from the contraption, and Jacob focussed on those lines, just trying to find some hint of a word or anything to tell him someone was watching. The sick material couldn't be focussed on for too long, it bit away at sanity and warped in the air, always bending as if everything might just be an illusion. Before it snapped back hard, whipping Jacob's mind and the black talons tearing further into reality than before.

Jacob tried to pretend it wasn't true, but he wished that maybe Ellis would come back and save him, just like they had a long time ago when they became friends. He tried to stop himself, but he held his own hand in the growing darkness, gulping under a growing and heavy fever. The ground rumbled with a horrid punch, and Jacob searched for something to hold onto, staring at the sea of wings which flapped in the air, dripping and spitting acid at him. He rolled along the ground, grunting at the blow which hit him, pushing as hard as he could to accelerate hard through the space and away from the beastly, grunting monstrosity which was coming closer without stopping.

The Burning King's laughter was a huge boom, as he pulled on two thick lengths of glowing wires. One was thick and wrapped right around his arm, burning a black and ochre patchy tone right along his muscled chest. He was huge, and Jacob's hands rumbled heavily while he tried to slow time. The line of spittle from a craning monster above was a sign he had nearly stopped time. It wouldn't stop the rising panic though.

The King ambled toward him at his normal pace, smirking by how simple it was to beat back what Jacob thought was power. Jacob summoned harsh whooshes of wind to crack against his wide chest, and they burned black as those shadow-strikes when they flashed off him, and rode right up his leathery wings, seeming to make them grow where they should have wounded him. It collected into an aggressive sonic boom. Jacob launched himself out the way with a rushing leap through a nearby window, shattering the glass.

As it descended and twinkled, the huge claw of the King in his beastly form grasped his body and time collapsed back upon itself. The cackling sea erupted with a slap of claws and the scraping of hooves against the floor, still praising their lord.

The people had become ochre puppets, barely holding up on their strings, and even in the explosion of that window, they didn't back away. Jacob was pulled away from the explosion as he watched those subtle figures – barely visible in the sun – march and sing toward their new-found God. Slowly the whole crowd with a violent swishing of their heads became translucent and walked to the same groaning hymn. For those that fought back, just a puff of ash was left of their body.

"This is your demon." The Burning King bellowed, having caught Jacob bodily by the hair again. The ground rumbled underneath his words. Jacob could feel his claws growing larger, squeezing at his ribs and choking him. He struggled as much as he could, the King held him higher. With a slam, he thrust the coiled leash around Jacob's throat, pulling his face up to stare into those deep, black eyes which echoed with the depth of some hungry valley, and his panting face was a tired, pale remnant before that gaping anger.

The other cable pulled the King's huge body back, rocking them both back a little, sending a punch across the city, pushing the ground up. Something huge was coming. The King pushed himself up by one ugly, wet flap of his wings, and they hovered unsteadily. The black horrors swelled under a mist of ochre that swept through the yawning crack, and Jacob could just about stay conscious. He focused on the ugly fangs bigger than his arms opening as the King prepared to say more, unable to prevent himself smiling.

"There is only one of them left now, the other rotten child is lost. They are the curses which rid you of this pure world, and he must not escape. We can all smell what he is, but I will make those powers you fear the end of him. Watch and enjoy." Jacob could feel the heavy chuckling right through his body in horrible waves, the immense claw straining closer toward him. He forced as much of his powers as he could summon, trying to take the air and the earth away and absorb some of the overpowering strength from the Burning King.

He was overwhelmed by that valley of hunger and suffering, and without realising what was happening with his sheer exhaustion, the long nails drove themselves into his arm, dragging itself along a prominent vein.

Jacob screamed without control now, feeling the acidic whiplashes of that gross touch roll through him like the harshest tides, striking out hungrily with a lashing tongue.

His skin stretched and popped, and Jacob buckled to the ground, dark sweat blocking out his eyes. He slammed his hands onto the battered remains of the black ground, the soil spitting up not hot magma but the ochre sickness. He was left coughing and wailing, feeling his back wretch up with a shaky fever. He sweated thickly, could barely stay up as the earth boomed and flashed an electric explosion right along the city, destroying every pane of glass, and punching the spines of all the buildings.

The blades of glass rained down, exploding through the beasts, and so many of the Mirroring exploded under the shards. Their fragments scraped together again, yelping and crawling, the black distended pieces roared back to life while they still wandered closer, even as they were reborn.

The ground swelled again and shook, the heavy vibrations pounding along the air in terrible shockwaves which gripped the shadow-forms, but Jacob wasn't focussing on any of that anymore. He had a chance and the smallest of spaces. He was not looking back.

Around him, the ground popped and boomed, exploding in one volcanic bellow, and this time magma tried to erupt across the earth. The King feeling it's strength, feeling a thrilled rush, with a booming laugh looking down and pointing with those huge talons at

Jacob. He still tried to crawl away, coughing as the acid still rolled through his body.

The King stared down at Jacob, craning his neck down as the King's muscular body tried to bend down as much as it could. Jacob was rampant with adrenaline now, every small crawling step he could make, the inky poison slipped from his hands and burned away at the ground, hissing on the growing heat. Jacob saw the King's shadow move just a little and instead of trying to run took him by surprise.

Jacob slammed a fist against the descending arm, and it looked so little against the stonework strength of the King. His punch would have bounced straight off if he was only mortal, instead the black corruption seeped right into his hand. The heat was sweltering, and the earth around them rocked under this assault, but Jacob was focussed on one thing.

Jacob jumped up, slamming his other fist right through one of the Kings eyes as he bowed. With one thunderclap, Jacob disappeared in a spinning assault of Earth, hiding under the dusty remains of the Burning King as they blew away. Jacob was freed of all the pain, and with that sprinted away from the steaming land, shooting from one geyser which launched a boulder up, and further away, running as fast as he could to the whispering trees nearby.

Distracted by the sheer force of his master approaching, the King could do nothing more to chase Jacob now, he knew more suffering was coming deliciously soon.

-

Deep underground, a battalion of earth sprites had been marching against the coming flames, absorbing the raw melting heat, and battering ancient axes against the furious fires. Within the burning miasma though, something else was smashing reality, cursing the assaults of everyone that disappeared inside the thrusting fist of magma.

They were born to keep the land settled and safe, and something horrific was decimating the world and cursing it. These soldiers had been slumbering, and now they were called awake once more.

Two solders hunched under another underground assault, leaning against the melting walls of an old shelter. They stared at each other under heavily furrowed foreheads and grunting at an oily illness they had not tasted since before their last great rest. Thousands of brothers were running past these two, these old hands in the wars who could remember a time before the words of "mountain" or "river" were spoken. They had spent all this time hoping and enriching roots where they could. The only beings left old enough to still know the face of the Eternal in all her starlight, gold beauty while they made their dutiful pledge.

They were the first farmers, and now they were armed for war, the earth and magma rolling along their thick arms, sharpening the edges of every joint. The lava around them was alive and speaking. Even in the huge sea of light and fire that surrounded them, they were still both so sensitive to the ancient whispering. This mountainous creature of fire and rage was pushing up among a treeless hell. They had hope though among the sickness.

A purple light they had seen around every Sprite Lord, or those blessed callings in the madness down here. They whispered *Eden* in their own language with the sound of creaks and clacks pounding among the two of them. They laughed as their last defence melted away, the heat burning away at their toughened flesh.

It seemed there was nothing left, old friends staring at each other's eyes with a certainty this was just the right place to be. Even if it was the end. The dazzling purple light shot down and into them both, the light filled with messages of fear and a pain from something they thought had been crushed to death a long, long time ago. The sea of flames swelled even more, striking right into the brothers. That wrath was echoed by a gluttonous, fat yodel with a sound like mud scraping along violin strings and a rotting mouth chewing down on a small creature's bones.

The echoing sound was so heavy, they could feel their bodies vibrate and crack apart but still hold together. The two old sprites screamed an old battle-cry as the wall and floor melted before them in a sea of feeding heat.

"Mountain-stride…" they yelled, the name of their most ancient father. The old name stretching out as they hopped across the scraps of rock, never flinching only holding their firm and worn faces against the sheer white light which faced them, feeling the armour melt away.

The sea of sharp shadows was coming through when they should have just died in this blessed place.

Every single sprite could feel the approaching pressure of that insurmountable power, like a flood of flames you can only destroy by desecrating the forest. The only thing was that the very lava they were surrounded by was the weapon this power had learned to use.

The mass of fire fought and grasped at these spiked sprites, each one exploding under the pressure of that acidic lava they could not have taken more of. This unending burning launched from the talons of the King's master they could see this close now. Facing death itself. The two brothers clacked ancient axes together as they leapt through the short gap between them and that sheer bright sunlight. It throbbed with that same deep echo, that rampage of flames burst from the monstrous reality of what the Burning King really was.

Thick wires of smouldering jelly and spitting sparks wrecked the floor, decimating the floor in heavy cracks. The two brothers slid great axes along each other, reaching into a head butt and yelling as loudly as they could among the roar. The immense squid head extended down under the magma, but with that horrible scream racking out in one dense smash, the world exploded in smelt wedges of rock.

-

Jacob had a rush of madness pushing past him, screaming mouths of silver crafted on the side of one tower. He pushed through the scrapyard which remained of a traffic jam, splashing into and out of a flurry of cars and spitting up in a mass of horrible ash. He spat the smoky remains, rolling in the air and crashing down to the floor, catching his old and wounded hands right through the thorny hedge at the entrance of a yawning forest. He groaned in exhaustion and ran as quickly as he could.

The soft scent of flowers blew up over his torn body, and he limped forward, following what sounded like the soft echo of the whistling song Ellis had learned just a few weeks ago. He felt his lower lip tremble at the smell of moss that took over the bloody stench. The green shimmer under the daylight was another memory of those sweeter times.

Blonde hair shimmered around a distant tree.

Jacob hadn't realised he was doing it, but he started to jog just about, having to lean against a tree as he went, but with those wooden hands as they gained this power, he rose and kept pushing further into the sweet hope maybe all this suffering was about to end. He knew now there was nothing all the sprites in the world could do against that swelling madness.

Jacob felt exhausted, barely breathing but pushing forward still. Before long he was standing before an opening, looking at the mouth of a deep tunnel which swirled with a purple sparkle.

The first thing that took his eye though was a sharp, white block of ice. He stepped forward faintly, striding faintly across the soft ground and not making a sound. The hunter's instinct there without hi needing to think about it. He couldn't think or notice a thing, the fact no birds sang was strange, but he didn't sense it at all. Even the sprites had gone. Any tree that was left was a spy or the ruined husk of a blessed, ancient being.

An ice cube in the middle distance was a smoking mass, hung up by a long wire. A stark white light in the dank shadows. Jacob caught the shimmer of blonde hair disappearing down the echoing tunnel. He stepped forward to try and reach into those depths, but the ashy smoke he had been coughing away twirled about and tripped him. The floor smacked him in the face, and he pulled himself against the tree, breathing hard in the growing smog from sudden biting cold.

The ash was a horrible smoke, and it racked through his bones, the acidic touch seeming to reach its activator now. Jacob buckled, his flickering eyes catching something which made him catch a sharp breath in sheer panic at the picture that stood in front of him. Two tiny hands were flopped in front of the water-sprites face, the glowing sprite Ellis had nicknamed "Mum" must have been trying to protect itself from the attack. The smoky air was that white glow, it was the ashen smoke collapsing and growing stronger with every second.

The smog started to coil around his arm, chilling his blood and fusing his hand to the cube, pulling at his legs and chest. The dense airlessness strangled him into silence, and he flailed at this strengthening grip. He tried to move away, and it fought back, growing all the stronger from any movement in the trap. As strange searchlights glowed and boomed above him, the strand of blond hair fluttered in the air. It was clasped in the ugly scorched hand of the Ash Queen. Her mind was now captured again, and she couldn't help but smirk as she ambled down the tunnel, clicking her fingers together and closing the gate.

Jacob stared up, the unbelievable mass of the Burning King raining lava onto the miles of this forest in his cruel freedom. He knew how horrendously those screaming trees would echo down to the last Sprite Lords, those ancient Eternal, and Ellis so far away now. Jacob wished only the others had found some way to keep away from this attack. Though the trees began to burn on the edges of the massive forest, and the earth itself swelter, he tried for as long as possible not to let his suffering show, still with his heart racing trying to stand defiant and strong. "Ellis", he whispered, racked with guilt and pain.

The tunnel's scratched door was sealed closed, but he scrambled against it, pounding at the door without logic while the Ash Queen disappeared into a remnant of smoke herself. He could just about hear her voice chuckling as she wandered away. Jacob could see the smoke's grasping silhouette coming closer, and searched hopefully for a gap between the swooping ash. Half-formed beasts groaned out of the blackness, and he breathed in shakily, trying to find some power to stand tall again.

The Ash Queen woke up from a Mirroring possession, shaking her head and staring in a tear-filled gaze down at the scrap of hair she had made appear from her own powers. An ancient shortcut was open to her in the black depths of these tunnels, and she took the path gladly, knowing just where that blessed Ellis would have gone. The trees sent thanks to her as they wandered from the great forest, hiding under her own whispers of ash. With all her strength she kept walking, in her mind the last fragments of sanity sprinted from an approaching see of flaming, ochre hunger.

The Burning King was unleashed, and he became the pain and flames which descended under his command. The whole world was going to become his, and any crumble of blackness for him would have just been noise to the burning of the trees. He would have been blind to their silence, to the reality of them being just ordinary trees. Witnessing only the glory of his own power. As she cried at the loss of Jacob, racked by the terrible turn this journey had taken, and overwhelmed by the pain of the world all around her. Just about able to hold back the golden gold which tried to burn right through her flesh and hair. She disappeared, skulking in the tunnels. With her disappearance, the forest thinned to its real size, and the roar of the Burning King exploded in a sea of vengeful hate. The air itself laid burnt, but nothing thought or needed to breathe in his world anyway.

-

"Howwwwwwwwwwwwwwlll", the sharp note bounded along the swelling river, echoing with a higher note every time it hiccupped over another stone. Ishmael slapped one great hand onto Beast-Shadow's furry white mound of a back, punching the air. *Everything I had built grasping onto life* Ishmael thought.

Ellis snapped back to life, catching the warmth of the connection which still held strong right to Jacob. It was impossible to tell if they were in the real world now or not, they had travelled so far away from anywhere Ellis recognised. The moonlight glowed as a distant red hue, reflecting in a deep pool. When Ellis was last anywhere near the sea, Mum had been alive, and they couldn't help but keep looking for that little water sprite they'd made friends with and found some fun together. Just a twinkle of that sweet memory when Jacob's hand wasn't there to answer a reaching hand. She still wasn't there either, and Beast-Shadow growled heavily for just a second before he remembered Ellis had been sleeping there. It was impossible to ignore the tense hackles on everyone with the world dying all around them.

They had run for miles while Jacob suffered. Every second Ellis had spent in their nightmares had been spent tearing and running after Jacob who seemed to be swirling in flames and darkness. Whatever Ellis did, the darkness didn't move, and there the dream would fade, the two of them drifting further and further away again. No matter how much it pulled at Ellis to see Jacob safe whatever it took, Eden had made plans for these desperate times. So, here they stood in the darkness, waiting.

The world was more important. Ellis just had to repeat it enough to tell themselves it was true. Even in this strange world, with all the madness and danger, it was impossible to forget Jacob.

Ellis had healed some victims before they had fallen

asleep, every one of them became a light while they ran and hid from the devouring darkness which took Jacob away. With a shake of Ellis's head, the dream disappeared in the bleak night.

They stood, looking the other way, and glowing in the moonlight as the palest figure around. Eden grabbed one drooping hand as the wait stretched on, tutting under her breath as Ellis pulled away, hoping somehow, she could help create a small escape and focus their mind. Ellis had learned somewhere along this separation knowing their hands were just for Jacob, wherever he was.

"The sickness of our great enemy spreads in three ways, my son, as it always has." She whispered, her soft voice just dancing above the sound of the delicately lapping waves. She was ever so close to Ellis, who had been gawping at the way the red light deformed as it knocked into the pattern of pebbles. They looked at Eden and noticed deep burn marks on the leaf-work of her long hair, sharp cracks which traced up her nails, but most of all the way she paused between each word, smoky eyes blinking slowly to find the perfect thing to say, gasping breaths pushing out small fingers of smoke from the fires raging inside her.

"One, we cannot stop. It is the very heart of the person. Most are far too weak to face off against the Queen's sweet tones, and they allow themselves to break. Vanity, greed, selfishness, she feeds on your needs and breaks you down into a shell that can accept anything. Even total possession." She breathed deeply at that one, and Ellis wondered if she could sense the Queen just a few steps behind them, whimpering for some reason, and shaking in the cold.

Ellis didn't want to tell the others, but they knew one thing; the Queen wasn't the same. There was the same kind of disease coming off her that had destroyed all those people in Greenview, but it seemed to be swirling around her and striking down instead. It was somehow part of her and not, both at the same time. Ellis pushed their focus away. It was true how hard it was to look at her for any time without being pulled in.

Eden pushed at their cheek, hoping to grab Ellis back. She could feel that gross pull she had sensed in Misty and so many more before him. Maybe they would be the ones to destroy her corruption and free the world. When they ran away from the rest of the Sprite Lords and all their companions, those left behind were lost. They shared a gaze, and Ellis coughed the illness they had caught off the Queen which would never leave her.

Eden did not want to think that something, like a deformed reflection of the Eternal, might have created that sickness when life itself was born. For a moment, the darkness felt like it was one great open mouth, infinitely hungry.

"The second lies in the air, and Whisper has gone where we cannot follow high up into the clouds to find his people who have hidden in the storms and the clouds, just as I had hidden for so long." She looked down, shaking on her thin legs for a moment, but smiling at the sweet thickness of the air, gulping at its richness.

The world suddenly seemed blessed again. Ellis did the same, tasting the salt of the water and a tingle of energy shoot through them.

The moon had disappeared behind a cloud, the water started to glow in strange patterns like oil plays when it spills. "The air takes time though, it only seals their fate. The third is the water itself, and this is our worst pain. Everything flows back to Ishmael, all of life came from the fall of rain – RUN!" Her voice squeaked, and she pushed Ellis to the ground, though they flipped from the blow and stayed in the air as they started to run, looking for where the enemy was coming from.

They looked up at the arriving clouds, the way the moon shot through it was fading away as thicker, angrier clouds fought for control. Thunder started and was swallowed up by what could only have been Whisper. Ellis pleaded for their victory against this assaulting darkness, small golden flickers rolling up from their worn hands and the scraps from their hair.

Ellis for one second stared with far too much sadness at the tatters of their hair, just remembering snatches of a moment where that first huge beast had been scrambling through the forest in rage toward them. A shadow twirled and ate through the sky, sprinting without remorse to lash out at Ellis, dying against the golden light. It had just enough strength to touch Ellis once at the top of their skull and burned away from the glow.

The warm stench of its breath faded away as Ellis's focus returned to the glowing lake, staring up and feeling the healing part of them push up into the air and all that darkness. The rain was just starting, and the water fizzed off a bright lance of light as it penetrated deep into the heart of the storm clouds. Ellis closed one fist, forcing the next thunderclap to stay within the clouds, holding onto all that force and feeling their body swirl with this furious energy. Something told them this was a conjuring call, and they had to do anything they could.

Ellis glowed like moonlight, fizzing at the rain as it fell. This was no ordinary rain. The golden light pushed through the darker clouds, and Ellis shivered from the cold, the wind rustling in what remained of their torn hair, and still they pushed on. The rain stung, Ellis couldn't think about themselves anymore. There were people to help. A sea of darkness pushed through the lunar murkiness, and Ellis thought it was the Ash Queen unleashed, against the healing powers losing herself just as much as that rotten King had.

The squirming dark waves became clearer, a mass of gnashing black beasts. Ellis tried to pull themselves away, not forgetting the last time they had met these beasts. Rushing behind them, right out of what Ellis had thought was a cloud, Whisper boomed with a quake of rushing air, reaching out to find the sprites he hoped were up there somewhere.

The sprite lord was miles across, like a huge cloud which had arranged itself into a monstrosity. This one was a swirling torrent of wind, every touch of air an inescapable tornado. The furious wind tore at the feathers and the sickening black corruption up there.

Ellis pushed the healing strength behind it, shrinking back from the acid rain which was falling stronger and stronger.

Another cloud smashed into them, a tide of ochre air clashing against them all, and for the smallest second, Ellis had everything suspended. The burning spit of an engine burned away at Whisper's wrath, and while the fire still burned, Ellis could see the imprisoned air sprites in swirls of fog, their focus fused to their panting, panicked faces.

They tried to push that healing power against this tide. The eruption of ochre destroyed the needles of light, beams of scorching Serpentine searchlights burning away at the darkness and revealing great long monsters which stretched and spat streams of that ochre acid, burning through the clouds and tornadoes Whisper could summon. *Twins they cannot be apart. The gap may be too far too see. I still know the beat of your heart. Oh, brother, you thought they had taken me. Well, it has taught me new art. There is a lot of air here which deserves to be free.*

In one seismic quake, all the healing light was absorbed by an immeasurable breath. The figure of Misty erupted out of the space between spaces, a shrunken figure grabbing onto Whisper's hand as the wrathful gaseous wave disappeared with every memory of a shadowed storm.

Ellis whimpered on the floor, the acid rain falling heavier and heavier with predatory vengeance. The Golden light swelled from Ellis under this pain, grouping around Eden, Beast-Shadow and Ishmael who himself had started to fizz and burn. Ellis fell to the ground, and without thinking rushed into the sky, pushing the surface of the lake with them, and Ishmael guffawed as he rode the little wave up with them, feeling the rise of war's victory swell across his breathy heart.

A plan. Yes, of course we can. No time to rest and get a tan. The war will end its span. For one true reason, Ellis, those healing hands. Misty was right beside Ellis, her whole face a smile, as they looked at each other, without needing to speak, they all took a breath in anticipation of a great strike to come.

Ellis was trying desperately to free the poor sprites before a vengeful Misty destroyed them all in their blind passion. They could see the air twinkling under the moonlight as it was dragged out of every beast, and every eely monster swirling in the shadows. They stopped, the air of those sprites struggled and tried to run. Ellis pulsed with light, but the air was swirling without control, and the healing light faded against this maelstrom.

The remaining beasts grew wild in their fear, launching black waves of bladed hate toward them, shedding their fangs and feathers along a sea of conjured acid. They were being used as a single weapon rather than the free people and animals they had once been.

Ellis tensed at this, trying to fall or find some cover. A heavy slap, the sick scent spread across the air. In a heartbeat, every member of the enemy was gone. The ash shed away, falling and disappearing in the fragile light. "Thank you", Eden whispered, squeezing Ellis's elbow as they descended together. Ellis and Misty had combined into a furious cleansing wave, and for the first time the Burning King had been forced to surrender.

The Ash Queen laughed, buckling under an onslaught of the Burning King's assault across every nerve. For one second the real picture of who she had been appeared, the newest victim of the Burning King's seeking torturous claws. False memories faded, and real life came back. She couldn't help but gawp at Ellis while they all landed together. Though she tried to run toward them, that same flaming curse she could not forget raced at her, the puppeteering of the Burning King grabbing around her hair and threw her against the nearest tree.

She would never lose their tracks though, never lost hope.

21: A HIDDEN SAVIOUR AT THE VERY END

Mother animals are happy to raise anything, though it is used against them sometimes, it does bring out some strange moments. There are children that are found sometimes which have been raised by wolves, a gorilla has adopted a kitten before and many other strange relationships. If someone cares for you, it doesn't matter who they are, the care is the most important part.

Nothing stopped the acid rain, as it crashed, the strange sharp whispers echoed strangely against the ceiling of this underwater world they had escaped to. Each of them had stepped below the water without question, following Eden as she stepped through the waters. *You must save Jacob* it seemed to whisper, but the flow of the water was against Ellis. Whisper was closing the tunnel of air behind them as they walked down the depths of this opening to the sea. This far down, it was impossible to swim to the surface.

A few times the Sprite Lords had tried to discover what might had happened. Ellis didn't know any more than them. If it was another power they had summoned out of the madness of this world, they hadn't felt anything, they were still struggling with the golden twirls which had tried to heal the shed ash.

They knew the Eternal were more powerful and more ancient than even Ishmael. The light was unmistakeable just like its powers, and it was impossible to know whether this really spoke of the time the Eternal would finally return and save them all. Ellis was leaning heavily on Beast-Shadow's back as they pushed further and further into the heavy darkness.

Twice now, they had stepped calmly of a sheer edge with Eden, down and down and down, ever further into the darkness. They brushed dusty sand off the floor which hadn't been disturbed for ages. They followed jellyfish which seemed happy to bob as electric lights, marking the path for everyone. Ellis sat upright too high on their seat, splashing into the ocean, and spitting the water in its huge swirling weight.

Whisper adjusted automatically, the rushing hugeness disappeared into the continual echo of all that pressure around them. A thousand times heavier than the sound you get just as you swim below the surface, a pressing that pushed at their skin, squeezing heavily, and each step as they fell became even more hard.

A school of fish swam past, swimming of a thermal Ellis saw in the mad, winding waves. They all came to a routine stop again with almost military precision. Beast-Shadow howled again as the only note through the dense ocean. The pulse of its note echoed across the sea just as it had every time before, and the jellyfish started to swim away in the direction of an even greater, danker depth.

They pushed on, unknowing of the days passing. At times, in the heavy black silence, there was just the waft of striking fins nearby. It was like a swell of storms, and more than once they had to lean against a sharp cliff while huge mouths swiped past, and Ishmael disappeared into the waves to calm and distract the beasts with waters echoing strangely in what might have been a mating call with Ellis's help, checking the route. He swam and pushed away with just a finger to the cliff edge, but the force still shook rocks loose.

As the boulders clattered all around them, in the immense darkness Ellis had never felt more afraid, but that only lasted a second. The overwhelming pressure of all these events rushed at them whenever they rested, and it disappeared again with the rush of all the energies around them. Before long, they were glowing just as they couldn't help but glow now. Everyone leaned into a cliff's shelter to eat, hiding from the tumbling rocks as well as they could. Ellis pushed anything that looked dangerous away, struggling under the weight of the water.

Soon enough, another white wave announced the arrival of Ishmael again. He slumbered at the back of the group and his sheer energy pushed them on again, for a moment each time he would lean over the small form of Ellis and groan as the healing shimmer of gold enriched his battered arms once more. It looked like he had been digging at the rocks in a desperate attempt to find something. Eden was the only one that remained calm whatever this was would still be there. Ishmael would whisper something in the first language, and a purple glow popped like a firework to shoot their silhouettes against the huge cliff. He just hoped something else was listening.

The heavy shadow pressed on them all, but Ellis kept

the light going as much as he could, and while they ate at the roots of Eden's making and found some broken rest. The press of the immense beasts would approach them again, but down here there were monsters Beast-Shadow summoned just by the strength of his newfound companions.

Huge beasts smoking with that ochre curse circled down toward the only light in these shadowed depths, miles below the shimmering surface. The Serpentine swam with them, swiping and boiling the water while they fell, swooping with snapping jaws and flaming wrath amongst a cloud of smoke and flames. Amongst it all, just the beacon of a tiny light was their prey. The Ash Queen rendered false pictures of the huddling camp desperately, but the King's slaves could smell their way through the lie. She could not conjure a mask to breathe with, this water had something else inside it.

The light twinkled under the starlight of the golden city only Eden and Ishmael could remember, as faintly as a man might recall his first word, but a joyful idea filled with a glowing sweetness you would never replace. Ishmael stood in prayer for just a moment while the others fell asleep. He caught the golden light as it faded while another day disappeared. "Gabriel…" he whispered, wandering if the Eternal truly had come back in their hour of most precious need, that perhaps the very bringer of light would save them in the darkness.

-

The only light they could see was the wrath of the Burning King in his endless hunger. The crowd pushed down under an encircling attack, lances of shadow pushing down to the small orb of light in a fragile path of rock. The earth sprites worked to keep the tunnellers away. The floor exploded as they burst through, feeding and feeding on the remains of Ishmael's people.

He had been working to call them, and now they had arrived. They were ancient and calm beasts, the very soul of the oceans, scales and fins glowing with the brightness of that very first light incarnate. In waves, the beasts sped up as they struck, opening a flurry of daggers and claws. Seeping acid, they hungered at the thought of all that flowing blood to come. Pushed on by the hope of victory. The ochre swarm squinted hard as the tiny orb of light was eclipsed by great beams of cold-white. The Guardians of Ishmael's home awoke. He had found the sacred throne.

The ancient corals of the sea crackled and yawned open with an echo of sonar, awaking the memory of old, angered whales. The darkness turned into a sea of open mouths, combining in a swooping turn to attack right at the deepest field of the horde. The acid spilt but disappeared quickly within the pulses of white, gold and purple, pushing from spears aged long before anyone had learned to speak a word.

Ishmael awoke the Guardians with explosions, running down among the rocks as it dropped down for them, just the memories of Mountain-Stride rumbling amongst this birthplace of the Gods. They stepped down, far below the biting maws of those immense whales. While the sprung trap bit and swirled, devouring those beasts, it would bring more of the Burning King's Wrath. It was just what Ishmael wanted. In the echoing depths, they each stepped down onto the floor where first life had been born.

"You may relax", Ishmael breathed out, his body solidifying again as he balanced to the ground. They had passed through a golden shimmer of ice which shed just a little snow as they cracked through the old shield. They could feel no pressure now, just a serene land which still held those first gulps of breaths all those years ago.

The coral cracked heavily, like old joints breaking as something woke. Faces squirmed out among the flittering fish, sprites turned wild. The old, sandy rocks stretched high as steep cliffs up the other side. Stepping out of their old resting places, two old Guardians groaned and pushed the water away as they stood to either side of the panting, open-eyed group.

The tiny collective stared up at the two colossal Guardians. They were covered in great lengths of old moss, growths of sand forming the echo of their muscle, which they stretched as they still seemed to grow beyond seventy feet high. The whales sang above, Ellis in the cold light felt their pain, knew the sounds were the rawest screams. Even if Beast-Shadow howled to keep them close, there was only so much pain they could take before they ran into the endless black. The ground below them began to glow, a mist of purple pushing off both giants. As they strained to stand tall, the very oceans were cleansed in a bloom of blinding white mist as their spears smashed into the floor.

The runes below them bloomed with huge letters, each one shaking the sea and pounding right up to the stars themselves. Everyone echoed back ten-fold with the warm gold bloom that had been shimmering from the first echo of Gabriel's words to calm light itself. It had been with them forever. A sweet scent Ellis had nearly forgotten wafted in the soft air, as for once the Ash Queen was free to become her true self. The Burning King was far too distracted by all this loss. He would still not be merciful though.

-

The Ash Queen buckled under the blows of her King, and that sickness had been rolling up her throat was a horrible pain. It ordered her to come back and take him into her arms, to get away from the suffering the rest of the world bled. That pain had driven a hate for the green fool she had never seen. Blinding her in its wounds, making her more and more angry, more and more driven. Now she had seen a kind mother caring and feeding her friends.

The Queen was remembering, but the King was trying to knock that out of her, trying to wound and break her down again. She was supposed to tempt them close to the fires and along the river, where a crowd of beasts waiting. The trap would be finished, and the two of them would finally be free to rise as the Gods they should have been when man was born below them. She couldn't remember any of this now though, it all just sounded like a fuzzy dream hiding behind the ash of something else.

She coughed heavily, drinking in the water she had been feeding on for days now, and as it always did, the bright light of that water glowed in her. The cancer which had grown in her snatched at her stomach every time, making her weaker with every second. With a lashing of golden light, the cancer swirled out in thick black lines of slime. It burned away to tiny flitters of smoke. Her illness died, a different obsession for that blonde, innocent face glimmered, and this time her smile didn't have any malice inside it.

This time it didn't have the hunger to hurt him. This time she wept as in her mind's eye, the twinkling face of a baby giggled, and she remembered everything. That beastly mass of tentacles formed of two arguing enemies wrapping itself around her. It collapsed into a blistering moment of pain which warped and distorted everything for so long. As that suffering lashed across her, one particularly ugly beast was blessed to think it was the very Burning King it had worshipped for so long. Even that beast whimpered with the pain of transformation though.

The reaching flames scorched the nearest trees, an old water-sprite exploded in front of the flames in a sea of turquoise, trying desperately to save her while she sprinted. She could not remember that moment as she woke back up again, but she had worked her first talents to hide the scorch mark of a heavy paw-print. The monstrous monarchy had hidden deep in the city, and from then, she had lived a life of fear and servitude.

The echo of that monster's raw echoed, the Unholy, the true visage of the great enemy away from any stupid King or weak Queen, awoke. Without any of its allies left, its full power was freed. It was an immense creature in the darkness, blocking out any memory of the skyline. The creature the Burning King had been trying to unleash in a moment of glory, driven mad now it was bellowing with a sound like the scream of the very earth itself.

Heavy blows of magma slammed into the flowing river, boiling the ocean and with it every Sprite Lord the Unholy so despised. It spilled oily waste as its laugh boomed. Just in the distance as another day rose, the Unholy could see the smoke from a distant power plant, and knew even if the enemies made him skulk underground again, they were weakening their own world without its help. It squinted heavily, shattering its huge weight right through a skyscraper, anchoring up as it watched the scalded remains of Serpentine limping away.

The Unholy had been waiting and playing with the minds of everything involved in this great game, now the enemy was coming. Everything had become so early, far too rushed for the enslavement to finish with overwhelming numbers. They were still far too weak, but they had no time left now. Everything would be unleashed. It was the part of the game when all the small pieces had disappeared, and only the strongest pieces remained. Stretching itself miles across, every violent, electrified tentacle searched for prey. The great, crested head burned through all the remaining minds, and animals faltered to the ground under the assault.

The Unholy was hungry, and in its driven hunger and obsession, it had not wandered why that one women had struck out to it as the Queen. As the bright day-stars glowed in the new day, for the first time, the Unholy felt a fear and panic ruin its war cry. A shockwave of waste burned across the cityscape and the forest, smashing off the ocean and electrifying it, feeding on the ancient tree-sprites in a smouldering smoky air.

The Queen slumbered and skulked in that ancient tunnel, leaving her entrance open with the picture of Jacob held there, hoping somehow Ellis would make it out of the boiling pool, and pull themselves away from any danger ever again. She ran through the tunnel as a ghostly whip of ochre searched for her, disappearing just as it crackled against the nothingness where she had been.

The Unholy had its servants, and they prayed together, every one of them writhing in pain, and an ochre mess of squelching air flocked together, pulling them closer. Most of them waited though, far away and still holding other pieces of this game together. Keeping ancient secrets hidden, pretending ruins remained where the great monuments to the Eternal still pulsed. There were so many more weapons to play. For now, it focused again, knowing where Ellis would be, where they would all appear.

Screaming in fear, the Burning King flailed and kicked with what strength he had left. The burning of that raw speed tore through strained muscles, and though beasts tended to him, one wing drooped weakly against his heavy-set shoulder. The acid burned still, and he hid in the ruins of the skyscraper. He could not look up, for fear he would just be devoured as so many of the flying beasts were, while the humungous Unholy decimated everything before it.

A whip smashed with a high snap against the concrete, and the Burning King was alert, cowering a little and then with a small explosion defiant. The tamer stood there, runes glowing along his hood, dark lines of red that spoke to the beast of darker times. With the curve of one skeletal finger, the Tamer summoned the Burning King toward it. A troop of loyal soldiers grasped a torn banner, some shaking while they shed young, already breeding and preparing for the next war.

They knew how to skulk and plot, and as the Unholy was lost in a rabid rage, they followed the scent to a monument that could tear apart the fabric of humanity. Tear them down so they might no longer know technology or peace, but only to hunt and survive. The crowd chuckled together as a horde of beasts abandoned their true master, freed in the very trap the Unholy had weaved.

-

The light grew stronger, the earth itself crackling. Ellis was already ignoring the Guardians around him, the staring eyes of the beastly horde, nor the turning storm clouds that rose in hurricane forces toward the burning smoke in the distance. This time, they knew just what that smell was, it was far too strong to deny. Nobody ever forgets the way their mum smells, and as they giggled in a way they hadn't for what fell like an unbearably long time, Ellis already disappeared down and through the secret pathway.

The light fought against them, the Unholy had built these paths only for those rotting under its control, and Ellis was assaulted by a rain of wires, the stench of burning hair scalded them. The echo of Jacob's muzzled face yelping. The world melted away with the shimmering silver of that nightmarish future. Jacob's scorched hand was in front Ellis, but their glowing power was driven now. Instinct drove them through the tunnel with unblinking pace. The pounding fists of gold struck through the nightmares, the memory of their mother fading away again. Ellis wasn't letting go of that scent

That sweet perfume whipped past Ellis's nose, and they hit harder against the swelling maze. The black mass of spider-work slime plotted in their way, and though it melted, Ellis tripped and fell further into the shortcuts, a hundred different places glowing below them. They pushed further forward toward that smell, but the Unholy had learned just what it was now, and the tunnel laughed itself, rumbling gutturally, chewing on the delicious child who fought to find a way out. Ellis couldn't see anything, ran blindly through the violent dark. Buzzing tunnels of wiring started to strike at their wrists.

A heavy smack of shock racked through Ellis and a coil of electricity strangled their light, launching Ellis to this other world under the breaking dominion of the Unholy.

The ground boomed above, the message of just where Jacob was waiting pummelled through the Sprite Lords and each of them prepared for their final sacrifice, not caring what horror awaited them.

Ellis stumbled through the destructive madness, the twirling ash and a swirling sweet scent. The scent of Mum's perfume. They grasped with their golden and healing hands as strongly as they could, just to hold onto whatever was left in this chaos the moments when the darkness flittered away, and they could just about see a way forward. The rushing panic was quick, but they couldn't help running forward and grabbing onto any shaft of yellow light, just hoping that maybe this might be the time they would finally be close to their mother.

Over and over a Mirroring would flop to the ground without any resistance, shimmering and crying. Ellis would grasp at them feverishly, healing with the force of sunlight. The uncontrolled power of Ellis's healing strobed into the next figure they touched. Rocks exploded which reflected too much light.

It was never their mother though, and as the world around them exploded with the earth shattering under fire. They shimmered with the new golden light, and the surviving beasts rampaged forward, mad and hanging onto the tendrils of the commands. Their gnashing teeth disappeared into smiles and confusion, the bloom of golden light falling behind Ellis. Every healed person a scorching pain on the flesh of the Unholy. Every survivor was lifted in a ball of enriched air, and gasped at the beauty of being freed.

The Unholy commanded the devourers through the carving roots of Eden. She tried to heal as much of the forest as she could. She skulked under the shadows, swallowing away the pain. The smoke was rising, and with each time it rose, the golden light froze its progress. The sheer fury of the monstrous tentacles burned against its own strikes, and the world buckled again. A shockwave of wrath shattered where the people had been running, destroying any survivors it could notice. The sea of enslaved people began to wince from the sharp light, trying to run away and back into the darkness. Knowing somehow it protected them.

There had been a rain of gold lights slamming down onto the swelling black oil, but now it began to fade, and while Ellis ran, following Jacob's frail trail, along a tide of aggressive wind. The scraps of broken cars reformed under Jacob's swirling strength, and now the mirrors were free of ochre eyes.

No, another trap flicked on, and in a talon of slime. Ellis was pulled from another journey in the psychedelic light, pulled deep down in the madness of her throne.

Ellis slammed into the ground, their groan echoing down a strange, long, gaping tunnel. They tried to push their light out, but the very walls were dripping with a sickly ochre, and they could feel their own energy being fed on over and over, their shadow fading away while the tunnel grumbled hungrily. The squelching nearby grew louder.

The Ash Queen sat on her throne in front of Ellis,

captured again. She was burning just a little down her shoulders, and laughing as she breathed a sweet perfume. The laugh quickly rose to a shrill cackle, the steps began to wriggle. She stepped down from the throne as the Mirroring unwrapped themselves from her chair to become her small troop. Ellis looked around them, trying to find someone to grip onto, some fragment of light or joy. They could only see their reflection. A tired, wounded and panting child stood there, whimpering. Nobody would dare to Mirror them.

"The world is ruining itself, you are hurting them. Forcing them to do something they just don't want. The wires through this world have shown me one thing. Everyone wants to consume more and more. They will never give to anyone if they have nothing to gain." Every word whipped at Ellis, knocking them further back just enough to see the wriggling wires which fed and moved closer and closer to them, wriggling with their own mind.

"I have left two humans alone on their own, enough food to share between them." Her whole body shook, she pushed out a hand of cracked claws to fight some assault only she could sense. "They turn wild, destroying each other. That is the most natural way of things. I have freed the rabid thing that survived. STOP THAT!" She bellowed, as Ellis moved closer without fear, walking through the wires which tried to assault them, but bounced right off the power of their gaze. Blocks struck Ellis as they tried to move closer, but they fizzled away to nothing.

She spat fury and pain, launching a wave of fire, but

Ellis glowed against this attack, without any idea why, focussed on the inner good they saw everything. Ellis caught the smallest hint in the eyes of that beastly woman, the Ash Queen touched their healing hand, grasping it and smirking ever so slightly, warmed.

The walls rumbled with the cataclysm of this touch, the ashes soaring around in a tight tornado which burned fitfully. Ellis kept the darkness away. The sharp needles of electric wrath bore through the lights, and with another swiping hand, the violence was over, the snapping roar dead.

The strength of the Unholy turned with gross joy. Ellis shrank away, diminishing down under the digesting black. In a sharp strike just like the first attack of the beast but a thousand heavy ochre claws, they were hit hard.

Mum stared down at Ellis with a gleaming tear in one eye, and in one tug taming the wrath of the waiting beasts. The darkness didn't stop descending. Ellis knew then those ancient tales of the Eternal and the painless joy of their childhood was the same blessing. Her arms shimmered with those old tattoos of bright white Ellis had always thought were drawn on, but knew the old runes they really were. Without a word, Mum whipped the darkness away from her. A horrid scream echoed behind them as they disappeared from the tunnels and free.

The beasts buckled without their master, hearing the lashing of Tamer. They needed a strong master, perhaps now it was time to run and plot once more. In its unstoppable rage, the Unholy had nothing left but suffering to bring. If it would not have victory, it would have a parting meal.

-

Words and songs were built on those gigantic golden runes. They sprouted life, and a calling to all those who waited and held onto the dying world at every sacred monument that still stood. Not all of them were as protected as Ishmael's.

The two giant Guardians stretched and pushed the sea around them in their strength, summoning it just as they lord could. They had stood before the first light of life, and here they stood below its solar flares again. Each had been gifted by a segment of its power, the edges of their foot-long fingers shimmering in this shimmer in the moonlight. Their eyes were torches.

The light was more powerful than the day, and they could all feel the pain of the forests and the sprites all around them. This time though, they could feel them like extensions to their hands. Guardians did not feel sadness, they only gained fuel for a wrath that shook through the stonework of their souls.

Beast-Shadow howled again in a haunting tone over and over, searching for Ellis, calling for all those who had gone, and something else that pulsed with an energy far too bright to be of earthly descent. Beast-Shadow grasped that hope, his tail wagging too fast to see clearly. The group rose, and none could ignore the rune constellations as they glowed, the light touching only those who were free of the grasp of the Unholy.

"We are blessed… My mother… The Eternal…" Eden whispered, nodding her head to the sky and kissing her hand toward it, clicking in their old language toward something.

-

The shadows were biting and ravenous, filled with an unending splatter of ochre eyes and oily skin. Each time they came near, Jacob pushed back up his defences. It had thrown the door of that tunnel together as a desperate shelter, smashing into the trees remains together to hide behind as much as he could get. The smoky ice had worked its way against him for a time, but his hand was fused with some burning flicker of those flames. In one heavy strike, he had pushed himself free of its grip.

It hissed back at him for a time, and the smokiness forced him to hide under the ramshackle shelter. The water sprite glowed as the only tiny beacon of light. They both stared out, crouching while the darkness grew even deeper, and watching what had been smoke step through the moonlight unnaturally. Trees crumbled and squished out there, and no matter how hard Jacob tried to save it, the water sprite faded.

He swiped with his hands through the fading picture, each time seeing less and less of his own hand, feeling the sick blackness drive through his hungered body and feed at everything with a gurgling laugh. The water sprite pushed out the little light it always held in the centre of its body, smiling as it looked up through a crack in their shelter.

Jacob grabbed the light. His hand formed shakily back, repairing the shelter just as the assault of shadows and beasts smashed against the loose slats again. Jacob grunted, feeling his failing strength as he pushed hard against the roots, kicking back in fear as he saw them writhe too.

The days merged together, squinting in bright light, not knowing if that was worse than the writhing black mystery. He jumped at every noise, fighting and hiding and panting, all memory of Eden and Ellis, any idea of comfort was impossible to summon in the chaos.

Jacob had tried before to crawl away and leave the shelter behind, but the darkness had preyed on him. His raw speed let him escape snapping jaws or driving blades. He would shoot past in an explosion of scraps to repair the shelter as he rolled.

He looked up as he kicked this time, staring at the guardians as they strode through the forests. Waterfalls shimmered in the light behind them, over their shoulders. Their glowing water flesh silenced any assault, no matter how huge the flaming spheres were, or the seas of black wrath.

A mass of wings smashed through one face, crashing into each other and biting the only flesh they could find. Jacob couldn't hear a sound among all his kicking and panting, working tirelessly to fight the coming tide of darkness.

An immense sword smashed and sang high, twinkling for one moment. The shockwave of its calling knocked away his shelter. He was open to the gargling void, focussed at him. The birds smashed through the huge giants, but they did not even look down, and he realised those waterfalls were alive. Exploding whirlpools smashed down at where fire reached up and was squashed among the ginormous legs, the two figures decimating the nets of ochre without pause.

The floor was popping and barking in vengeance. Another gold, shimmering shot of light crashed to the ground and lit up what was a sea of strange beasts, growling and clicking at each other. They slammed half-built paws to the ground and yelping at the Unholy who tightened every leash he had left. A Serpentine lashed out and struggled, pulsing wires shooting out of its remains. It all turned to shadow again, and then a beam of white brightness blinded Jacob for a second, forcing him to roll backward, rolling backward and punching straight into a plume of sweet perfume.

They crashed to the ground together, just as behind them, the Unholy unlashed its final contortion. Jacob coughed, "Mum", just as he had been allowed to call her in those last months. He scrambled to protect himself, noticing in a flicker of clarity the leaf-work of her shoulder tattoo. Open-mouthed, he allowed her to pat his fists down, and push them firmly against his hips. She looked at him just as she had all those times before, pretending she could be firm.

She had the bright blue eyes of Ellis, the long blonde hair was there. The sharp, harsh war-dress of the Ash Queen still hugged her figure. Jacob couldn't help but laugh, so glad to see a friend amongst all this. They embraced, and Mum giggled at being picked up, it was the perfect symbol of her freedom. She blinked hard, shaking her head hard sheer joy of it, before she laughed too.

The wrath around her had gone silent.

She twisted her hands around, and with one gesture, that same warm, golden light flashed from her hands, smashing every burning remnant of the trees together, healing him and throwing the beasts back amongst a tide of icy hate. The snap of their bones as they were pushed back echoed, and she giggled to herself, there was the dancing high note Ellis hadn't been able to help but copy. When she laughed now though, the wind listened, and the answering howl chilled Jacob in its sharpness.

The cracking of those bones didn't stop though, and the cursed, sick light of the last loyal Serpentine beams struck behind Jacob and Mum. The whining hoots from these mountains cascaded over one another, and a crash of burning waves crackled in the distance. Both leaned forward though, trying to stare at what was happening down at the underbelly of the Unholy. They felt the sickness of that horror's shadow creeping forward. They couldn't help but back down, instinctively hoping Greenview might save them. The whispers of control still working, given enough time, everyone would break down. The tide of chaos had beaten them, and the grass they were running along boomed under someone's control.

The earth struck up as a field of wolves smashed

through the darkness, followed by a mass of charging bears and birds of prey that shot through the trees, hiding from the sea of wrath that swirled above them all. Splashes of violent water splattered around their feet, twirling and caught by cursed air it smashed through the faces of the slobbering beasts who foamed at the mouth.

The black faces bit at the trees, kicked and bellowed, trying to charge. They couldn't as the light froze them, A claw, a root, a branch, a fang, or a blast of harsh waves knocked them down. They kept running back, sprinting hard and trying to recover, the air throwing them back to their end.

Mum grabbed Jacob's hand and pulled her out of the forest, the sheer power of her push pulling ahead of the Sprite Lords attacks. He was the first one to notice just what was wrong. The beasts were running from behind them, scrambling in the tangles of electric darkness to run back.

They weren't afraid, they were buying time.

The gurgling noise, and the snaps of bones echoed against the respawning forest. The sound died, Jacob swallowed the sick in his throat. They were all together, and Jacob did not know Beast-Shadow in his native, furred form. He could feel the warmth between them, caught the happiness in their smiles, the scratch of tears at the Eternal shimmering amongst them. Every sprite-lord crossed themselves, kneeled or curtsied, enraptured for just a moment.

Under Mum's command, they pushed hard, away from

trees and tentacles that struck at the writhing darkness. Jacob didn't know how far they had gone. He slammed against the hard side of a van, rolling down to the ground with tarmac arms, crashing through a building and rolling bodily against the office chair of the reception.

Somehow, they had looped back to the city

The flow of wrathful air smashed at them all as they landed, their shadows fighting to catch up. They stood among the burning ruin of what had been the throne of the Unholy. Together, in a break of calm they stood, staring down at the chaos, the screaming void down there in the depths. The Eternal was the only one that knew this was far from over. The world was infected. She shook her head, knowing something was wrong. Ishmael, Misty and Whisper had not joined them, and combined Eternal remembered the chaotic madness of their father. They winced as the cleansing rain began to burn them. The waste of the Unholy. The last great oaks groaned in the way, surrounding them, and they climbed together, Mum lighting up the ground, and heavy thorns pushing out among the old tree.

They sat on the shoulders of those trees, heavily dented faces gasping out of the trees shadow. They ochre but stood strong. Other trees scraped from the flames of that massacre, though they had been looking for a river and quiet, finding themselves staring at the steel ruins. The deep smoke wafted heavily around them. Jacob was glued to the horror in the distance, not free of its assault. A black mess which seemed to have been ripped right out of his nightmares scraping life together in the forest from the smoke and ancient traps sprung at once.

-

Ishmael roared out of the ocean, Misty and Whisper at his shoulders bringing a tsunami and hurricane to this demonic horde. He had seen Mountain-Stride fall so long ago, it was impossible that those earth sprites had fallen. The ground itself fed on every part of his call, digesting the shore's sand into a mess of blades. Lava exploding from the Unholy, and every strike smashed against the corals, and around them the oceans, and everything they could bring were summoned.

The sprites boomed in joy at the glory of a call without the disease of the Unholy, weeping as they rose with the sight of the Eternal's runes in the night sky. These proud warriors were glad the oceans dropped above them.

They sprinted at the sea of creatures which screamed and exploded in the white-water whipping. Feathers flocked around his face, but he cleansed every ochre scrap. He grew in power, showing himself as a father of all life, snapping at the whirlpools with a flick of his wrist. He grew layers of muscles to reach his most powerful form.

He choked, the beasts he thought destroyed writhed through him, chewing and spewing their acid amongst him. The flaming rocks pummelled his brothers, and it was all he could do to stand up as he faltered and faded to his mortal form, sending a tide of ice through their bodies. They did not disappear, they absorbed the water, swelling with fattened stomachs, and chuckling mouths. As much as they could chuckle through that water.

Encouraged, the Unholy pounced with its sea of steel tentacles, wrapping itself around those two guardians as they rotted. All their flesh turning to ochre sands and sick slime. Ishmael sacrificed them, pushing his shrinking fists down to the grasping ground. He looked up at the looming squid-like mass of the Unholy, the carnivorous shadow coating him. From every length of shade, a jaw, claw, paw, spike, hackle or burning eye exploded again.

A thousand beasts scrambling and running toward him, freed from their hiding places inside the dying Guardians. Swelling from every human they had turned, every child which had disappeared around the country, devoured, the Mirroring were unleashed without control.

He felt something brush his back, flinched and raised a spear of white-water. Under the sparkling, crystalline gaze of Ellis who sprouted from the ground itself, and he was calmed. Ellis smiled, trailing a length of dead wires which had spread through the ground. Though ochre shadows bit at Ellis's body, nothing could stop their glowing body, and as they reached out their second hand, Mum appeared beside them, taking both their spare hands. Ishmael trembled with freed emotion. He was teleported under Mum's power to stand with his brothers as he fell. The word *Mum* echoing just a little as they disappeared.

Together Ellis and their Mum grasped those fidgeting

wires together, feeling the sharp, wrathful paths of them. These silver lengths reached down and into the whole world. As they travelled through it though, machines deep in the earth snipped those wires and it shifted to appear to only be local to this city, the light dancing through the hellish ruins still echoing with so many deadly memories. As Ellis and their Mum cleansed the pain, healing the limping survivors as much as they could. Eden worked to try and bring back the remains of those burning trees.

The light of mother and son flowed over itself, strengthening, slamming life where decay had stood, wiping every memory of the horrifying pain away. They grabbed at the remains of those Mirroring, pulling the real people back into their lives. Every one of them was exhausted, straining and leaning against the trees shoulders, worn and scarred from so much running.

Ellis could not heal every survivor, and their light dulled while the stars boomed her gentle golden fingerprints across the land. The bejewelled, dazzling touch fizzled, the Eternal's scent rolling across the wind.

There was no energy left for rhyming, and Beast-Shadow gave up trying to howl, wounded at the silence that laid in reply now. Each of them winced as small flecks of Ash flickered and danced around them, spelling out some old curses. Jacob couldn't care to think about what it was, staring at the symbols and feeling a horrid heat rising across his head. He buckled to the ground, fixing his eyes on the sharp star of the Unholy as it buckled and flailed toward the ground.

An ochre shadow flashed, and the abysses of eyes he could not forget was right in front of him, the spirit of the Unholy as it started to tumble down. With one last, vengeful strike, a single needle of bloody acid bit through Jacob's heart. His burned back slammed onto the floor. As always, Ellis was closest, and he heard the soft noise of it cracking in his ribs, resting with him. Maybe they would lie together just like they always used to on the grassy mounds before. The veins of black spread up Jacob's neck and he coughed thickly. Ellis panicked, pawing at his hand to squeeze it hopefully, trying to feel his warmth, some last fragment of the most precious companion they had ever had.

Nothing grabbed back. Jacob held their eyes open delicately, forcing himself to focus for one more second while the biting shadow took him away. With no time left, and two rushing hearts, Ellis and Jacob kissed softly, holding what remained close. He disappeared, for once having no time to think. Ellis reached out a hand to Jacob while he faded to a smoky memory.

Their hand passed right through the weak silhouette. Both hearts fluttered rampantly without control. Ellis couldn't help but think Jacob had been the only person who could ever tear their eyes from a bird in flight. Now they couldn't watch as a butterfly landed on Eden's shoulder.

Ellis fought, and wouldn't let any memory escape, squeezing their hand tight, just their nail digging in. For one moment, a warm hand squeezed so tight, and they hiccupped a cry.

Ellis gripped onto every memory they had together, and in the truest sign of their birth yet, saw the whisper of his outline up in the golden towers of a beautiful city that had been twinkling in the corner of their eyes for so long.

Ellis

The air whispered, and they looked up through teary eyes to see a small silver cloud wave once as it faded in the rising sunlight.

EPILOGUE

Death is all that lies below. That is all the people should have remembered. All they should have ever done, but time eroded their faith in nature. They looked beyond, and harvested the world. The Eternal could feel it, they cursed the land in their vengeance, knowing the earth was ready to hatch. It was still diseased though all the Sprite Lords had managed was to imprison that ancient mess.

Hell was the lesson you shouldn't sin. People made caves, but they would dig no further. Tribesmen and wildernesses held monuments, each a key to seal the underworld and every memory of that corrupted tomb. Man had forgotten, they had thought themselves smarter. Already the military were here, speaking of a disaster. Where skyscrapers and beasts had been, just the remains of an aeroplane and a thousand confused survivors remained.

The whispers had invented a plane crash, and while the true heroes skulked in the remains of a forest, Mum turned away, prepared to purify those monuments, force the seals closed again. She could smell the dying world, and tried not to weep. This day did not need any more tears. The truth of that horrifying first war rushed back to her with the reflection of her home in the sky.

She stopped thinking about that hellish world of reflections. The birthplace of every Mirroring, surrounded by flames and torture, metal and clanging bells. She stepped forward, out of the fires and on a serene road running away from Greenview, and she could just about see the mountain in the distance. She knew the Sprite Lords would hide, heal and fight to keep as much of the world alive as they could. The clouds of her own whispering still hung over them, and all at once she was alone again.

She forced herself to stop thinking about those reflections, to stop thinking what Ellis might do if they knew what could be possible if they followed. She started to form the air around her, ready to disappear here and reappear where the golden beam of light rested. Miles away. With a last fleeting look at her dearest companions, she lurched forward, and a curling flash of purple surrounded her.

The flurry of furious wind, the scream of weary muscles, it was familiar and comforting to be running again, down amongst the wilds and the secrets built upon falsehoods desperately tensed against the frame of an old trap.

They hadn't moved an inch.

With the rag of someone else's jumper pushed over their hand, Ellis gripped their mum's hand, shaking their head with commanding force. Their eyes were still tearful, but their glow and power would not weaken. Looking down at their hand, they thought *together,* as the Sprite Lords nodded together.

The tale continues in part 2

Made in the USA
Middletown, DE
15 November 2017